"PLEASE, BRAM . . ."
MARGUERITE BEGAN.

"I have one or two things that I should have told you. Long before now. I would like to say them quickly. Before I lose my courage yet again."

His grip grew tighter, as if he feared what she had to reveal.

Feared? Could it be possible? Could the strong, indomitable Abraham St. Charles actually feel enough for her that he could *fear* what she might say?

Her thumb rubbed against the soft linen of his shirt in an uncontrollable caress, a reassurance. But she did not feel reassured herself. In the next few moments, she could be responsible for undermining all that had been built between them in the last few weeks.

"You asked once why I married you years ago."

"Tonight you said it was because you . . . fancied you loved me."

"Yes. In part."

The silence of the room pressed into them both, then she continued. "But I didn't tell you the whole truth. . . ."

Books By Lisa Bingham

Silken Dreams
Eden Creek
Distant Thunder
The Bengal Rubies
Temptation's Kiss
Silken Promises
Sweet Dalliance
Sweet Defiance

Published by POCKET BOOKS

SWEET DEFIANCE

LISA BINGHAM

POCKET BOOKS

New York   London   Toronto   Sydney   Tokyo   Singapore

This book is a work of fiction. Names, characters, places and incidents are products of the author's imagination or are used fictitiously. Any resemblance to actual events or locales or persons, living or dead, is entirely coincidental.

An *Original* Publication of POCKET BOOKS

POCKET BOOKS, a division of Simon & Schuster Inc.
1230 Avenue of the Americas, New York, NY 10020

Copyright © 1995 by Lisa Bingham

ISBN: 0-671-88712-2

First Pocket Books printing July 1995

10 9 8 7 6 5 4 3 2 1

POCKET and colophon are registered trademarks of Simon & Schuster Inc.

Cover art by Bill Dodge

Printed in the U.S.A.

Chapter

1

Baltimore, Maryland
October 1865

To say that the wedding was to be the event of the
season was an understatement. The first amber fingers
of dawn had barely tickled the horizon when delivery
men began pounding on the doors to St. Jude's
cathedral, heralding a pilgrimage of artisans, florists,
and craftsmen that would not ease until the ceremony
began.

It took six wagons to bring the flowers that had been
cut and arranged to decorate the vestibule alone.
There were roses and daisies and chrysanthemums
and ferns. White wicker baskets and arbors were
stacked one behind the other near the doors, offering
those who entered the illusion of walking through a

veritable garden. An entire bolt of gold silk had been stretched from the rear doors to the nave. Over three hundred beeswax candles had been inserted into fifty candelabrum. Twenty spools each of gold and scarlet ribbon festooned the benches. The floors beneath the pews had been scattered with fresh rose petals, the altar adorned with a bower of blossoms. Outside, sixteen liveried servants had been hired to manage the guests' carriages while another two dozen surreys and broughams had been ordered to bring the immediate family to the chapel.

The details surrounding the events at St. Jude's were among the simplest to arrange and the last to be completed. After all, the interchange of vows would be the briefest part of the festivities compared to the luncheon, reception, and ball to follow. The Rothchild Hotel had been in contact with the bride and groom for nearly a year. Meals had been planned for months. The hotel scullery had been jammed to the rafters with all sorts of delicacies—meats and fishes, nuts, vegetables and candied fruits, pastries and breads.

Not all of the work remained below stairs. Valets and chambermaids were run to a near-frazzle, since three floors had been reserved for foreign guests and another two for those who would travel from out of town. Prior to the visitors' anticipated arrivals, linens had been aired, carpets cleaned, and silver polished by the legion. Once the guests checked in, baths were drawn, fruit baskets delivered, luggage toted, and wardrobes freshened. No expense had been spared, no comfort overlooked.

Such measures of hospitality were not completely

unexpected. After all, gossip about the happy couple had begun long before the bride's private steamer had docked in New York a month earlier. Invitations were at a premium. Less than one hundred people had been asked to attend the ceremony, while no fewer than two hundred were to be included in the evening's events. To receive a hand-engraved, gilt-edged invitation was the *coup de grâce* of the season. Not only because such lavish entertainments were unheard of in a nation recovering from a war, but also because the bride was none other than the reclusive French artistic model Marguerite Merriweather DuBois.

For four years the name M. M. DuBois had become synonymous with the astounding portraits and sculptures fashioned by the great Frenchman Francois Joliet.

The haunting, chestnut-haired, dark-eyed, ethereal woman who appeared over and over again in his work was believed to have been a product of Joliet's imagination. A composite of his mother, a dead sister, and a tragic lover. Then a French periodical had broken the news that M. M. DuBois was a real woman. They had even managed to photograph her during a trip she'd made to Versailles.

The unveiling of her identity had been shocking enough to receive international attention since Francois Joliet was a realist through and through, portraying his subjects in a way that made even the most liberal critic's eyes widen. He'd developed a reputation in the art world by remaining completely aloof of proper social mores. Somehow, he was able to capture the true emotions he found in his models into unyielding stone or flat canvas. And none of his creations was more well-known than those he'd done of M. M. DuBois. With this woman, Joliet shunned any sorts of artifice or cultural trappings. His paintings were studies of pure emotion. Often his interpretations were raw, at times primitive, occasionally denigrating, but always honest—proving almost painful for the viewer to see so deeply into Mademoiselle DuBois's soul. The feminine heart was to remain hidden. Pure. The whole idea of a woman allowing a man to see her that way was shocking. Completely and utterly shocking.

Polite society would have shunned her if not for the fact that after her "unveiling" she had been heralded by kings, honored by aristocrats, and proclaimed the most influential beauty of her time by such renowned names as Henry James, Queen Victoria Regina, and the American suffragette Elizabeth Stanton. So instead of being snubbed, Marguerite DuBois was met with the anticipation of visiting royalty.

From the instant her betrothal to a prominent Baltimore family had been announced, talk ran rampant in the city, spilling from the highest levels of society to its more elemental roots. Men were drawn to ascertaining whether her beauty was real while women ignored her less than suitable occupation to concentrate on the latest French fashions she brought with her. The most common lady's maid knew that Marguerite's bridal gown and trousseau had arrived upon the *H.M.S. Hillary,* kept shrouded in muslin, and guarded around the clock. Dressmakers the world over were waiting for its debut. In-home seamstresses were preparing to copy affordable facsimiles for their customers. Milliners had stocked a greater supply of

Venetian lace and pearls—because it was believed that Marguerite's headdress would be made of those things—as well as exotic feathers and velvet flowers for bonnets and hats.

In order to record the event for those who could not squeeze into the narrow streets, sketch artists and newspaper photographers had slept the last two nights behind the velvet cords that were meant to rope off the gawkers. The police had employed an extra shift. Business for blocks around St. Jude's became frenetic, nearly panicky, especially once the anticipated day arrived.

Soon the flow of delivery men began to subside from the church itself, and the traffic transformed from hacks and wagons to the elegant conveyances of the guests. As the church clock tolled one, half-past, two, shops were closed, chores abandoned. A breathless excitement shimmered in the air like fairy dust. The cold was forgotten, strangers became friends, as people for blocks stopped, waited, listened.

And then it appeared. A black carriage bedecked in lilies of the valley, ferns, and white roses.

She was here.

M. M. DuBois was here.

"Close in the ranks, men," one constable shouted. "Just in case."

Just in case.

From inside her carriage, Marguerite heard the statement and felt a shiver of unease. She didn't know why exactly. She only knew that as the coach and six pulled to a stop beside St. Jude's and she absorbed the strains of the organ melting through the doorway, a cool finger traced down her spine.

"Is something the matter, dear?" Aunt Aggie asked, her cheeks pink, her tiny body fairly trembling from anticipation.

Marguerite shook away her disquiet and shot the diminutive woman a quick smile. "No, no. What could possibly be wrong?"

What indeed? her mind echoed. The event was to be lavish beyond belief, a fairy-tale day. So what if her motives weren't spurred out of love? So what if appearances were deceiving? What did that matter? She was about to wed a wealthy man. An *incredibly* wealthy man who had insisted on paying for this elaborate celebration. To make an alliance with such a generous man was an accomplishment for any woman —and with each day that passed, Marguerite was learning that it was far more satisfying to marry for money than adoration. Once before she had made a mistake in that regard.

Marguerite did not repeat her mistakes.

"Has the carriage stopped?"

She started at Nanny Edna's question. The woman was old beyond belief—nearly a hundred—deaf as a post and oftentimes senile, but since she had been Marguerite's nurse, Marguerite wouldn't have dreamed of leaving her out of the festivities.

Edna smacked her cane on the floor of the carriage, her lips pursing and folding inward due to the lack of front teeth. "Drat it all! Is anyone there?"

"*Yes,* Nanny Edna!" Aggie shouted, touching the old woman's hand. "We've *arrived* at the *church!*"

"Church. What church? I'm not dead yet."

Aggie and Marguerite exchanged wry glances. "No, Nanny Edna. It's Marguerite's wedding day."

"Wedding?" she echoed, enunciating each syllable with extreme care. Then her jaw quivered as if she were actually chewing the idea. "Don't tell me that St. Charles fellow has come back?"

Edna may as well have dropped a cannonball in the carriage. The St. Charles name was not mentioned by the DuBois—had not been uttered for as long as anyone could remember. Not since Marguerite's disastrous elopement with Abraham St. Charles five years before. Not since her father had retrieved her mere hours after the ceremony. Enraged by his daughter's hasty actions and the way Abraham St. Charles had ruined her reputation, Edmund DuBois had thrashed Bram with his quirt, and sent Marguerite home to France, all the while railing on and on about her flagrant lack of propriety—with an American, no less.

Edmund had never forgiven her for her disobedience, disowning her within weeks of their arrival in Europe and forcing her to fend for herself by becoming an artist's model. He'd died with a curse of the St. Charles clan on his lips because the family had shattered all hope of his allying Marguerite with a powerful French family that could further his career.

"*No*, Edna!" Aunt Aggie bellowed. "She is marrying Algernon Bolingbrook III."

That particular piece of information must have left a bad taste in Nanny Edna's mouth because she smacked her lips together with great vehemence. "The fool with the ridiculous collection of pistols?"

"Nanny Edna!" Aggie cast a glance at Marguerite in case the older woman's words might have caused offense.

Marguerite didn't even bother to shrug. Algernon was a difficult man to get to know, vague at times, too stoic, too involved with his guns and his own weak wit. But he was rich. What else mattered? Not love. Not passion. Her family was teetering on the brink of financial ruin thanks to her father's poor investments. Her work brought in some money, but not enough to support all of those who looked to her for sustenance. Although she'd never allowed money to be the basis of a personal relationship in the past, now she had no other choice. She must find a way to provide for her family. She *must*. Algy was willing to offer her an allowance as well as the freedom from prying eyes that she craved. She had only to marry him and tour the United States for one brief year. Then he'd promised to take her home. To France. She could last that long. It was only a year. A year . . .

As if sensing a measure of Marguerite's disquiet, Aunt Aggie leaned close to pat the general location of her knee beneath the yards and yards of fabric that had been crammed into the narrow space.

"Don't let Edna upset you, dear. Algy is a good man, and you're a vision. A real vision to behold."

Marguerite was sure she was. Since dawn, she had been poked, prodded, coifed, and constrained. She hadn't taken a good deep breath in hours and wasn't likely to get one soon. In her opinion all this nonsense was completely unnecessary and bordered on bad taste, but Algy had insisted on a show.

A three-ring circus worthy of P. T. Barnum himself, more likely. But she hadn't had the will to deny him what he'd wanted. Not when he'd financed the whole affair. Not since he knew her motives for marrying him were entirely practical and businesslike. He didn't care as long as he could lay claim to "the most beautiful woman of the decade." He wanted an entreé into European society to further his businesses, and Marguerite was more than willing to help him, since she would gain so much from the match. Life had been so uncertain, the thought of knowing that she and her family would have a warm home and regular meals was worth enduring a fuss. Was even worth becoming Algy's showpiece.

She fought a bitter smile. To think that she had sunk to this level—marrying a man for purely economical reasons. She had once been so idealistic, so romantic.

So completely wrong.

But not again. Her emotions would never get the better of her. Not in this lifetime. The poets might spout reams about the power of love, but they'd obviously never tried to barter it for something to eat.

"Come along, ladies," she said, infused with sudden energy. She brushed at her skirts and stiffened her spine. "Let's get this nonsense over with."

Aunt Aggie's eyes widened at Marguerite's lack of sentiment, but she didn't chide. Marguerite had not confided her true reasons for marrying Algy, but Aggie must have sensed that Marguerite was not in the mood to temper her tone. "Jitters," she mumbled under her breath. Elbowing her husband, who slept in the corner of the carriage, she proclaimed, "Wilson, get up. It's time."

He snorted, slapping at the unknown offender. With a grunt, he woke completely, righting the spectacles balanced on the tip of his nose. "Hmph? Whfph?" he muttered through his enormous whiskers.

Aggie tapped his knee with her fan. "Wake up, you old fool. It's time for you to escort Marguerite into the church."

"Hmph. Rmlmph."

Uncle Wilson rarely spoke in anything more than incoherent grunts—not because he wasn't an eloquent man. To the contrary, in fact. But when Aunt Aggie was around, she invariably did all of his talking for him, so he hadn't bothered to speak his own mind in years.

Opening the carriage door, he clambered down, jumped from the carriage block, then turned to extend his hand to the women inside.

A bevy of footmen rushed to help. After Aggie's feet were firmly on the ground, a groomsman came to escort her into the church. Another pair of men untied Nanny Edna's rolling chair from the back while a third servant reached inside, scooped her from her seat, and lifted her free. Before the young man could get her settled, she poked him in the ribs cautioning, "Don't get cheeky, young man. I might be all but dead, but I know a pinch on the rear when I feel one."

The servant nearly dropped her in surprise, but Uncle Wilson waved the old woman's objections away in patent disbelief of her claim. The men rolled her to the stairs, then carried her, contraption and all, into the church.

Noise from the waiting crowd rose to a deafening pitch. Marguerite shivered again. There was something wrong. She couldn't place her finger on what it might be, but even shielded by the carriage, there was something that waited, watched, making her feel . . . vulnerable. Afraid.

Afraid?

She tilted her jaw at a militant angle. Marguerite DuBois was never afraid. She had a job to do, a duty, and by heaven, she would do it with flair!

"Young man!" she called to one of the servants.

The boy rushed to peer inside.

"Will you inform the bridesmaids that I'm here and they should give the signal to begin?"

"Y-yes, milady," he stammered in a thick brogue. She didn't have the heart to inform him that she had no ties to the aristocracy. Her father had been a Parisian diplomat, plain and simple, her mother, the daughter of a Baltimore lawyer whom he'd met on a business trip.

Uncle Wilson offered an outstretched hand. The time had come.

Obviously sensing she was about to emerge, the noise became even worse. Gathering her skirts, she stepped onto the carpet-covered carriage block, and from there to the runner that had been extended to the front door of the church. The cool air brushed her cheeks, and she breathed as deeply as she dared, considering the tight lacing of her corset, while flash powder exploded and the crowd cheered.

On cue, Algernon's six sisters rushed from the chapel in a rustle of ivory satin. Other than assigning a palette of colors, Marguerite had allowed them to choose their own gowns—with somewhat hideous results, in her opinion. The Bolingbrooks might have plenty of money, but that did not mean they had good taste.

"Yoo-hoo!" the oldest, Regina called, running forward in a puffed and tasseled creation her own

11

dressmakers had sewn. Marguerite had only met her once and still had trouble concealing her reaction when Regina's lips spread wide over the most prominent, crooked teeth Marguerite had ever seen.

"You're here!" Aurelia exclaimed, making Marguerite revise her position on Regina's teeth when she grinned widely. In fact, the rest of the Bolingbrooks' dental patterns didn't bode well for any children the family might conceive.

"You're a vision," another sister sighed.

"An absolute vision!"

"Algy will be so pleased."

The ladies gathered around her, one bringing the huge spray of lilies and roses that was her bouquet, the others reaching to help her remove the cloak that covered her gown.

As soon as the garment was drawn away, a chorus of gasps erupted around her. The activity on either side of the velvet cords became frantic as onlookers pressed close to get their first glimpse. Artists sketched furiously to capture the moment.

Because Regina was nearest, she was the first to absorb the full effect of Marguerite's ensemble.

"Marguerite!" She whirled to plant herself in front of Marguerite's skirts, holding her hands wide as if that act alone could form an impenetrable barrier to prying eyes. "Your gown. It's been torn!"

Marguerite didn't even bother to reply.

"Oh, Marguerite," one of the other Bolingbrooks sighed in dismay. "How awful. What happened? Did you fall?"

Marguerite fought the urge to laugh. There was nothing wrong with her dress. It wasn't torn. It had been made exactly to her specifications, influenced only by Joliet's urgings: "Don't cow to that lot, Marguerite. Don't let them think that you are ashamed of who you are or what you've done. Make a statement early on that you will not bow to their silly little codes, to gossip, to innuendo. If you will do that, they cannot hurt you."

She'd taken his advice without pause. With the aid of several fashion designers, she'd planned each hairpin, each fold, each ruffle. After all the renderings, the measurements, the fittings, it took nearly six months of labor to complete, but the final results were more satisfying than she would have ever believed possible.

A tiny wreath of porcelain orange blossoms circled her head, simple, dainty, elegant. From that fragile coronet, a swathe of Venetian lace studded with pearls fell over her hair, down her back, and extended twenty feet behind her.

The gown itself was also deceptively uncomplicated with a low rounded décolletage. Her shoulders had been left bare and were draped in silk net berthe embroidered with roses in the palest of pinks and yellows, the center of each flower adorned with a pearl. The bodice was tight, form-fitting, enhancing the fullness of her bosom and the tiny circumference of her waist. Below, twenty yards of heavy ivory satin had been draped with thirty yards of embroidered net. The fullness of her skirts had been drawn to the back, as per the current mode, where the fabric was bunched and puffed over a bustle and decorated with silk flowers, ribbons, and ruching. Beyond that, a train extended for a good fifteen feet. But what had caused the most attention was that the skirts had been split in front, revealing a pair of trousers, à la Amelia Bloomer, ivory-clocked hose, and tiny satin slippers, every detail completely bare to examination.

"Oh . . . oh . . . oh . . ." Esmerelda—the youngest of the Bolingbrooks—panted, her eyes nearly popping out, her mouth gaping in distress.

Marguerite ignored her. Deciding that she'd endured their fussing long enough, she took her uncle's hand, grasped her bouquet, and began to walk toward the portals.

Immediately, the Bolingbrooks scurried to form an impenetrable wall of flesh, as if they could prevent her from making such a spectacle by their mere presence, but with a nod of her head, Marguerite signaled to Aunt Aggie to give the orchestra permission to begin.

At the first gold-toned strains, the sisters were forced to take their places in front of her or invoke even further scandal. Marguerite's lips twitched in amusement. Aurelia's face had turned beet red. Camellia was close to swooning. Esmerelda still panted while Regina's lips pressed tight in order to brazen her way through this embarrassing encounter, as if she'd known all along that the bride would arrive in trousers. Trousers! The word began as a whisper, grew, repeated, pushing Marguerite forward like the chug of some giant locomotive.

Regina reached the doorway, and the music swelled. Strains of Mozart filled the air, imposing a sense of grandeur, majesty. Marguerite kept her head high, looking neither to the right nor to the left. Soon she would be Mrs. Algernon Bolingbrook III. Nothing else mattered.

"Hrmply. Rdlympy," Uncle Wilson mumbled. The crowds bothered him, she knew, but she didn't need him to repeat the words he couldn't bring himself to say.

She squeezed his hand. "I love you, too, dear Uncle."

He beamed, his bushy brows lifting to his hairline in delight.

They paused in the doorway; the company of guests arose, and the murmurs began. The shocked glances.

"Oh, my . . ."

". . . This is the woman who . . ."

". . . How can she possibly . . ."

". . . From France?"

Marguerite reveled in the whispers. Joliet had been right. These people who looked at her so curiously, so morbidly, with such patent fascination would soon be her peers, her neighbors, her associates. They had never seen her like, she was sure. Used to women who "knew" their place, fragile creatures, traditional social butterflies, she could tell by their reactions that they had rarely experienced someone so unmoved by society's dictates as she. She intended to use such a fact to her advantage.

Her uncle took a step, and she moved with him, down the silk runner, over the rose petals, into the church and toward her groom. He turned to watch her. Algy, balding, pudgy, grave-faced Algy. She knew the second he noted the trousers. His cheeks grew flushed, but there was also a glitter of pleasure in his eyes, as if all the fuss had excited him.

They joined hands at the altar, Uncle Wilson ac-

15

cepting the responsibility of giving her away with a "Mwldph" in the direction of the priest.

She handed her bouquet to Aunt Aggie and against all codes of propriety and custom, laced her fingers with Algy's, leaned close, and kissed his cheek. Then, taking her place beside him, she watched him with open affection instead of the stoic acceptance women were schooled into adopting at such events.

"Dearly beloved . . ."

She would make him a good wife, of that she was certain.

"We gather . . ."

With the business techniques she'd learned from her father she could multiply his millions into even more.

". . . To join . . ."

He would never regret having married her.

". . . This man . . ."

She would never regret having accepted his proposal.

". . . This woman . . ."

Their life together would be fulfilling.

". . . Bonds . . ."

They would never want.

". . . Matrimony . . ."

They would never need.

". . . Any have cause . . ."

She and her family would survive.

". . . Let him speak now . . ."

They would *survive*.

"Stop!"

The single word, spoken from the rear of the church turned Marguerite's body to ice. That voice. So deep, so dark. So unforgettable.

16

Boot heels rapped on the stone floors. Even through the layer of silk covering the aisle, the sound reverberated against the thick walls and high ceilings, sending a shiver to Marguerite's very heart.

"Stop this debacle. She can't marry anyone. That woman is already *my* wife."

Chapter

The voice came straight from her past.

Bram.

No. It couldn't be. He was dead! He *had* to be dead.

Marguerite knew that she should have fainted—any other woman would have fainted. It would have been the proper thing to do. It would have been the most delicate way of handling the situation. It would have given her some time to think. But Marguerite refused to be so cowardly. She turned, keeping her posture erect, one eyebrow lifting in that imperious way that she had practiced for weeks in front of a mirror in the hopes of discouraging pesky reporters.

Even so, she was not prepared for the sight of him,

her first love, her first husband, silhouetted in the light streaming through the open doorway.

Sweet heaven, had he always looked like that? Had he really been so tall, so lean, so . . . beautiful? It was ridiculous, but even from this distance, she felt sure she could see the color of his eyes, blue-gray with a hint of hazel. Did he still have that dark shadow of a beard that required an extra shave each day? Was his brown-black hair as thick, as soft, as rich to the touch?

"Margaret!" he called, holding out one hand. "Come here."

Margaret. Not Marguerite. He'd refused to use the French pronunciation, damn his hide. He'd insisted that by becoming his wife, she'd been made an American through and through. Therefore, her name would have to be American, too—as if she had no identity or choice of her own.

"Bram." The whisper escaped from her lips without thought. That gaze of his drilled right through her, willing her to obey his command, but she found herself rooted to the floor, thunderstruck. Never, in her wildest imaginings had she thought—even considered—that Bram St. Charles would appear here, today. Like this.

The wedding guests finished gaping and began to talk. Their voices grew louder and louder, bouncing off the rock walls and crashing in her ears, underscoring the scandal. When Marguerite had helped to plan the event, she'd thought to create a stir, a little interest, but never would she have willingly agreed to a scene of this magnitude.

The reality of the situation struck her again. No. No! It couldn't be possible. She wasn't married to this man. He was dead—was *supposed* to be dead. When she'd tried to contact him after a few months spent in France, Marguerite had dared to return to her father's house to ask his help. Livid at his daughter's inability to forget the man, he'd sent her to the American Embassy in Paris, where finally she'd been shown his name on the list of casualties at Bull Run. Her lips tightened ever so slightly. He'd been on the list of *Confederate* dead. After all his talk of valor and God and country, he'd defected to the enemy he had once despised.

He was alive.

The thought pierced her very heart. He had been alive all this time. Yet, if he'd been aware of such an error, he'd never bothered to contact her and convey the truth.

A trembling began in her knees, but she pushed it away. She would not be weak. He would not see her weak. He *must* not see her weak.

"Margaret."

When she did not respond, he walked forward, striding down the aisle in that authoritative way he had—one which reminded her of Caesar returning triumphant to Rome.

"Now, see here, my good man!" Algy piped up, crossing to stand slightly in front of her. "Just who do you think you are, bursting in on our wedding like this?"

Bram's expression was unrelenting.

"I am Abraham Lexington St. Charles, second son of Adam and Wilhemena St. Charles, and *I* am married to this woman. Legally. Lawfully. And morally."

"B-but that can't be!" Algy blustered through his

monstrous lamb-chop whiskers. Marguerite had been waiting until after their marriage to tell him they gave him a comical air. Like the pictures of walruses that Joliet had once given her.

She lay a calming hand on his arm, but like a windup toy, he was determined to have his say. "You've made some sort of error, Mister . . . Mister whatever your name is."

"St. Charles."

"Yes. Well. There's been a mistake. Hasn't there, my dear?"

"No," she replied faintly, then stronger, "I mean, yes. That is . . ." Bram pinned her to the spot with a look, and for an instant she couldn't think, let alone speak. Then she hurried to make light of the situation. "He *means* that he *thinks* he is my husband."

"But *I* am to be your husband," Algy whispered out of the corner of his mouth. "Aren't I?"

She patted his hand. "Of course you are, dearest. This interruption is merely a misunderstanding. My marriage to this man was a brief, youthful mistake. One which can be easily rectified."

To one side Regina Bolingbrook mewled pitifully and fainted onto Aurelia, but she, getting her first real look at Bram St. Charles, began to wilt as well. One by one, the Bolingbrook females fell like dominoes until they were heaped on the floor in a puddle of ivory silk and lace right at Nanny Edna's feet.

"Is it over?" Nanny Edna grumbled, squinting at the women.

"No, dear. There's been an interruption," Aggie explained.

"Thank God," the old woman muttered. "The whole ceremony was far too long for my taste." She huffed in irritation. "Tell everybody to sit down. It's most irregular to stand during a wedding."

Edna must have been overheard by at least the first few pews because the audience returned to their seats, row by row, like a wave ebbing away from the shore. However, Marguerite also noted that a majority of the guests sat on the edge of the benches, straining to catch the slightest sound.

Bram stopped a few yards away from where she stood, his hand held out. "Come along, Margaret. It's time for you to come home where you belong."

Where she *belonged?*

She didn't *belong* in his home, and she didn't *belong* to him. Even *he* would be the first to agree that any emotional bonds they'd once shared were long since severed. To pursue them now would be madness, utter madness. Their interests would be much better served apart: she to marry Algy, and Bram to . . . to . . . to do whatever he wished to do. Alone. Without her.

"Now, see here," Algy stammered. "How did you get in here without an invitation?"

Marguerite scowled at that new point. Bram St. Charles had *known* about her marriage in advance, not surprising considering the publicity. He must have anticipated every detail to create such an embarrassing scene. Yet, he'd purposely waited to confront her, purposely waited until the last possible moment to appear.

"Through the front door," Bram replied mockingly. "What with everyone's eyes on the bride, it was an easy enough matter."

Damn the man! How could he be so cruel! How could he purposely give her such a shock? This was all his idea of making her pay for the dent in his pride that her father had inflicted with his beating.

"You've collected your pound of flesh, Bram. Don't you think it's time you were going?" she murmured so lowly that only the tight knot of people gathered around the altar could have heard her.

But as she watched him, gauged the tense set of his body, she knew she was underestimating the situation. Bram hadn't come here just to cause a scene. He was intent upon far more than that.

No! a little voice whispered deep in her heart. A panicky voice that had been squelched since that day her father had come to help her escape from her precipitous marriage to Bram St. Charles.

How could this have happened?

Bram was supposed to be dead. And no matter how many times in those first few months she'd prayed the information the embassy had given her was wrong, the years of silence had proved otherwise. She'd never been contacted by the family and informed to the contrary—or by the man who stood here today.

That fact hurt her more than she would have cared to admit—that Bram had been alive and let her continue to believe in his death. That he'd let her forge through life believing a lie, and then, just when she'd found some measure of purpose, he'd returned to haunt her.

He shouldn't *be* here. He shouldn't be looming in front of her, his hair longer than she'd ever seen it, flowing past his shoulders, rich and heavy. He shouldn't be standing with his feet braced on the church runner, dressed in muddy boots, dusty gray britches, and a wool greatcoat that was well past its time—obvious remnants of a Confederate career.

The bitterness she felt tainted her tongue. Trust him to wear such a uniform months after the war had ended—as if it were a badge of honor, even though he'd fought a losing cause.

"Come along, Margaret. You've wasted enough time gawking. Come home with me."

"I have no home with you," she managed to say between stiff jaws.

"Haven't you?" Her defiance appeared to amuse him, and he planted one foot on the bottom step, his boot leaving a smudge on the silk.

At that moment she hated him. Hated him for spoiling this day, humiliating her this way. But most of all, she hated him for making her love him once—because she *had* loved him, heart and soul. And she would have continued to love him—if he hadn't chosen a more important cause in his eyes. War. A war she didn't understand or believe in. He hadn't understood how the very idea had terrified her beyond reason. So much so, that even after she'd left him and abandoned all hope of their being together again, she'd felt sick and empty upon seeing his name printed so clearly with the list of the dead.

"Marguerite?" Algy took her wrist. *"Do* something."

She jerked her arm free of his clinging hold. "Hush, Algy!" she snapped impatiently. "I'll take care of this."

"There is nothing to 'take care of.'" Bram's lips curved in a mocking smile. "A wife belongs with her husband."

"I am *not* your wife."

"We were wed."

"It was a mistake."

24

"Mistake or not, the fact exists that we are bound to each other in the eyes of the law."

"A law which can be circumvented very easily by an annulment—one I should have obtained long ago. I believe there is some sort of special contingency for a husband's desertion."

"I didn't desert you."

"This is neither the time nor the place to discuss this. I'll look into a dissolution as soon as it can be arranged."

"Why didn't you do it before?"

An annulment wasn't something she wanted to explain in front of a chapel full of people, but he didn't offer her a way to avoid such a discussion.

"There was no hurry to arrange such a thing at first. With an ocean between us, I knew you wouldn't be able to bother me. By the time I looked into the details, you were listed as dead and there didn't seem to be much point." She glared pointedly at the boot still resting on the silk runner. "I can see I will have to examine such matters again. You can rest assured that I will be quite thorough this time."

"No, Margaret. You won't. There will be no annulment." The last statement was flat and filled with an implacable certainty. "Not while I have breath in my body."

With that he drew a knife from the top of his boot.

The congregation erupted into a flurry of panic.

Regina, who had begun to show some signs of life again, swooned.

"You are my *wife*," he stated. "It's time for you to assume your position as such."

"Position! I am not some footstool to be moved about at your whim, assigned willy-nilly to one duty or another. I am a woman, flesh and blood, and I have a mind of my own!"

"Enough!"

His jaw grew taut, his knuckles white around the hilt of the knife, making her realize that she wasn't the only one who harbored resentments. Bram usually hid his emotions well, but this instant he was enraged.

As he ascended the last few steps, the blade glinted with the colors reflected from the stained glass windows. Algy's face grew florid, his hands balled into fists, but Marguerite stood still.

"Go away, Bram. You haven't been invited to these festivities—"

"The . . . *festivities,* as you call them, are finished."

The blade slashed out, cutting away a good portion of her train. She screamed, thrusting out an instinctive hand in protection, but Bram ignored her. He tugged at her veil, wrenching it free from her coiffure, and tossing it onto the floor. Clasping her wrist, he tugged her hard against his body. "You are *mine.* I do not share anything which belongs to me."

She opened her mouth to make a scathing comment, but the breath was knocked from her body as she was lifted and thrown over his shoulder.

Moving in long, ground-eating strides, Bram made his way to the rear of the church.

"Stop! Put me down this instant!"

But he paid her no heed—and as for the rest of those in attendance, not a soul tried to help her. As the door slammed shut behind them both, the last thing Marguerite heard was Nanny Edna exclaiming:

"Is it over? What a relief! Now get these people out of here and let's go home."

* * *

Bram paid no attention to the crush of onlookers waiting outside the church. Tossing Margaret onto the driver's seat of the bridal carriage, he climbed up beside her and made an audacious escape. His own mount—attached at the reins to the back—trotted along behind them.

Fifteen minutes later, after making his way to a hotel as far away from the church as possible, Bram threw his wife onto the bed and stared at the woman he had once pledged to love, honor, and cherish.

If only her own vows had meant something to her. But she'd offered him nothing more than hollow promises and an empty heart. She was a sham through and through. A beautiful facade.

Margaret flung her head back, pushing her hair from her eyes—long, dark lustrous hair that he had dreamed of during the war so many times he couldn't count the occasions. Over and over he'd envisioned having the strands twined about him in the throes of lovemaking. Now he wanted nothing more than to wrap them around his wrist and force her to look at him, to see what she'd done to him, all she'd taken away with her careless actions, her spoiled behavior. It had taken so long to confront her, he didn't think he could bear waiting for the answers he required another instant.

She glared at him, her indigo eyes black with suppressed temper, but he felt no regret for what he'd done to her carefully laid plans. She'd all but forced such measures. It was she who had been ready to commit bigamy.

"How dare you?" her voice was low, but growing louder with each word. "How *dare* you make such a shambles of *my* wedding day?"

He gave an affective sigh and shrugged from his greatcoat. "No matter how many times I try to remind you that *we* are married, you can't get the facts straight, can you?"

"What we had was a youthful infatuation. We merely compounded the error by trying to make it permanent."

"But vows *were* exchanged." He stripped off his dress blouse—a tale-tell gray garment with darker stripes to show where the military insignias had been removed. "As I recall, you could hardly wait for the ceremony—or should I say all the nights to follow. You said the lovemaking would be sweeter when you didn't have to worry that someone would find us entwined together in the gazebo."

Her huff of indignation did not dissuade him from continuing on his current course, and he began to unfasten his vest. "That was why we ran away to get married. Because we couldn't keep our hands off one another. Because you were so afraid we'd be caught and your father would beat you for surrendering your virginity to a mere American."

"Liar!"

"Come now, Margaret. Who's the liar? Let me refresh your memory. It was summertime," his voice grew low, deliberate. "Your father had come to Solitude to do business with mine, and he brought you along. You arrived in an open carriage with your hair tumbling over one shoulder, wearing a simple cotton gown. You set your sights on me the first moment you arrived.

"I didn't!"

"You did."

A flush had crept into her cheeks and grown quite pink, a very becoming effect.

"By the second day, we'd kissed. Within a week, we'd consummated our affections."

She opened her mouth, but he knew she couldn't deny it. The memories of their passion were so powerful that even now they filled the room with their phantom chords.

He touched her cheek, recalling each detail so clearly. "You must have known I'd be an easy conquest. I'd never seen such beauty before. Your eyes, your face, your skin."

He caressed each in turn as he spoke. "We'd only known each other for a few weeks when we were making our way to the gazebo on a regular basis for far more than a bit of kiss and cuddle. You keep insisting that you want an annulment, but you should have known such a thing would prove very difficult considering the intimacy we've shared."

Her lips tightened in embarrassment, and for some reason it weakened his anger a bit. She *did* remember. It was there in her face, in the subtle parting of her lips.

"You would wait until everyone at Solitude had fallen asleep." He paused to study her, to watch the color creeping into her cheeks. "You used to hurry down the back stairs and rush outside." His voice became gruff with remembrance. "I can still see you running barefoot through the grass, your hair streaming behind you, a hint of your bare calves peeking between the edges of that flimsy wrapper you used to wear."

The words died in his throat as his own memories

became too strong to deny. He could almost feel the slight weight of her body as she threw herself at him, twining her arms around his neck and peppering him with kisses. He'd been so in love.

So trusting.

So foolishly enamored.

Not until later did he discover that her adoration hadn't been real. If she'd cared for him even a tenth of what she'd claimed, she couldn't have abandoned him the way she had.

The thought brought him abruptly to his senses. The anger returned full force. She'd lied to him. She'd sworn her undying love. Then she'd gone home to France with her father on the very day she'd promised to be his forever.

"A few months of passion," he said bitterly. "That's all we shared before you were gone. You can't even claim that I took advantage of you."

"What?"

"You followed my every move with your eyes, as if each time we were together your appetite grew stronger. It was a heady experience for me. I'd had women before—"

"Lots and lots of women!"

"Three, and you know it."

She pressed her lips together.

"I told you about it all. I spilled my soul out to you, confided all of my dreams for the future—and what I said to you only made you want me more."

Margaret folded her hands primly in her lap and looked down. At least she hadn't denied what he'd claimed. But then, how could she deny what they'd shared?

Bram straightened, regarding her carefully, trying

to locate some trace of the woman he'd thought she'd been. One who had been carefree, filled with a zest for life. But he couldn't find her. Not in the form huddled on the bed.

"You lost your virginity to me long before our marriage, Margaret."

She did not argue such a statement.

"Then, hours after we wed, you were gone."

"I won't—"

"What won't you do?" he interrupted. "Admit the truth? That you didn't love me, never loved me? Damn it, Marguerite, why did you marry me at all? I've asked myself that question a thousand times. *Why?*"

She remained mulishly silent.

"It couldn't have been the sex—"

She gasped at his bluntness.

"—We were already doing far too much of that to worry you." He shook his head. "Was it Solitude? Was it the thought of living in a plantation house, your every need provided for, your every whim indulged. Was that it?"

"No."

But the rough whisper was not entirely convincing.

"Why, then?" He leaned close, forcing her to look at him. "Was it because my family was wealthy? Is that it? Life as a diplomat's daughter couldn't have been too cozy. Did you see my family's money and decide to find a way to capture it for yourself?"

"I didn't!" she breathed, looking genuinely shocked. So much so, he nearly believed her. Nearly.

"Don't play the innocent, Margaret. It doesn't become you." He noted the way her breath had quickened at the barely veiled insult. The pale

31

mounds of her breasts pushed against the neckline of her gown with each puff of air.

She was still beautiful. Even more so. She'd been a child then. Now she was most definitely a woman. "You knew just how to ensnare me. You drove me mad with wanting you.

"I thought we were in love, Margaret."

He cupped her face with his hands, tipping her head. Her skin was as velvety and fragrant as he'd remembered. Perhaps even more.

"You agreed to be my bride."

He stroked her lips with his thumb, knowing that they were just the right shape, just the right texture for kissing.

So how could they have told him such lies?

The old familiar anger burned deep in his chest. His grip tightened around her chin, forcing her to look up at him, to really see. "Then you betrayed me. You had me whipped."

"No!"

It was an automatic protest, but he didn't pause.

"We chose a day that was unaccountably warm for our nuptials. We slipped out of Solitude at dawn, taking two horses from the stables. It was a four-hour ride from my family's home in Virginia to Maryland, but we made it in a little over three. We chose a justice of the peace in a tiny border town—"

"Then you left me!"

"I left you alone for a few hours to rest and change your clothes."

She wrenched free. "Now *you* appear to be having problems remembering. On the way to our hotel, we were trapped in a narrow doorway by the crush of a crowd watching the drill work of a local militia. You were fascinated. It didn't even seem to matter that we were about to have our wedding night. Your attention was diverted, and your interest became overwhelming."

"It was part of a political rally in favor of the recent win for Abraham Lincoln!"

"Yes, but it was also the first time—the *first* time you had even intimated that your political views were potent enough to goad you into joining the army yourself."

"I'd told you my views on preserving the Union."

"Yes, but I thought you meant to support diplomatic solutions, not a war! It was our wedding day, and you wanted to stop at the enlistment office. Did you really think I believed you when you said you meant to give me so much time to rest and change? I knew you were going back to the office to enlist."

"So the minute I was gone, you slipped downstairs to the hotel lobby, sending a telegram to your father begging him to come get you."

"That's because I knew you would return with a paper saying you'd joined the army."

"I insisted that they give me a few-weeks leave before assigning me."

"How very generous. How very romantic! A two-week honeymoon before enduring years of the threat of widowhood." Her expression was a mixture of fury and anguish. "You'd just promised to love and adore me."

"And so I would have done."

"From the middle of a battlefield? You were going to desert me for your damned war, and you waited until *that night* to tell me! Why didn't you say something to me about your plans before the ceremony?"

"I didn't think it was important. I would have discussed it with you when I returned from enlisting—"

"—After the fact—"

"—But your father had already come to take you away."

"You were gone for over six hours! When Papa arrived soon after your return to the hotel room, I knew it was hopeless to try and talk to you. I wasn't about to stay and see us both killed for a country I'd been in less than a season!"

"That's a weak excuse, and we both know it. Your mother was American. She raised you to be more American than French."

"But I grew up in France. France! My mother died over a year before I visited your family. I felt no allegiance to your causes."

Bram leaned close. "You were my *wife*. That should have meant something to you. It should have entailed a few sacrifices."

"It did! Just as many as were required by you. I begged you to come to Europe, to avoid that damned war. I *cared* for you!"

He bent so close, she was forced to lean back on her hands. "You had an odd way of showing it. You walked out of that hotel room without a backward glance." The words echoed in the room. The accusation that had burned inside him for years. "You *sent* for him. We weren't even married a day, and you sent for him. Only hours before, you'd sworn that you loved me. Did you? Ever?"

She didn't answer, but her eyes were wide.

"Did you *love* me?"

"I cared—"

"Did you *love* me?"

"If you mean did I care for you beyond all reason, beyond all thoughts of well-being and safety . . . no," she blurted. "I found you appealing, witty, comforting." Her voice shook. There was a brittleness to her tone he had never heard before, one which made him think she was lying, but her words were just as he'd imagined they would be when he'd envisioned this confrontation in his mind.

"Then, why marry me?"

She took a deep breath, exhaling it slowly. "Because you had taken my virginity."

"Taken? You were a willing participant. Why leave as soon as we were married?"

"I would not be abandoned."

"Abandoned? How? I was enlisting in the army, not taking up with some other woman!"

"You were leaving me to fend for myself—for God only knew how long. So I did what I thought was best. I returned to France. At least *I* had the courage to admit the elopement was a mistake. One I should have thought through more completely. I didn't belong in your country. I didn't belong with you." Her eyes sparkled with something that—if he didn't know better—could have been tears.

"I see." They were the only words he could force past the tight band of anger that gripped his throat.

The room pulsed with a heavy silence. Then Bram demanded, "Tell me, were your reasons for marrying Bolingbrook considered any more carefully? You would be marrying an American. You would be forced to live here in the one place you evidently despised—a place that is still suffering political upheaval. Or did his money assuage your fears enough to convince you to stay? Was that why you really left me? Because you worried that—as the second son—I wouldn't inherit enough of my family's wealth to satisfy you?"

She didn't answer—not that he'd thought she would. Her expression was testimony to her own guilt. Money. Was that all she had ever cared about? Money?

His shirt had been left unbuttoned to the breastbone, and he began reaching for the rest of the tiny discs.

"What are you doing?" Margaret whispered. Her eyes clung to the skin being exposed.

"I'm taking my clothes off."

"Taking—" She blanched. "Why?"

"So that we can see to the unfinished business which lies between us."

"We have no 'business' together, I can assure you." She began scooting her way backward on the bed.

"But we do. Business your father postponed. Our wedding night. As I recall, it was at about this point he interrupted us the last time. You might not have been a virgin, but I still anticipated the event with some pleasure."

"My father—"

"Is no longer living. I know. The sketchy details of your life the press has been able to glean have been in all the papers for days." His fingers paused in the process of stripping his shirt away, and he grew a little more sober. "I regret that fact for your sake, but you'll have to forgive me if I don't mourn his absence. He was wrong to have helped you leave me." He leaned so close he knew she could not ignore his intent. "There will be no such delays this time."

Margaret's eyes widened. "You don't actually think that you and I . . . that I would *allow* you . . . that . . ."

"I am your husband."

"Nonsense. We were never really married."

"We repeated our vows before an officer of the court. I have the paperwork to prove it."

"You were listed as dead! I have a copy of *those* papers to prove it. I was told I was a widow. I have gone on with my life, and I'm not prepared to return to past mistakes."

"You don't have much choice. If you thought I was killed, I can't help that. The casualty papers you saw were evidently wrong. You and I are married and will continue to *be* married—'until death do us part,'" he mocked. "My *actual* death."

"But I don't even know you anymore."

"I'm trying to rectify that."

His hands moved to the buttons of his trousers.

"But I don't *want* to be married to you. My feelings for you were never strong enough to have lasted all these years."

"You should have thought about that when you begged me to marry you."

"I *never!*"

"You did. You took my hand, placed it against your breast, and—"

"I was a girl then. I can't be held accountable for such foolishness now."

"You can be, and you will be." He tugged the woolen underwear tops over his head and tossed them onto the floor. "I think it's time to see if the spark we once had still exists."

"No."

"You used to melt as soon as I touched you."

She lunged, grasping a ceramic chamber pot over her head. "Don't come any nearer. If you do——"

"You'll what? Beat me? Your father isn't coming this time, so you'll have to do it yourself, Margaret. Shall I go get you a quirt?"

She faltered, the pot dropping to the pillows. "You wouldn't hurt me. You never hurt me before."

"Something which cannot be said of you."

"I won't make love with you, Bram."

He didn't bother to answer. He merely sank into a chair to begin removing his boots.

"Come now, Bram." She said quickly, trying another tack, one that was less than subtle as her voice became silky in its effort at diplomacy. "I haven't seen you in years. If you wanted a marriage all this time, why didn't you try to contact me?"

"I was fighting in a war, remember. I couldn't come and go as I pleased. I couldn't try to track you down and bring you back. However, if you'd stayed here, in America, I could have arranged for leave and we could have worked things out."

"I told you before. I would not participate in your war. I would not stay and subject myself to such atrocities."

"Atrocities, hell. You were never in any real danger. As my wife, you would have lived at Solitude with a caretaker and guards. You would have been relatively safe until I returned to find a home of our own."

He rose and went over to her, forcing Margaret to lean back on her hands. "But you didn't listen when I told you that. You kept harping on and on about your blessed French citizenship. What you never bothered to acknowledge was that you were *married* to me. That fact alone should have fostered some sort of loyalty for those things which were important to me."

"I was only sixteen at the time. I was young, too impulsive, too self-centered."

"Yes, but you were old enough to accept the responsibilities of your actions. Your father, of all people, should have recognized that fact and left you with me." He came nearer and nearer, crowding her. "You were a brazen thing, Margaret. You fascinated me. You bewitched me. You held my heart in your hands and led me around like a bull with a ring through its nose. But I didn't care. I married you all the same. Then, hours after you swore your undying love, you were gone. You will pay for that."

Margaret tried to escape him, but his hands were planted on either side of her. With her back to the headboard, she was effectively trapped.

"I was sixteen," she said again, more weakly this time. "I didn't realize until later how selfish I'd been in running away from you."

"You could have come back to me. You could have written at any time."

"I was told you'd *died!*" Her voice cracked.

"But I didn't."

He captured her chin, forcing her to look at him. "I survived. Over half of my men were killed in all the years I was in command, but I survived. Do you know what kept me alive, what kept me sane?"

She couldn't speak, she couldn't think. He was too hard, too angry.

"It was you," he whispered, but the words were

more of a curse than a compliment. "The day you left, I vowed that I would claim you again. As soon as the war ended, you would be my wife."

His lips were so close, too close, causing her to tremble.

"I vowed that I would have my wedding night, and every other night entitled to me from that moment on."

Chapter

3

"Take off your clothes, Margaret."

His wife was trembling. Bram could see the way her breath caught in little jerks—a phenomenon that wasn't entirely caused by the tight lacing of her gown. Very tight indeed. Enough to make her waist look tiny. Enough to make her bosom press against her neckline so that only the fragile wisp of lace at the edge kept it from springing free altogether.

She was so beautiful.

Bram had forgotten—no, not forgotten, he simply hadn't taken into account the fact that, like a fine painting, the years would make her coloring even richer, her hair darker, her eyes less innocent.

"Come, Margaret. You can't be that averse to my company." One of his knuckles audaciously touched the curve of her breast, stroking the tiny trio of freckles that graced the side. He watched in fascination as a faint tide of pink she'd displayed earlier returned, beginning at that point and moving upward, ever upward to her neck.

"Do I embarrass you?" he asked softly.

"You embarrass yourself." But the retort had lost a good deal of its tartness.

"I believe my behavior has been exemplary considering the circumstances."

"You interrupted my wedding!"

"I had to. Imagine my shock in discovering that my wife was about to commit bigamy."

"You could have approached me privately."

"I wanted the witnesses."

"Witnesses?"

"I wanted everyone in Baltimore to know you were mine. There will be no going back to that man, Margaret."

"I want a divorce," she said stubbornly.

"I won't give it to you."

"You would live with a woman who hates you?"

The finger at her breast became more daring, skirting the edge of her décolletage, then dipping lower to trace the delicate embroidery.

"You do not hate me, Margaret."

"How could you possibly be so wrong?"

One corner of his mouth tipped in a wry grin. She was a feisty one, even in her ruined gown, locked in an unfamiliar hotel room, confronting her long-lost husband.

"You do not hate me, Margaret. Far from it. I sense deep in your eyes a spark of the old passion. At least we'll have that together."

"What you see is disgust."

"Desire."

"Impossible."

"Is it? Then why are you breathing so erratically?" He lay his palm flat over her left breast. "Why does your heart pound against me?"

"Sheer temper."

"Mmm. Perhaps a tiny bit. But hidden beneath your fury is a storm of another sort. Kiss me, little one."

That was what he used to call her. Years ago. He knew she remembered from the way a near-flinch crossed her features. Those delicate, heart-shaped features. He cupped her chin. "Kiss me."

"No."

It was a very weak refusal, and he took advantage of that fact, lowering his head, fractions of distance melting at a time.

"No."

He smiled. She didn't mean it. He knew that from the way she unconsciously clasped his wrist, pulling him closer, not away. Her lips parted and her eyes became hooded, dark, filled with meaning. He'd seen her like this so many times in the heated months of their liaison, but she'd been a girl, not the woman he saw now.

It took all the will he possessed to let her go.

"You're right. I shouldn't kiss you. Not yet. Not until we've had a chance to get to know each other again."

Her expression was a comic mixture of disappointment and disbelief.

"Maybe later. After a bit of supper."

"Supper?"

"You must be hungry."

"If it weren't for you, I would be dining at the Rothchild by now."

He stood. "We could still go, if you'd like."

"No." When he quickly dressed again and began tucking in his shirt, she took his arm. "I can't go back there."

"Why not?"

Her mouth gaped. "The scandal."

He leaned close. "Scandal never used to concern you. You used to relish it."

"Productive scandal, yes. I'm not averse to talk—"

"As long as it's said with a touch of envy, not pity."

She opened her mouth to speak, but when she found no proper reply, he chuckled.

"You haven't changed all that much. You're still a little wicked, still craving attention."

"Not of this sort."

He shrugged. "So sorry, but it couldn't be helped."

"Couldn't be helped?"

Bram ignored her. "I'll just let the desk staff know we'll be needing something to eat, then. I've got an errand to run, so I'll do it on my way."

He knew the minute he turned his back that she would try to escape. "Oh, and, Margaret," he added casually. "Just to make sure you stay . . ."

Moving with the quickness that had aided him well in the past few years, he slapped a pair of manacles on one wrist, fastening the other end of the chain to the

44

foot of the bed. "They're a gift. From my brother Micah."

"Oh!" Her squeal of outrage could have been heard three rooms away.

"I know it's an inconvenience, but you see"—he braced his arms on either side of her hips—"I don't trust you."

Then he kissed her, full on the mouth, passionately, before drawing away. "You still taste good, Margaret. Better than you ever did, in fact."

The door was about to swing shut when there was a whispered curse, a scuffle of shoes, and a spry gentleman slipped into the room.

Hearing the noises, Marguerite prepared herself for another battle, but it wasn't Bram who had returned. Instead, it was the wizened courtly figure of Francois Joliet.

"Francois!"

"Mon dieu! I've been waiting nearly an hour for that ogre to leave," he grumbled, straightening his vest and adjusting the swag of his watch chain. "An old man such as myself should not be reduced to skulking through the shadows like a common thief." He threw out an accusatory finger. "I have been crouched in that damned dusty niche with the horrible statue of . . . heaven only knows what . . . for far too long."

Marguerite jumped from the bed and rushed to embrace him, only to be brought up short by the manacles that bound her.

Joliet's eyes grew wide.

"Sacre bleu! What kind of games does this man play?"

She felt a hot tide seeping to the roots of her hair and hastened to explain, "It's his way of keeping me from escaping."

"Ahhh, so all is less than paradise. Just as I feared when I heard the row from the hall."

"You could hear us out there?"

"Mais oui. Both of you must learn to temper your tones, but," he hastened to add, "that is not why I've come." His gray eyes lost some of their sparkle, becoming grave. "I have a very important matter to discuss with you, and I will hurry. No doubt, after the scene he created in the chapel, your husband will be sending someone else to guard you before he goes anywhere."

When she scowled, he grinned. "What is the matter, *cherie?* Didn't you think dear Aggie would be ready to tell all once she returned from the church?"

"I thought it might take a little longer than this." She glanced at the door, trepidation welling within her. If Bram were to return and find Francois here . . .

"He is gone. For a minute. Now, I must speak to you about Jeffrey before that man has a chance to return."

"Jeffrey. He isn't ill, is he?" A dank terror, one that sometimes felt like her constant companion, tainted her tongue, leaving her weak and trembling.

Francois took her hands and he hastened to reassure her, his skin warm against her icy fingers. "Shh. Jeffrey is fine. I received a letter to that effect this morning. His nurse was satisfied with his health of late. That bout of whooping cough he had has all but disappeared." He paused before adding, "But I fear you have one slight problem."

Her fingers dug unconsciously into his skin. "What's happened?"

"They have left Paris."

"What?" The word was a bare puff of sound.

When she swayed on her feet, he hastened to lead her back to the bed and settle her on the edge.

"Babbette explained in the letter that they were able to obtain passage on a steamer bound for New York. They would have sailed at the end of last week."

Marguerite felt her mouth grow dry.

"When will they arrive?"

Joliet touched her cheek, pushing aside a wisp of hair.

"Too soon for your comfort, I am sure."

She shuddered, and Joliet offered a curt nod.

"I was right to have come to warn you. I told your dear Aunt Aggie I should."

What remained unsaid was that Joliet had wanted to attend the wedding but had abstained for appearances' sake. Marguerite knew there were some who thought it strange that an old man should be obsessed by a woman so much she appeared over and over again in his art. They did not understand that it was not her beauty or her figure that attracted him to paint her time and time again. It was what he termed the "secrecy of her eyes." Marguerite didn't know what that meant, exactly. But she did know that he had never asked her to do anything that she had not felt comfortable doing.

"Surely, you will be glad to see the boy," Joliet prompted, obviously concerned by her reaction.

"Yes. Oh, yes! I've missed him horribly. But I didn't mean to send for him for months yet," she whispered.

"Not with the grand tour Algy had planned for our honeymoon."

He frowned. "Babbette is a bit of a cheeky miss. I've told you that before. She's far too independent at making decisions concerning Master Jeffrey."

"I had thought to . . . work up to telling Algy about him, but now . . . I suppose there's no point."

Joliet's grip tightened. "You mean you hadn't told him about the boy?"

She shook her head.

"Marguerite!" His tone was that of a parent scolding a child. "How could you have done such a thing? Not only for Jeffrey's sake, but your own?"

"I couldn't tell him! He never would have continued with the marriage if he'd known I had a son."

"Well, that's a moot point now, don't you think? The boy's father has come back . . . and . . ." His eyes widened even more. "Don't tell me the St. Charles fellow doesn't know about him, either?"

"No," she admitted reluctantly. "I had only begun to suspect I was pregnant when I married him. My condition was one of the reasons why I refused to stay and watch Bram join his war." She threw her hands up in a gesture of defeat. "After living with my grandfather's and father's stories about the revolutions and wars they'd survived, I wasn't about to bring my own flesh and blood into that same environment." She dropped to her knees in a rustle of skirts, gripping his hands. "Oh, Francois, what am I going to do?"

He opened his mouth, then shrugged in defeat. "I don't know, *ma petite,*" he finally said. "I just do not know."

Evidently, he knew the dilemma she faced. It would

have been different if Jeffrey had been whole and healthy as most young boys.

But how did one explain to a man such as Bram that his heir, his firstborn, was a cripple?

Slipping down the back alley behind the hotel, Bram wound through the narrow collection of streets until he found the Macklebee Drinking Establishment. In the back pew he found the man he'd come to meet.

"Sheffield," he acknowledged, taking a seat on the dark bench. He made no mention of the man's title or his superior status. The Secret Service was a fairly new institution, but discretion was not a new concept.

"You made a bit of a scene in town today."

Bram's lips twitched in a poorly concealed frown. "The news is out, I suppose."

"I wouldn't doubt it if tales of your antics *preceded* you from the church."

"Gossip does have a way of traveling, doesn't it?"

"How's your wife?"

"Defiant."

"I can imagine." Sheffield cupped his hands around his glass. "When I gave you your orders to return to some appearance of normal life, involve your associate Jim Casey in your affairs, and make a show of spending a great deal of money, I said nothing about claiming your wife again. I thought you'd go back to Solitude alone, offering Casey a job." He sipped his whiskey. "Nevertheless, the fact that you're reconciled may help to give credence."

Bram leaned close. "I didn't do this for you, or the damned job; it's a personal matter, pure and simple.

What's mine, I keep. She's got nothing to do with this investigation, and I swear if you involve her in any way—"

"Easy, easy!" Sheffield cautioned. "I didn't mean anything of that sort. I just thought that having her journey with you back to Virginia might help our efforts. Make Casey drop his guard and think you're ready to leave the service for good."

Bram's fist dropped on the table. "I don't give a damn how her presence will or will not affect the next few weeks. I wanted Margaret back. So I took her."

"Of course," Sheffield hurried to add in a placating tone, tapping his finger on the glass. "When will you—and the missus—be heading home to Solitude?"

"Tomorrow."

"Does she know that you are taking Casey and three other men—ex-soldiers—along?"

"No."

"What have you told her?"

"Nothing yet."

Sheffield's tone grew glum. "I must caution you not to confess to her the true nature of your . . . occupation."

Bram shook his head in disbelief. "I'm not a fool, Sheffield. I made it through the war because I knew when to keep my mouth shut. I haven't lost that instinct. I might have played the charade of being a Rebel in order to gather information, but I'm a Yankee through and through."

"Just so long as you remember the precariousness of your situation. The shipment of gold you take with you to Solitude was originally stolen from a Union supply train. One which was guarded by Casey and a contingent of Secret Servicemen. If you hadn't stumbled over it's hiding place during the war, we would never have recovered it, never known Casey was a traitor."

"What makes you so damned sure it *was* Casey who took it in the first place?"

"Come now, Bram. You haven't gone as far as you have in the service by being naive. The shipment was ambushed, and Casey miraculously escaped injury—even as six other guards were killed. It was a planned event, a planned execution, to put it bluntly. The fact that the gold was found before he could retrieve it again—only two miles from your camp—clinches it."

He shook his head, taking another sip of whiskey. "As soon as the trunks are spotted, the traitor will surface to claim them." He pounded the table, reiterating, "And that traitor will be Jim Casey, on that you can rely. He is a spy, a Confederate double agent. He stole that gold and knows someone in our organization found it. All you have to do is let him see that person was you."

Bram scowled, hating this man, hating him for being so sure one of his colleagues had betrayed his ideals. But since he had no proof to the contrary, he would have to follow orders.

Without another word, he stood, but Sheffield caught him on the arm. "Take care."

"Of what? I go home, I settle back into my old life, lay a trap, and attempt to catch a man in the act of treason. A friend. A comrade."

The bitterness he felt must not have escaped Sheffield's notice because he stiffened.

"What has to be done, must be done," he muttered.

Bram didn't bother to respond.

"You have everything you need?" Sheffield asked.

Sheffield knew Bram was uncomfortable with the task ahead, but Bram didn't bother to reassure him.

"Yes."

"Ammunition, food . . ."

"I have everything."

"You've been given an expense account for any needs you might incur in trapping—"

"I don't want anything you have to give me," Bram rasped. Blood money. That was all it was. Thirty pieces of silver to trap a friend. One Bram wasn't even sure was guilty. "I'll handle my end of the job."

"I know. But you may wish to keep an eye out for unexpected complications. Casey may have enlisted some help from the rest of the men under your command, bribing them with thoughts of gold."

"Damn it, Sheffield—"

"Then, there's your wife," he said pointedly, ignoring Bram's outburst. He tossed back the rest of his drink. "Somehow, I don't think she'll prove to be as easily managed as you might believe."

She wasn't.

Bram purposely waited until dawn before returning to the hotel, knowing from experience that Margaret's temper burned on a long fuse. She couldn't go anywhere. Even if she'd managed to extricate herself from the manacles, he'd sent men to watch the door of the suite and both entrances of the hotel. They would have taken their spots within an hour of the order.

But when he entered, the first hint of light brushing the horizon, it was to the report from the soldier he'd stationed down the hall that not a peep had been heard from the room.

Not a peep.

A bad sign.

Taking the key from his vest pocket, Bram opened the door as quietly as he could, hoping that the cause of the silence was Margaret's sleeping.

It was a faint hope. She sat on the tangled covers of the bed, her clothing in disarray, her hair disheveled.

She glowered at him as he came in and unlocked the manacles. "It's about bloody well time you got back here."

He closed the door behind him. "You seem to have picked up a few British mannerisms."

"You told me you'd be right back."

"So I am."

"You told me you'd be bringing something to eat."

He held up the basket he carried. "So I did."

His responses didn't alleviate her temper.

"How dare you?" she accused, so softly, he hardly heard the words. "How dare you treat me this way?"

He set the basket on the nightstand, just out of reach, and shrugged off his greatcoat. Tossing it onto a chair, he prowled toward her, unable to completely dampen the emotions that burned inside him: deep-rooted anger, frustration, betrayal. Lust.

"Be careful how you tread, little one," he said, bracing his hands on the bed and leaning close. She smelled delicious, rumpled. "I am not in the habit of coddling my men. I will not coddle you, either."

Her eyes flashed. "Don't you mean your Rebels? Traitors? Isn't that how you've all been branded now that the war is over?"

His hand snapped out, and he grabbed a fistful of hair, pulling her head back. "Be careful where you tread, Margaret. You've been gone a very long time. There are many things you don't know."

Then he released her, swiftly, before the heat of her skin could convince him to linger.

Standing, he threw the basket on the bed. "Eat." He began to unfasten his shirt. He needed to wash and shave. Then they would be on their way.

Margaret handled the container quite suspiciously. "What is it?"

"You were so concerned about missing the hotel festivities, I managed to finagle some of the leftovers for you." He tugged his shirt free, not unaware of the way her eyes flicked to his chest. Did she see the scars there? Did she have any reaction at all to them? Could she guess they'd been made by deep saber wounds? Yesterday, she hadn't even blinked when he'd bared them to her.

"Leftovers?" she echoed faintly.

"From your wedding luncheon. Even though the bride disappeared, the groom's sisters—ever the model batch of hostesses—insisted that the out-of-town guests be fed. The hotel staff enjoyed the rest. I just returned from there. I even managed to persuade one of the serving girls to pack up a bit for the erstwhile bride. She was more than willing to do so. Probably relished talking to the staff about how you'd sent someone by for a sample of the food."

A slow fire ignited in her eyes. When her hand closed around one of the linen-wrapped parcels, he warned, "I wouldn't throw that if I were you. If you

54

do, it may be the last meal you have in a very long time."

She became docile again, but Bram knew it was probably not so much because of his warning, but because of her hunger. One by one she unwrapped the plates to expose smoked meats, breads, pastries, and finally a wedge of wedding cake. When she saw that, he heard a surreptitious sniff.

"What are you going to do to me?" The query was somewhat weak, and Bram felt an unwilling tug of sympathy.

"I'm going to take you home."

"Home?"

"To Solitude."

She frowned in confusion. "But I was told by my own father that *your* father died. Isn't it your brother's place?"

"Not anymore."

She stared at him aghast. "Micah isn't . . . dead, is he?"

Bram shook his head. "He's living in Ohio."

"Ohio?" She said the word in the same manner she might ask if he'd relocated on the moon.

Bram swung a chair around and straddled it. Once again her gaze returned to his body, following each movement, the food apparently forgotten in her lap.

Jerking her attention back into line. "What could possibly have captured Micah's interest in Ohio, of all places?"

He rested his arms on the ladder-back of the chair. "A woman. He remarried."

Her brow creased. "But he and Lili . . ."

"Were in love," he finished. "Unfortunately, Lili died soon after you left."

"Oh." It was a bare puff of sound.

"It was very hard on him."

"I can imagine."

"Then when he was hunted during the war—"

"Hunted!"

"As I said, Margaret. You've no idea what happened to us these past few years. You were insulated from the truth. You ran to safety where your only contact with reality was a set of newspaper headlines and gossip."

"I think I can imagine—"

"No," he interrupted harshly. "You can never imagine what war was like. Not without living through it. But you were too much of a coward to stay with the rest of us, weren't you?"

He stood abruptly. "Eat, tidy your hair. We're leaving in twenty minutes."

"Twenty minutes? But I can't. My family . . ."

"I'll send word where you've gone."

"No." She jumped to her feet, causing the food to scatter across the bedclothes. "They depend on me. I can't just leave them here without means."

"Your father may not have been overly wealthy when he died, but he must have had a pension of some sort to provide for them."

"My father died a pauper. All of his moneys were claimed by creditors."

"I could tell you I'm sorry," Bram said. "But it would be a lie."

"What about my aunt, my uncle, Nanny Edna?" she asked when he didn't speak for some time. "They have no one to take care of them but me."

"Is that why you prostituted yourself with that artist?"

"I never! Francois Joliet has always treated me with the highest respect."

"Those paintings are indecent."

The fact that he had seen them caused her to pause in her tirade, and he was sorry he'd ever brought up the subject. It wouldn't do for her to know how much he'd hated that his wife had posed for such . . . intimate portrayals.

"There is nothing wrong with his art. Why do you speak about it as if I'd bared my backside and lain on a couch?"

He grabbed her wrist, pulling her close so that she would not mistake his warning. "You may as well have done so. To reveal so much about yourself to anyone other than your family is despicable."

She wrenched free. "It was *for* my family that I did it. It was the only way to pay for food, clothing, and a place to stay."

His eyes narrowed. "You fell so short of the mark, didn't you, Margaret?"

"What do you mean?" she asked suspiciously.

"Yesterday you meant to marry into wealth, to live a life free from care. But I interrupted your plans, forcing you to return to a world where money is hard earned and carefully saved, not frittered away on silly whims of fashion."

He must have hit a nerve because she began to tremble. A curious expression slid over her features, one that was far more disturbing than any he'd seen in Joliet's masterpieces. It was as if he'd physically slapped her.

"What about my family?" she whispered.

She was so still, so pale, so tiny. Bram didn't have the heart to push her any farther. Taking a deep breath, he released her arm.

"Tell me where they are, and I'll see to it that they have the means to live here in Baltimore for a while." He eyed her sternly. "But only if you behave."

Chapter

4

"Wilkins!"

After leaving his wife's room and the hotel Bram strode into the sunshine, barking at one of his men to come forward. He handed him a slip of paper. "There's a wagon loaded and waiting at the livery. I need you to retrieve it for me."

"Yes, sir!" The young man tugged a battered hat over a thatch of sandy-colored hair and hurried to obey. Swinging onto a dappled mare, he galloped down the street, heading for the opposite end of town where Marshall's Livery was located.

Bram watched him go with narrowed eyes, feeling a curl of unease settling deep in his stomach.

If he was going to stop Sheffield's schemes, they would have to be stopped now, before Wilkins returned, before he came back with a wagon full of Union gold. Otherwise, nothing could ever be the same again. Bram would have to watch each man with suspicion and try to determine if Casey—or any of the other men—showed an above-average interest in his belongings.

Especially the trunks that had been re-marked in such a way to unsuccessfully cover the Union identification stencils, thereby providing the first bit of bait for the trap.

"Where's Wilkins going?"

Bram had to will himself not to stiffen when Jim Casey approached, stopping just a little behind him so Bram couldn't see his face in his peripheral view. Not that he needed a reminder of what the man looked like. After all the years together, all the campaigns, Bram could have closed his eyes and summoned Jim's lanky, curly-headed frame more easily than that of his own father. It had taken time for Bram to work his way into a position of command in the Confederate Army. Once there, he'd arranged for his men to be given "scouting" assignments and had liberally laced the squad with Secret Servicemen. Those that remained with him now had been some of his best officers.

"I sent him after a wagon of supplies."

"Supplies?"

It was a casually uttered question. Bram couldn't tell if there was more than a curious intent behind it.

"Some things my wife will need."

Casey shrugged as if it were no concern to him.

"We could make the trip to Solitude in a day, you know."

Bram shook his head. "By horseback, yes, but the roads are in horrible condition and Sheffield has requested we stay away from the trains to keep from advertising our move during this last mission for him. We'll be lucky if we can make it in two days with a wagon—especially one loaded as heavily as ours will be."

The bait was subtle and slipped easily into the conversation, but Casey made no sign of having even caught the significance of what he was being told—that a woman who'd been kidnapped from a church with little more than the clothes on her back would now be taking a wagon loaded with trunks.

Sheffield is wrong, Bram told himself for the hundredth time. This show of lukewarm interest wasn't the action of a traitor. He wasn't uneasy, or suspicious, or upset.

"Let the hotel proprietor know we'll be leaving in the next half hour," he ordered.

Casey offered him a jaunty salute. "Yes, sir."

Bram watched him disappear into the hotel and make his way up the inner staircase scarred by spurs and sabers and soldier's boots.

Sheffield had to be wrong, he told himself again. But try as he might, the seed of suspicion his superior had planted could not be quelled so easily.

A hot October sun streamed through the window over the landing as Marguerite was escorted from the hotel room. She would have groaned if the action would not have been so telling. In her opinion the

Indian summer they'd been experiencing was lingering far too long—especially if she was going to be forced to travel in it. She could only pray that Bram had arranged for a carriage of some sort. A *covered* carriage. One that would not allow her to be seen by any gawkers who might want to catch a glimpse of the famed M. M. DuBois being taken away in shame.

Damn, Bram St. Charles. She would never forgive him for what he'd done to her, how he'd ruined her carefully made plans for the future.

"This way, my dear."

She could have ground her teeth at his falsely solicitous tone as Bram led the way, his hand gripped firmly around her elbow while two other fellows—also in faded Confederate uniforms—brought up the rear.

"Who are we traveling with?" she asked, indicating her guards, but he purposely chose to misunderstand her.

"No one. I've seen to your aunt and uncle as well as to your dear Nanny Edna. They'll be taken care of until I give you permission to send for them."

At that tidbit of information, she came to an abrupt halt, causing him to tug on her arm and the men behind her to rest their palms on the butt of their weapons.

"Permission? *Permission!* No! I'm not going anywhere without my relatives. They can't stay here, with the talk, the innuendo." Her toe tapped impatiently on the floor. "You'll send for them now and bring them with us. It will grow unbearable for them here."

"You should have thought about that earlier when you asked me to make arrangements."

She glanced at the guards—a gaunt man of about forty with curly dun-colored hair and a short bandy soldier of about fifty. It pained her that Bram was intent on forcing her to air their dirty linen in public.

"I didn't realize that you intended to storm St. Jude's, now did I?" she hissed as softly as she could.

"You should have known I would come for you."

She stamped her foot in frustration. "I thought you were *dead!* I told you that. Now you must send for my family. I won't go anywhere until you have."

"You will, and you are."

She mulishly dug her heels into the carpeted runner. "No."

He swiveled to face her, bending so that they were eye to eye. "You will. Either by force or under your own power. I don't care which."

"I'll scream," she threatened, but he didn't appear the least bit cowed.

"Go right ahead. Anyone bothered by the action will take one look at you in that wedding gown, realize who you are, and turn the other way. After all, a husband's rights are absolute in this country."

"How incredibly boorish."

"I don't really care."

"I thought that your beloved United States was based on a creed of freedom. Isn't that why you stayed to fight the war?" She offered a small mocking sigh. "Oh, but forgive me. I forgot. You swore you would defend the *Union* to the death, but it was the South you fought for."

Marguerite felt a small thrill of pleasure when her remark caused him to glance about for fear they'd been overheard.

"What changed your ideals so quickly, hmm?" she pressed.

"Enough!" His voice was tight. "You're coming now. With me."

"As I recall, sometime during your precious war, Lincoln released the slaves," she retorted as he tugged her down the hall.

Bram halted again, pulling her close so that she could not mistake his anger. "Yes, Margaret. He freed the slaves. But he didn't free *you*. Until I see your own personal emancipation proclamation signed by President Johnson himself, you'll just have to follow my orders."

"Never."

He pinched her chin, forcing her to look at him. Marguerite realized she may have baited him once too often.

"I don't think that you've absorbed the seriousness of your predicament, Margaret."

"Oh?"

"You keep claiming that you're overly concerned about your aunt and uncle and Nanny Edna, but you haven't quite grasped the fact that they *will not* be coming with us today—and the class of lodgings I provide for them in the meantime depends on your manners and your compliance to my wishes!"

He had her cornered with that remark—if he only knew how much. Despite the airless heat of the hallway, Marguerite felt a chill enter her bones at the threat. Her family was everything to her. Everything.

Bram must have sensed her acquiescence, because he inquired, "Are you feeling more docile?"

He made her sound like a milk cow.

"Yes," she ground out between clenched teeth.

"How about a little smile?"

"Oh, really," she snapped in irritation.

"A smile, Margaret," he said firmly.

She offered him a grimace. It was as much as she was willing to give.

"We'll work on that in the future."

Marguerite would have been more than happy to have kicked him right in the shins, but she didn't. Instead, she yanked free and flounced ahead of him down the stairs, her chin tilted defiantly, her shoulders squared.

Despite her show of bravado, she trembled in delayed reaction. Irritated with her own display of weakness, she pushed the sensation away with a righteous sense of pique.

The whole situation was absolutely humiliating. And the only person responsible was Bram. He'd refused to show any sort of chivalry, any sort of gentility, any sort of softness. He was determined to punish her for the crimes that he thought she'd committed, and Marguerite didn't know how to stop him.

Marguerite had spent most of the night fuming and plotting and planning, hoping to come up with some sort of solution that would allow her to walk away from this man and all he intended to do to her.

All her time had afforded her was a monstrous headache and the realization that there was no way out. Bram had seen to that. By confronting her in the midst of her wedding to another man, he had effectively sealed her social doom. She was now rich food for gossip, good prey for jokes and crass remarks. All because her husband, the husband she had thought dead and lost forever, had shown the unmitigated gall to be alive. If she left him now, after he had made such an effort to claim her, it would be Marguerite who would be branded the heartless one.

"I know what you're thinking," Bram murmured, snagging her waist so she had to walk abreast of him.

"You couldn't possibly."

"You're wondering how you got into this mess."

"I know how I got into this mess. You put me here."

"Ah, but I was only trying to prevent you from making a horrible mistake."

"Only from *your* point of view could it be considered a mistake."

"I think the law might disagree."

"The law would have forgiven my marrying Algy. After all, I had official documentation to prove you were dead—documents given to me by the American Embassy in Paris."

"A clerical error, I'm sure."

"A miscalculation on the part of the Union Army, if you ask me. Someone should have shot you long ago."

"That's not very gracious of you."

She stopped in her tracks. "No. No, it's not." She gestured to her ruined gown, "But I think I have just cause for *my* attitude. My wedding was to be the event of the season. Now, the whole affair has become nothing more than a farce. I have been kidnapped, manhandled, starved, and verbally abused."

He appeared truly offended by that remark. "I brought you something to eat!"

Her hands balled into fists. "I did not fit into this gown by having the most filling of meals the past few months. I haven't had anything but bread, vinegar, and water in weeks. I need proper food and regular meals now that my wedding is over."

"Vinegar?"

"A . . . dieting aid."

He made a face. "How revolting. But you really can't complain about my treatment. I fed you this morning."

"With the leftovers of my wedding feast."

"I thought you would appreciate the thought behind it all."

"I did not. And I do not appreciate what you're doing to me now, taking me heaven knows where, separating me from my family and my dear Nanny Edna."

He sighed with impatience. "Don't you think you're a little old for a nanny?"

"She isn't here for me; I am here for her."

"And so you shall be, once you've settled into our home at Solitude."

"Solitude! In Virginia?"

"Yes. In the meantime I would be more than happy to get you another meal if that will improve your disposition."

"It will not. The only improvement would be if you left me here—alone—and did not bother to return."

"I can't do that."

"Why?" She was suddenly fervent. "*Why* can't you just leave me to lead my own life as I wish to?"

He bent over her, so very near, his body honed to a whipcord leanness that she had never remembered. . . . It was somehow disturbing, intimidating.

"Because I have been through hell, Margaret, literally and physically, and I'm bound and determined to start living my life the way it was supposed to be. With a beautiful wife and a brood of handsome children." With that parting remark, he pulled her down the hall to the front door . . .

Never knowing how his words had shattered her to the very core.

Chapter

5

❦

Children.

Handsome children.

Marguerite huddled in the corner of the carriage, her eyes closed, feigning sleep. For hours she had remained motionless, barely daring to breathe, hoping against hope that Bram wouldn't speak to her, wouldn't look too closely. She could only pray that when the phrase had burst from his lips, she hadn't disgraced herself with some sort of visual reaction.

She would not have it.

She would not let him pity her.

At sixteen, Marguerite had been such a fool. Such a pretty little fool—and she would be the first to admit it after all she had experienced since. When her father had invited her to accompany him on a business trip to America to investigate breeding stock for the French garrisons from Adam St. Charles, she'd been so excited. She was going to see her dear mother's homeland. She was going to visit exciting new places and meet terribly handsome young men.

So she had. Within minutes of arriving at Solitude, she had been introduced to Adam St. Charles's three sons. Micah, the eldest, was so big, so quiet, so obviously in love with his bride, Lili. Jackson, the youngest, so brash, so vibrant, so impulsive. And then the middle son. Abraham Lexington St. Charles.

Bram.

Even years later, she could remember the way the breath had been stolen from her body the first time she'd set eyes on him. He'd been tall and lean with coffee-colored hair and a smile that melted her bones. Whenever he walked into a room, she went hot, then cold. He possessed every thought she had, every dream—and despite what he might think were her reasons for her marrying him, it had been out of love and love alone on her part, not money. Never money. Until the fear she'd felt about a war erupting around her had overshadowed even that emotion, until she discovered she carried his child.

Soon, it had become as natural as breathing to let him kiss her, touch her in places where no man had ever dared. In hindsight, she supposed the emotions between them were far too fiery, overcoming them both before they took the time to think. When he'd kissed her, she should have demurred. When he'd touched her breasts, she should have been shocked.

When he'd laid her down on the bench of the gazebo and made love to her, she should have run. But she'd stayed. She'd stayed and conceived their son.

Oh, heaven above, how it still hurt so much to think of all that boy had suffered with his ill health and crippled body. Little Jeffrey. Tiny. Sweet. So innocent of the sacrifices she had been forced to make on his behalf. She'd known she was pregnant before she and Bram had married. It had been the reason she'd pressured him into eloping before her father's scheduled departure. But after the ceremony when Bram had gone on and on about his intentions to fight, to join the Union forces, to help end the war—to die if necessary . . .

She hadn't had the strength to stay. As much as she had loved Bram, she refused to consider giving birth to a baby in the midst of such turmoil.

So she had returned to France and kept her son.

And relinquished her husband.

"Margaret?"

Marguerite jumped, her eyes flying open to confront the very man she had been thinking of. No. Not the same man. This Bram was older, hardened. Unforgiving.

"What?" It was a bare puff of sound.

"We're going to have to stop here."

"Here?"

He was leaning back in his seat. She realized she'd been so deep in thought, she hadn't even known they'd drawn to a halt.

"Jim Casey thinks we've got a problem with the axle."

"Jim Casey?"

He pointed to the lanky man who'd followed her down the hotel hallway.

"We're only an hour by horseback from Kalesboro, and another quarter hour from Solitude, but we'll have to stop here at this inn. It will be another day's journey by wagon."

She leaned forward enough to see around the edge of the window, but what she found was far from reassuring.

The sign that hung from the portico did proclaim the building to be an inn, but other than that, such evidence was scarce. A barren yard had been rutted with wagon traffic and pockmarked with hoofprints left by some long-ago rain. What plants and shrubbery that had once lined the stone foundation were gone, nipped down to the roots by the goat that was tied to the railing. The building itself was beginning to peel in spots, especially the shutters and window frames, and one entire wing had been obliterated by what must have been cannon fire."

"You want to stay here?" she murmured.

"It's the most comfortable place unless we go on to Kalesboro."

"I see," she said weakly.

"You'll be fine here, Margaret. We'll have supper and rest for the evening. In the meantime I'll have the wagon checked and repaired if necessary so we can rise early to finish the last leg of the journey to Solitude. I would like to get there as soon as possible."

You'll be fine here.

Fine?

Was he mad? She had lived in some humble surroundings in her life, but never anywhere that looked as if a good gust of wind would topple it completely.

She watched him for some sign that he was teasing her, but found none.

How many times, in the dark of her room, had she tried to wipe the image of that face from her mind? Jeffrey had inherited those eyes. Those striking, penetrating, hazel-colored eyes, and it made her miss her little boy all the more. He would be here within a month—two weeks if all went well. But if this hotel was anything to go by, each mile they journeyed south took them a little deeper into disaster.

"Margaret!" Bram said impatiently, stepping from the carriage and extending his hand. "Let's go."

Reluctantly, she complied. She had no choice. Until she could find a way out of this situation, she would have to concede to his wishes. At least on the surface. Then she would have to leave him. If she didn't, she would never be able to survive the emotional pain involved—Jeffrey would never be able to endure the strain of such a home life. The thought of spending year after year with him, remembering what might have been would be unthinkable. Especially since Bram could have prevented it all by coming with her to France, by abandoning his war games.

She ducked from the carriage, becoming conscious of the curious glances she received from passersby. Belatedly, she remembered how she must appear to them with her bedraggled hair, her torn gown, and rumpled ivory trousers.

Bram didn't notice the attention they garnered. He slipped an arm around her waist as if he were escorting her to a Sunday social. Leading her inside, he made arrangements for a room. One room.

Marguerite wanted to argue, but she held her

tongue, refusing to fight with him about the arrangements. Not here. Not until they were alone.

"Will you also arrange for a bath to be brought up for my wife?"

At the last instruction, she blinked in surprise. A bath. How considerate. She wouldn't have thought that Bram could be so kind. Marguerite frowned. Not that it changed her opinion of him, of his selfishness in bringing her here this way, in his bullheaded stubbornness. It simply was an unexpected surprise.

"Wilkins, Casey, get a room on the same floor for you and the others. Erickson, James, I want you to unload the supply wagon and check those rims as well. You can put the contents in the room connecting to my own. Then you'll need to take turns guarding the outer door. We can't have anyone stealing my wife's pretties."

Pretties? What pretties?

When Marguerite opened her mouth to deny that she had any "pretties," Bram's fingers dug in her arm and he dragged her away.

"Ow! I only wondered—"

"Hush, Margaret. Not now."

Her limbs were stiff from the long, bouncing ride in the carriage as she followed Bram up the stairs and down the dim hallway. She wondered how it was possible that in the space of twenty-four hours she could feel so weary. So old.

Bram stopped at the last room, inserting the brass key.

"Not the Bridal Suite, I'm afraid," he remarked as he opened the door and looked inside.

Marguerite ignored the comment and reluctantly

followed. To her infinite relief, the chamber they'd been given was clean, if a bit spartan, with white-washed walls, an armoire, a bureau, a changing screen, and one bed.

One bed.

Only one.

She felt her fingers curling toward her palms, her whole body growing tense. Was this where Bram intended to see that his "wedding night" was consummated? In *this* hotel room? Tonight?

"There's been a mistake."

The door closed, and she stared at Bram. The harsh evening sunlight streamed through the window, underscoring the chiseled angles of his face. He looked so hard. So embittered. As if the battles he'd fought had engraved themselves into his very soul.

"No, Margaret," he said firmly. "There is *no* mistake. Tonight, you and I will sleep together."

She kept her jaw firmly closed, refusing to be drawn into an argument. However, she was determined that before the evening was through, he would change his mind. She couldn't make love to him. Not now. Not like this. It would open up all the gates to the past, all the little memories she had locked away.

There was a soft tap on the door, and Bram opened it to reveal a pair of men holding a tub. They were followed by a half dozen of the inn's staff members carrying steaming pails of water. In minutes her bath had been readied and the servants had withdrawn.

Immediately, Marguerite became aware of the close quarters. And more. Who she was—a woman—and just what this man intended to be.

Her husband.

He stood a few scant yards away, the only real obstacle between Marguerite and the door. She knew that she should make some effort to escape. He hadn't reattached the manacles since they'd left Baltimore. She must try something.

Her muscles began to tense. Time stretched into eternity as she calculated the distance to the door, the placement of the key.

But then she made the mistake of looking at Bram once again. Her heart began to pound, her mouth grew dry. For so many years she had thought him dead. She'd hated him for that, for dying, for the ultimate symbol of a relationship that could never be salvaged. Until that time she'd felt a sliver of control, knowing that—if she chose—she could confront him again, demand his respect, demand his empathy. But when she'd received word of his death, she'd been faced with the awful fact that the past could not be repaired.

"You would not be able to go far enough, Margaret," Bram murmured, as if he could read her very thoughts.

She willed herself to run whether it be to the door, the window—anything to get away.

"You will stay with me."

A sob caught in her throat as she recognized the truth she had tried to deny. It didn't matter what he thought she'd done to him. It didn't matter that she had reasons of her own for returning to France. Bram would not let her go. Not now. Not ever.

"At last we are beginning to understand each other," he said, confirming that he'd guessed the nature of her impressions. It was a disturbing sensation. As if she lay as naked to him emotionally as he was determined she would soon be physically.

"Come, Margaret. The water will grow cold."

"Marguerite. My name is Marguerite."

"I have never liked that name."

"Nevertheless, it is the one with which I was christened."

He didn't reply, but she refused to give in. He must know from the beginning that she would not cow to him. She would not simper and preen and build her world around his wishes. He might keep her by his side, he might trap her into his bed. But never again would he be given the ability to hurt her so completely. She had a right to her own identity.

He didn't relent, not by so much as a flicker of his eyelids.

"Let me go." The words dragged from her very soul, fearing that if he made her stay with him, she would be lost forever. He would drain every ounce of strength from her, every ounce of individuality that she had created in his absence. He would mold her into whatever he wanted her to be. She would not have the will to prevent him. He was so strong and intense, one look and she became putty in his hands.

He moved toward her, his gait slow and deliberate. He had probably made a wonderful soldier. She was sure that he could have walked just as stealthily behind enemy lines had the need ever arose. He had the grace of a jungle cat. Like the black panther she'd once seen in a Parisian menagerie.

"Do not fight me, little one."

She nearly shuddered beneath the onslaught of the familiar endearment. The images came swift and strong. Solitude. The emerald hills dotted with Thoroughbreds. The stately brick house. The gardens. The gazebo. He'd taken her virginity there—or rather she had given it to him, willingly. He had only to touch her to make her forget who she was, what she'd been taught, what was right and what was wrong.

He stroked her cheek, and she started. This was no dream. This was real. He was real.

Although she damned the sensation, a tingling began at that tiny point of contact, spreading down, ever down, until it pooled in a tight ball of need deep in her loins.

"Shall I call you Marguerite? Hmm?"

She couldn't answer. Had she known how her own name sounded on his lips, she never would have demanded such a thing. That lazy Virginian drawl added a lilt to it, an intimacy, that should have been positively indecent.

His fingers splayed wide, plunging into her hair, dislodging what few pins remained and causing the tresses to fall around her shoulders.

"Do you know, there were nights when I thought of you like this? Not as you were, not as a girl, but as a woman, your clothing disheveled, your lips moist and parted."

"No."

"Yes, I thought of you. Night and day. First with anger, then hate." His grip tightened against her skull, becoming almost cruel. "Then, I began to imagine what you could be, what you would be, when the war was over. When you were mine."

He gave her no warning, pulling her close with the hand that had slipped to her nape. His head tilted and his lips covered her own, hungrily, passionately. Angrily.

She tried to fight him, pushing against his chest, but it took only a wisp of time for her to fall into his spell—just as she had so many times in the past.

His arms wrapped around her, pulling her close to him, reacquainting her with every inch of the body that she had vowed to forget. He was harder than he had been, leaner. She sensed a checked violence in him and a strength of will that was more than capable of carrying out that threat. It frightened her, more than she would have liked to admit, even as she found it all inexplicably exciting.

He shifted, drawing her closer, taking her weight so that she had to grip huge clumps of his jacket to maintain her balance. His tongue moved insistently against her mouth, bidding entrance, forcing her to obey. Then he was lifting her into his arms.

The firestorm inside her blocked all conscious thought except that of getting nearer, nearer. Her own mouth became greedy, accepting his challenge and returning it. It had been so long since she had been allowed to be a woman, to feel this way.

She had no concept of where he was taking her until the backs of her knees touched the edge of the bed. Dear heaven above! What was she doing? This was the man she had sworn to hate, the man who had abandoned her for the glory of war. A man who had felt no compunction about ruining her plans for the rest of her life. She'd been right to leave him so long ago.

Marguerite began to struggle, wedging her hands between them. But he was stronger than she, in more ways than one. She knew by the fire in his eyes that he had set a goal for himself. He would bed her tonight.

"Decide," he rasped between clenched teeth. "Now or later. But you will be mine."

She was tempted to surrender. As he had said, he would have her, one way or the other.

But not yet. Sweet heaven, not yet.

He must have read the answer in her eyes because he let her go, bit by bit. Her overskirts and trousers rubbed against the bedcovers, her toes touching the ground as he allowed her to stand on her own.

"Are you such a coward?"

"Yes."

Her honesty seemed to please him in some small way.

"Turn around."

She could not completely control her trembling. Bram had changed from the boy she had known. She couldn't read him as easily as she once could, but she obeyed him nonetheless. He had granted her a small reprieve. She would not endanger that condition.

Bit by bit, she turned, the motion difficult in the cramped space he had allowed her between him and the bedstead. She felt him bend, touch his lips to her shoulder. Then, the faint *ching* of metal against leather caused her to shiver in warning. In the corner of her eye, she saw him take a knife from his boot.

Did he mean to kill her? Here? Now? For the crimes she had supposedly committed?

Her heart pounded so hard against her chest, she was sure that he could see it. But if he did, he made no comment. The tip of the knife touched her, low at her back, so sharp it momentarily pricked her even through the layers of clothing she wore. Then, without warning, it slid up her spine, slitting her laces and causing her dress to gape even as her undergarments were left intact. Issuing a startled squeal, she clasped the bodice to her breasts when it would have fallen to the floor.

Bram stepped away, leaving her room to breathe. "Go take your bath, Marguerite."

Marguerite. Not Margaret.

Unsure of how she should proceed, she didn't move. Bram gave her a second, then nudged her in the direction of the tub.

"Go."

She stumbled forward, stopping only when she reached the side of the tin basin. There she stood, waiting for the sound of his footsteps to retreat to the door. The noise never came.

Turning, she eyed him questioningly. He must have read her silent query—she was sure that he had, but he didn't bother to allay her fears. Instead, he shrugged from his vest, laying it over the foot of the bed. Then he reached for the buttons to his shirt.

Her mouth grew dry as, inch by inch, his flesh was exposed to her gaze. Firm masculine flesh dusted with a hint of black hair and crisscrossed with scars of varying degrees of pink and white.

"Dear God." It was a betraying cry, one that revealed her disquiet, the first uttered proof that she'd even noticed them.

Bram looked at her with dark eyes, expressive eyes, before demanding, "Did you think that I would escape the war unscathed?"

She stiffened, sensing that she had lost her resistance somewhere along the line, her will to ignore the evidence of such scars. The instant he'd kissed her.

The second he'd allowed her to choose at least one element of her own fate.

He turned more fully into the light, causing the sun to reveal the old wounds with even more garish thoroughness. "Well, Marguerite? Did you ever wonder what had happened to me? Did you ever consider that I would return to you with the marks of saber wounds on my back?"

"I was informed you were dead, if you will recall."

It was obvious by his frown that he *had* forgotten. "Did you cry when you heard the news?"

Marguerite didn't answer. She couldn't. How could she possibly explain the emotions she'd felt that day. The bitter pain, the betrayal, and the infinite relief that he would never know what secrets she'd kept. He would never know that she'd borne a son. It was better that way. So much better.

"I think you should leave now," she said with as much dignity as she could muster.

"No. I want an answer."

"You will not have one. I intend to take the bath you so graciously offered."

"Fine." He sat on the bed, reclining in the midst of the feather tick.

"Don't you think you should leave?"

He shook his head. "I'm your husband."

"I wish to bathe in private."

"Your wishes are not my concern." His eyes grew even darker, more piercing. "Remove your clothing, Marguerite, and take your bath."

She opened her mouth to rebel, but wisely refrained. She could tell by the set line of his jaw and the tense stance of his body that he would like nothing better than an argument. It would give him the excuse he needed to strip the rest of the clothing from her body, and drop her into the water. But she wouldn't give him the satisfaction.

Her hands fell to her sides, and the dress slithered to the ground in a rustle of silk and satin and lace. His knife had not cut through all the layers. Except for the prick of the blade against her waist, he had severed nothing more than the dress itself.

She stood motionless, trying to breathe, to remain calm as his gaze raked from her bared shoulders to the mounds of her breasts pushing against the sheer fabric, to the fitted hips of her trousers.

After she was sure that she could move without revealing the shakiness that had invaded her body to the core, she unfastened the tiny shell buttons of her corset cover and shrugged from the garment. Next, she unhooked the trousers and stepped free. When she straightened, she wore only a pair of gossamer drawers, a camisole, and the grosgrain corset.

"You've changed," Bram murmured, more to himself than to her.

She didn't answer, praying that he wouldn't guess the changes to her body had occurred due to childbirth. She was unhooking the busk of her corset. The binder dropped to the ground, leaving the wrinkled silk of her camisole exposed to his gaze. Since the garment was fastened at her waist and above her breasts with two narrow ribbons, Bram's attention zeroed in on the flesh the gaping fabric revealed.

He sat up, but she stopped him when he would have crossed the room.

"No." Her command was soft, but implacable.

Tugging at the ribbon at her neck, she slid it free. Then the one at her waist, and last of all, the tie of her drawers. The silk fell from her body without a whisper of sound, leaving her completely naked to her husband's gaze.

His inspection was hot, intent, as tangible as a caress. "You are so beautiful. More beautiful than I ever imagined."

She remained motionless, refusing to cower beneath his regard. Then, at long last, she said, "Just remember, Bram. You were the one who forced me to abandon our marriage and return to France. I begged you to come with me."

"At what cost? That of my honor?"

"How much honor can be found in fighting for a cause for which you had no convictions? At least I remained true to what I thought was right. I didn't secede from my own code of values as you did, Bram."

Without another word, she turned and slipped into the water, feeling the sting of its heat against sore muscles. But even as the warmth began to seep into her body, nothing reached the cold center of her heart. That tiny core of want which had been there since Bram had chosen his love of war over his love for her.

For long, tension-fraught minutes, there was no sound at all. She wondered what Bram was thinking, what he was feeling, but she refused to face him again.

The silence of the room grew, intensified, nearly pummeling her with its strength. Then she heard a muffled curse, the stamp of Bram's boots, and the slam of the door.

Marguerite's eyes closed and she drew her knees up, resting her head against them.

He'd gone.

But for how long?

How long until he returned to claim the retribution he'd been imagining for five interminable years?

Chapter
6

"What are you going to do with her, Bram?"

When the voice came from behind him, Bram quelled the instinctive reaction he'd had to reach for the knife hidden in his boot. He'd been leaning against the landing rail, staring down, clenching his jaw to keep from shouting in frustration. Casey's simple question made him realize that he'd grown tense enough to shatter in the company of his own thoughts.

"Well?" Casey prompted.

"I'm going to restore her to her place as mistress of my home," Bram said to the man who was the closest thing he'd had to a friend in years. Tall and lean—to the point of gauntness—Jim Casey had been his second-in-command, following him through more campaigns than either one of them would care to count. But none of those missions had been as vital to Bram as the one that he'd undertaken alone at St. Jude's. Stealing his bride back from another man.

"Does she know that there isn't much of your home left?"

Bram's hands tightened into fists. He'd been back to Solitude only once since the war's end—when he'd been trying to find Micah. He'd all but stumbled over the rubble and ruin that had once been his home. His pain and fury had been so great, only one man had been able to persuade him to move on.

Jim Casey.

He'd understood.

He'd been his savior that day, keeping him from riding off, guns drawn, ready to shoot anyone he could pin to the crime.

Damn it. It didn't matter that Sheffield thought Jim Casey had turned traitor. Bram didn't believe it. He wouldn't believe it. And he would prove Sheffield wrong.

"She doesn't appear overjoyed to see you," Jim commented.

"I suppose."

"Does that surprise you?" Casey propped one hip against the stairwell railing, which Bram had been gripping as if it were Margaret's throat. No, not Margaret. Marguerite.

"She's my wife," he insisted for what seemed the hundredth time.

"She's just a girl, if you ask me," Jim remarked.

Bram eyed Casey with patent disbelief. "Then you obviously haven't taken a good look at her."

The man chuckled. "As if I would. You'd slit my gullet if I stared at her too long or too hard."

Bram's gaze narrowed.

"Be honest, boy," Jim said softly. "You feel a lot more for that gal than hate."

"She abandoned me."

"Yes, she did. And your head will remind you of that time and time again." He grinned. "But I'm sure another part of your anatomy isn't thinking so far into the past." He grinned. "Now, why did you send for me?"

Business. It never failed to intrude.

"I need you to watch her for a few hours."

Casey frowned. "I thought you just told the boys to go ahead and turn in for the night."

"I did. But I've got some personal business to tend to—some extra supplies to gather—and I need someone to watch Marguerite, and I'd like to spell the other boys from their guard duty on the adjoining room with its trunks."

"Personal—"

"Will you do it? Or should I ask James?"

"No, no. I'll do it."

"Fine."

Bram was halfway down the stairs when Casey spoke again. "There isn't anything wrong, is there?"

He shook his head, glancing up at the landing above him. "Not at all. What could possibly be wrong?"

But even as the words were spoken, he thought he saw a trace of disquiet deep in Casey's gray eyes.

Marguerite waited an hour before stealthily opening the door to the hotel room and peering out.

"Evening, ma'am."

Her hand flew to her breast, and she swiveled to find one of Bram's tall, rangy companions leaning his chair back against the wall, watching her beneath the brim of a hat drawn low over his brow. A pile of shavings lay at his feet, a knife and a block of wood held loosely in his hand. If not for the greeting, she might have mistakenly assumed he was dozing.

She gripped the too-large shirt she'd stolen from Bram's saddlebags and tucked into the waist of her trousers. She knew she must look a ridiculous sight with her half-dried hair and odd combination of clothing, but she kept her head at a proud angle, nonetheless.

"So, you've been given the task of guarding me while my husband is away, hmm?"

He grinned at her forthright challenge and nudged his hat into its proper position with a careless prod of his thumb.

"Yes, ma'am."

"You're Casey?"

If he minded the lack of proper formalities, he made no sign.

"Yes, ma'am. At your service."

"I doubt that. Otherwise, if I asked you to look the other way, you would oblige me. You aren't about to do that, are you, Mr. Casey?"

"No, ma'am."

"I didn't think so." She leaned a shoulder against the door in what she hoped looked like a casual pose. If she couldn't escape, at least she could get some answers.

"Tell me, Mr. Casey. Why are you traveling with my husband?"

"Most of us are just heading home."

"So long after the war's end?"

"Not everyone was released from the army the first day of peace."

"But you fought for the South. Weren't the Southern armies disbanded right away?"

"Yes, ma'am."

In Marguerite's opinion their conversation had gone back to its original topic.

"So why are you just now going home?"

"We had some business to see to."

" 'We'?"

"Your husband, me, Wilkins, Erickson, James . . ."

"And this business was . . ." she prompted.

"Finished," he supplied, purposely misinterpreting her.

She sighed impatiently. "Mr. Casey, where is *your* home?"

"I haven't got one."

"But your family—"

"Was from Indiana."

She stared at him in astonishment. "But that's a Northern state," she blurted without thinking. "Why ever did you fight for the South?"

He remained silent for a second before saying, "Money. Pure and simple."

She frowned. "I don't understand."

"You will, Mrs. St. Charles. The boys and I may have been kept on the losing end of things, but we managed to collect a souvenir here and there that could be sold at another time or place with a great deal of profit. We all became quite good at the game. Especially that husband of yours. He's got a cache of funds he hasn't told anyone about." She must have looked shocked because he added, "Not even you."

His eyes narrowed. "What do you think he has hidden in those trunks? There's no 'pretties' in them, and we both know it. If there were, you wouldn't still be dressed in the remains of your wedding gown and I wouldn't have been asked to guard that room."

He waited then, waited for some kind of response, but Marguerite found that she felt loathe to say anything at all—no matter what her own disquiet might urge her to ask this man.

After a long stretch of silence, Marguerite backed into the room, closing the door and leaning against it, somehow weak.

Money.

Had Bram given up all his ideals for a *profit?* The thought was too preposterous for words. He'd fought a losing battle. She'd seen enough of the aftereffect of the war to know that the South was on the brink of economical ruin. Even the North worried about the upcoming winter. Casey must have said such a thing to bait her.

But why? He was a stranger to her. Why would he wish to mislead her?

She closed her eyes, pressing her fingers to the ache in her temples. She wouldn't think of her misgivings anymore. She couldn't.

She couldn't bear it if Bram had really changed that much.

Bram stopped at the head of the stairs, clutching the dress he'd traded from the innkeeper's wife in a bundle under his arm.

"Evening, Casey. You can turn in now, if you want."

Casey yawned and stretched, folding his knife and

putting it back into his pocket before kicking the shavings he'd made under the chair.

"What is it tonight?" Bram asked, pointing to the block of wood. Casey was notorious for carving wooden animals that no one but he could identify. He'd never been very adept with a knife.

"Duck" was the man's curt answer.

Bram glanced at the rough shape. In no way did it resemble a duck or any other kind of fowl.

"Looks good," he lied.

"I'm improving," Casey said, then with a nod, went to his own room, leaving Bram to feel uncomfortable and vaguely guilty.

But what could he do? Until he had evidence one way or the other, it would only upset Casey to know that his honor was in question. Best to keep the doubts to himself and pray that they would never have to be spoken.

Waiting until Casey had disappeared completely, he took the time to unlock the door where the trunks were being kept. Allowing the lamplight from the hall to flood inside, he examined them closely enough to determine that they had not been touched while he'd been gone. The tiny shirt fibers he'd put on the tops of the lids gave evidence to that fact. Yet, he could not deny that, at some point, the stenciling on one of the lower trunks had been carefully chipped away to reveal the rest of the Union identification code beneath.

Someone had been curious enough to double check the trunks' original markings.

Casey?

Or another of his men?

Sighing, he thrust the thought away, closing and

locking the door. It galled him that his mind came back to that issue of guilt over and over again, as if obsessed by the possibility. Why couldn't he concentrate on more agreeable topics?

Such as the fact that his wife waited for him.

And tonight they would make love.

Turning to his own room, he forced the blacker thoughts of betrayal aside, his uneasiness being doused by a wave of anticipation. He would think only of his bride.

Opening the door, he slipped inside. Marguerite was in bed, the covers drawn up to her chin. It was a weak attempt to avoid the inevitable. Bram knew that she wasn't sleeping; he wasn't even sure why she'd bothered to pretend. Her body fairly radiated with tension, and he was sure that somewhere along the way, she'd forgotten to breathe.

Thanks to the bargain he'd made with the innkeeper's wife, he'd traded a pound of white sugar for the dress, a hot meal, a shot of whiskey, and a nice tall glass of well water—a luxury to him after so many years of drinking from creeks and riverbeds that were often tainted with the taste of blood. It had helped him to shed the anger that had driven him from Margaret's side.

Stripping off his greatcoat, blouse, and vest, he noted the tray on the bedside table, and saw that his request for a meal had been obeyed. Thick slices of bread, meat, and cheese had been sent up to his bride as well as a pitcher of milk and a plate of cookies. Judging by the crumbs on the plate, she'd been hungry.

Had she really drunk vinegar in order to fit into that blasted gown?

He studied the ivory creation—which he'd all but butchered with his knife—draped carefully over one of the chairs. Why had she starved herself? The dress was beautiful, to be sure—his lips twitched in amusement—and certainly daring, considering the trousers exposed underneath. But there had been no reason to subject herself to such asinine dieting tricks. She was so tiny, so wraithlike. Why exaggerate the effect? As far as Bram was concerned, it was simply more evidence that Algernon Bolingbrook III was a fool. He should have seen what she was doing and put a stop to it.

Bram's hands moved to the buttons of his shirt, a flicker of impatience settling deep in his loins, but he pushed it away. He had all night to avail himself of the pleasure that he knew he would find in his wife's arms. He didn't need to rush things.

He took his time in divesting himself of the garment, all the while watching Margaret—no. Marguerite. With each passing second, he wondered how long it would be before she showed some reaction to his nearness. It had been difficult for her to hide her emotions wherever he was involved—and Bram had not been that much more successful at concealing his own. They had only to enter the same room for a throbbing awareness to fill the air. It was a wonder that they'd been able to keep their original affair a secret. She only had to look at him to make him hard.

In that respect, nothing had changed.

The shirt fell to the floor, and Bram settled onto the edge of the bed. He had to give her credit for continuing with her ruse. Even when the weight of his own body caused her to roll toward him, she kept her eyes closed, her body quiet. She had braided her hair and tied it with a prim ribbon. He wondered what she'd managed to find in the way of an equally prim gown. He hadn't brought her anything to wear earlier, but he had no doubts that she would have made some effort to dissuade him from looking upon her favorably.

As if that were possible. He might be angry with what she'd done to him, but he could never deny that she also inspired a fierce passion in him that he had never encountered with another woman, no matter how hard he'd tried to make it so.

Knowing that the rein on his control was growing tenuous, he rid himself of his boots and his trousers. Then he returned to the same spot on the side of the bed, watching, waiting, aware that soon she would have to abandon her charade.

When she didn't respond, the corners of his lips quirked in an unwilling smile. She would hold on to the bitter end. Damn, she was a stubborn thing. She always had been. Her dainty figure might belie a certain fragility, but she had never needed him. No matter how much he'd wanted her to.

Guessing that if he left the evening's events up to her, he would be sitting on the edge of the bed until morning, Bram decided to take the initiative. His hand slipped beneath the covers until he encountered the supple arch of her foot.

She started, giving up the game before it had ever begun, her eyes springing open.

"Oh, good," he murmured. "You're awake."

It was obvious that she wanted to offer some sort of pithy remark, but he began to rub his thumb against her in a circular fashion, causing her eyelids to flicker ever so slightly. She had sensitive feet. Tiny feet that grew sore after a long day spent in narrow kid slippers or boots.

"You've been gone an awfully long time," she said. It was meant to be an accusation but somehow lost its sting as it emerged.

"I had some last-minute details to arrange as well as the payment for our room."

"I hope those preparations included some clothing for me."

"Yes."

Her eyebrows rose. "Really?"

"The wedding dress is lovely, Marguerite, but I'm ready for a change of scenery." He moved up, caressing her ankle, her calf.

"Bram, no." It was a bare whisper of protest.

"I gave you the evening to grow used to the idea."

"But—"

"I had a bath and food sent up to your room, so you can't complain that I've neglected you."

"We're strangers."

He cupped the back of her knee.

"No. We're not." He refused to hear any more of that line of defense. "We know each other more than most newlywed couples."

"We aren't newlyweds."

"That doesn't mean that we can't act that way. I once caught my father chasing my mother through the orchard. They were laughing and giggling and kissing. It didn't matter that they'd been married twenty years or had three sons. I vowed then and there, that someday I would have a marriage like that." His tone hardened. "I thought I had chosen carefully. Now I discover that I will simply have to make the best of what I've been given."

"Do you actually expect me to fall at your feet in adoration when you say things like that?"

"I don't expect anything," he said, his hands splaying wide over her thigh. "I've learned to take things as they are handed to me."

In one lithe movement he lay down beside her, pushing the coverlet to the floor. Beneath it, she lay dressed in her pantalets, petticoat, and corset cover.

"Very creative, but highly unnecessary," Bram said.

Her hands crossed over her chest. "I will not take them off."

"Fine. I've found my way through more layers of clothing than this, if memory serves." He kissed her shoulder, the hollow of her neck. "Do you remember the first time? You trembled in my arms, but your skin was hot to the touch. We were out in the gazebo. It was dark. You wore a white gown with yards and yards of taffeta ruffles—not exactly the best choice of clothing considering the noise it made every time you moved." His tone grew dark. Husky. "You aren't wearing taffeta now."

Her eyes had grown dark in her distress.

"Nor is there anyone to hear even if you were."

With that, he leaned over her, kissing her, his tongue plunging deep into her mouth.

She mewled a small protest, pressing her fists against his chest in an effort to push him away, but he would not be dissuaded. He'd waited years for this. A lifetime. He wanted to drown himself in her sweetness, he wanted to immerse himself in the noises she made, the feather-light touches. He wanted the memories of war and hardship to be erased and the passions of youth to be revived. He wanted this woman.

Marguerite.

Her name escaped from his lips in a soft whisper even as she relaxed against him and her eyes grew wide.

"You want this, too, little one. You know you do."

She opened her mouth, but did not refute the statement. They both knew it would be a lie.

"We aren't children anymore."

He touched her cheek, her chin. "We never were. What we felt together was not a youthful fantasy. It was real. Real."

Then he was holding her close and kissing her again. Her hands wrapped around his neck, tightly, fiercely, as if for once she refused to think of the consequences of her actions. There was only this minute. This passion.

The effect on Bram was staggering. It had been years since he'd touched a woman, any woman. Now to be holding the object of his imaginings was completely unnerving. He was inundated with the sweet scent of her hair, the lingering traces of soap and supple feminine flesh. He couldn't absorb the sensations fast enough. He was so hungry for her, for her touch, for her lovemaking, that he became a desperate man, struggling for control so that he wouldn't mount her and take her now, this instant.

Rolling to his back, he pulled her over him, hoping that the action would allow him a few minutes respite from the storm of desire. But as her breasts pressed into his chest and her hips settled over his, he knew he'd miscalculated. There was something even more fascinating about seeing her this way. Over him, on him, her limbs tangled with his own.

He fumbled with the thick braid that fell over her shoulder, wanting to free it—*needing* to free it. His fingers became impatient in their efforts to comb it loose until the tresses hung thick and dark around his face. Just as he'd remembered. Just as he'd dreamed.

Her eyes grew wide, dark, piercing his very being.

"Was this all you ever felt for me? Was this all I ever did for you?" Her hand splayed wide, roaming over his chest, his ribs, his hips. "Was it?"

He knew what she was asking, and he could no more deny her the truth than stop breathing. "No."

Her head bent and she nipped at his shoulders, then kissed lower, lower, before drawing his nipple into her mouth and sucking.

He arched beneath her, knowing that he couldn't hold on. It had been too long. Too long.

Twisting, he pressed her onto her back and settled over her, working feverishly to find his way beneath the layers of clothing. Finally, in frustration, he rent the delicate silk, baring her to his gaze.

She was beautiful. So beautiful.

Too beautiful.

Then he was lying over her, reaching for her, readying her.

"Sweet hell Almighty, forgive me, but I can't wait any longer."

Then he was plunging inside of her, absorbing the way her body held him so tightly, so completely. He clenched his teeth together, trying to wait, trying to allow her at least a minimum of pleasure. But it was too late. His body was beginning to tremble fiercely. The delicious sensations were building, building, until they crescendoed in a throbbing burst of passion. He closed his eyes, pushing to the hilt within her, his hands clenching into the pillows, his entire body tensing as he felt his seed spurting deep in her womb. Again. And again.

When at long last he could think, breathe, he pushed himself away from her, tenderly wiping the hair from her face.

"Marguerite?"

She didn't answer. She merely gazed at him with dark, fathomless eyes. Then, wriggling, she disengaged herself from him, moving to the far edge of the bed. Clutching the covers to her breast and rolling to her side, she whispered, "Good night, Bram."

"But . . ."

"Good night."

There was a finality to her tone, and even though he might want to explain, he could tell by the stiff set of her back that she would not allow him to kiss and cuddle her until they could begin their lovemaking again. Not tonight. Lying back on the pillows, he flung an arm over his brow and sighed.

Damn it.

Damn it all to hell.

Why did life have to be so difficult?

Chapter

7

He'd gone.

Marguerite blinked against the morning sunshine streaming through the hotel window, and focused on the door vibrating on its hinges. She knew it was childish but she'd purposely feigned sleep until she heard Bram leave. She didn't want to talk to him yet. Not until she'd had a chance to repair her defenses.

Easing the covers back, she rose to her feet, grimacing at the shredded remains of her undergarments. Bram hadn't taken her gently the night before—and what shamed her to the very core was that she hadn't been offended by the fact. His evident need had been as heady as an aphrodisiac to her.

Standing, she gazed at her reflection in the mirror,

seeing the pink cheeks and wild hair. She looked like a wanton, brazen hussy. And she didn't care. She honestly didn't care.

The thought was astounding. She should be furious at him for treating her so roughly. She should be railing at him for all he'd done, for the way he'd ruined her life not once, but twice. But she didn't. She wasn't. Weakly, she sank back onto the bed.

No.

No!

She couldn't still be harboring some tender emotion for this man. He had killed all of that long ago. She was angry, yes, frustrated, yes, irritated—beyond measure! But she couldn't . . . care for him.

Could she?

She covered her face with her hands in an effort to avoid the sight of her own longing, but it did her no good. Deep inside, where she couldn't turn away from the truth, she realized that she continued to harbor feelings for Bram St. Charles. Feelings that had nothing to do with antipathy.

What was she going to do? She couldn't allow this to happen. She couldn't surrender to him, become the docile creature who had once nearly given him her soul. She couldn't allow him to steal the identity, the strength, that she'd developed over the years without him.

And Jeffrey. How could she ever explain why she'd kept him a secret after Bram had come for her?

She refused to think about it. She was just tired, that was all. Once she'd had a decent night's sleep and time to think, she would laugh at this moment of weakness. She would push it away as some sort of mental aberration.

"Here."

She whirled at the deep male voice, startled to see that Bram had entered the room without making the slightest noise. Automatically, she wrenched a sheet from the bed, holding it to her as some sort of modesty screen, but she knew in an instant that she needn't have bothered. The way he was studying her made it quite clear that he remembered just what she had looked like, bared to him.

He threw a dress her way and she caught it, the sheet falling to the floor.

"Put that on. I'll be waiting for you in the hall."

Thankfully, his words gave her the excuse she needed to look away, to avoid the intensity of his gaze and all the memories that caused them to glow with an inner heat.

"What is it?"

One brow rose mockingly. "A dress."

"I *know* that," she retorted with a thread of irritation. "What's the meaning of bringing it to *me?* Something that clearly belongs to someone else. Where did you get it?"

"That's none of your concern."

Her chin tipped to a proud angle. "I think it is. I think I have a right to know if you've stolen it from some clothesline before I go parading around town in it." She shook it free from the wadded ball it had been in for obviously some time. "It's easy to see you didn't buy it ready-made," she said, indicating the signs of wear and the mismatched buttons.

He misinterpreted her remarks. "What's the matter, are you too fine a person to wear calico?"

"Not at all," she said between clenched teeth.

"Then get into it. Now."

"I merely—"

"Get dressed, Marguerite! It's time we were going."

He turned on a heel and strode from the room, slamming the door behind him.

Sensing that his temper was short and only partially directed at her, she sighed and began to wash. Donning her pantalets and camisole, she put on the corset and corset cover, then stepped into the gown, throwing her ruined petticoat over the rumpled bed.

The dress was far from flattering. Whoever had worn it before had been much larger. Taller, broader, longer in the arms. She was forced to roll up the sleeves and use her hair ribbon as a makeshift belt. Gazing in the mirror, she realized she looked like a refugee. Well, at least in that regard, she should fit right into this country.

When she opened the door, Bram was waiting for her. He took one look at the wedding gown she clutched to her chest and frowned. "Leave it here."

"I will not."

He marched toward her, attempting to wrench the garment from her hands. "Damn it, Marguerite. You're *my* wife now. *Mine.*"

"So does that mean that I should suddenly become a wasteful person? The fabric of this dress has plenty of wear left. There's no need to throw it away."

"I will not have you in that gown again."

"Fine. But I will keep what remains of it, nonetheless."

His lips tightened, but he didn't bother to argue any further. "Let's go," he said, taking her elbow and ushering her down the hall. "We've already wasted most of the morning."

When Marguerite stepped outside, there was no

carriage awaiting them at the line of supply vehicles. As if the change in clothing had been a symbol of things to come, the vehicle that awaited her was another rough wagon crammed with trunks and furniture.

"What's this?" she asked, gesturing to the caravan of supplies. She'd been too distraught the day before to take much notice or ask many questions.

"We'll need some things once we get to Solitude."

She opened her mouth to ask further questions, wondering why they needed a table and chairs when Solitude had an abundance of each, but one look at Bram's dour expression changed her mind. Later. She would inquire later when his mood had improved.

"Let's go."

If it improved, she corrected herself when Bram led her in the direction of the wagon. Sighing, she supposed that she would have to bite her tongue for a while. Bram had become almost hostile in the last few minutes, as if their intimacies of the night before bothered him greatly.

And so they should, she thought. He'd taken her with no thought to her own wishes on the matter. He'd drawn her into his arms, kissed her, caressed her, filled her with a flurry of sensations and . . .

Stop it! Just stop.

Marguerite prayed that her cheeks had not flooded with a wave of color due to her wayward thoughts. It wouldn't do for Bram to know that she was thinking of the previous evening. Of his body warm and hard, pressing into her own. Of his hands, rough and calloused and curiously intriguing.

Marguerite! Stop! She had to put her mind onto other things. Such as Jeffrey. Her son. Their son. If for no other reason, she should be trying to find a way to reason with this man so that she could approach him with the truth.

Soon. Once they reached Solitude, his mood would improve. She knew it would.

"Bram?"

"What?"

His reply was curt.

"How long until we arrive?"

"On horseback, it would take a little over an hour. But with this wagon—even after the repairs—it will take two, maybe three or four hours, depending on the roads."

Three hours. Could she possibly endure that much time with Bram's ill-humor?

The time did pass. Slowly. For the most part, Marguerite sat stiff and proud on the wagon bench, crammed against the side of her husband, and hemmed in by a ladder, a metal gutter, and a coatrack that extended far beyond the edge of the conveyance on her side of the seat.

Sighing, she rested her elbow on the crude ladder and stared at the passing scenery, remembering that day so long ago when she and her father had taken this same route to Solitude. It had been summer then. The scents of hay and freshly cropped grass had hung richly in the air.

Looking back, Marguerite couldn't fathom how a girl so young, so rash, so . . . so *silly* could have journeyed so far in the time that had elapsed since then. Not just in miles, but in experience, knowledge. The sacrifice of love, convenience, and her father's approval.

"How much longer?" she blurted. The land was

somewhat recognizable to her, but changed, so very changed, that she wasn't sure if her instincts could be trusted. Where once the roads had been smooth and scenic, now they were rutted and scarred. The woods on either side had been thinned—probably for firewood.

"A few miles."

She mulled that over with a gathering sense of unease. The journey so far had been an eye-opening experience for her, one that she wouldn't soon forget. Her gaze fell on a couple trudging in the opposite direction, a bundle of possessions strapped to their backs or carried in baskets and canvas sacks. Refugees. Black, white, alone, in small groups. She'd seen a dozen such instances since they'd left Maryland, heading south to Virginia. But none had affected her as much as those she had seen today.

She hadn't expected the signs of the conflict to be so evident. She hadn't expected to see people wandering, looking for homes, months after a truce had been declared. But she had only to look at the ravaged features of the couple they passed to know the conflict and suffering, brought on by the years of battle, would take a great deal of time to mend.

"You didn't think it would be like this, did you?"

She started when Bram spoke. Looking at him, she studied the blunt angles of his cheekbones, his jaw, as he stared straight ahead at the mules that pulled them toward home.

"No."

"Weren't your reasons for returning to France to avoid all this?"

"Yes." But even when she'd imagined the worst, imagined being left a widow, she hadn't comprehended the true extent of what could occur. Somehow, she'd always believed there was something too beautiful, too charmed about the area around Solitude to allow any real vestiges of pain to dwell here. Even when she'd been led to believe that Bram had been killed and that she would never return, she had imagined this place as it had been, covered in verdant grasses. A fairyland of promise.

The wagon shuddered to a stop at the top of a slight rise, and she looked from the hard set of Bram's features to the valley below.

"We're home, Marguerite. This is Solitude."

"Dear sweet heaven above," she whispered, a horror such as she had never experienced before seeping into her veins.

It couldn't be. This . . . this *ruin* couldn't possibly be Solitude. Could it?

Her fingers dug into her skirts, as if to confirm the fact that this was not some dream but reality. The image that she had carried with her for years, that of a stately brick building with white terraces, neatly trimmed gardens and hedges, stables and barns and corrals filled with Thoroughbreds . . .

It was gone. All gone.

The house had been pulled from its moorings, collapsing into a pile of rubble. Other than the barn, which had been scorched at one end, the outbuildings were unrecognizable, the gardens obliterated and burned to ash.

"How?" She barely managed to force the single word from her tight throat.

Bram looked at her intently, his eyes seeming to kindle. "Did you actually think that Solitude would escape unscathed if there was no one here to protect it?"

She didn't answer right away, knowing that whatever she said would be misinterpreted. How could she explain that she hadn't thought Solitude *could* be hurt, that some magical quality would always protect it? To see it so savaged was a blow, both physically and emotionally.

"Hiyahh!" Bram urged the mules into motion, bringing the wagon down the hill to what had once been a drive of crushed shell, through stumps of brick that had once been the imposing front gates of Solitude.

With each inch they traversed, the sick feeling of regret and disbelief that settled into Marguerite's stomach grew stronger and more overpowering, until she actually pressed a hand to her waist in an effort to prevent the rising nausea.

She had so many memories of this place, so many images that lingered in her brain like fresh ink, never fading. Over there was the spot where the terrace had been. She remembered stepping outside for a breath of fresh air one evening, only to be followed by Bram. He'd been so tall, so handsome, so overpowering. She'd had no compunction about letting him kiss her.

The wagon drew to a halt, and after a slight hesitation Bram climbed down, holding his arms out to lift her free.

She barely noticed the way he helped her, the way he gripped the tender flesh under her arms. As soon as her feet touched ground, she brushed past him, her too-long skirts rustling ominously on bare ground. Ground that had once been covered with rich grass.

Automatically, her eyes skipped from horror to horror. The stables where Bram had shown her the colts, first taking her hand. The creek bank where they'd shared a picnic, and he'd kissed her neck. The paddocks that had once held a dozen mares. The fence she'd gripped when Bram had stood behind her and caressed her breasts. The gazebo where she'd willingly surrendered her virginity and ultimately conceived their son. Gone. All gone.

"We'll be staying here for now."

It took several minutes for the words to sink in. When they did, she turned to stare at Bram in disbelief. "What?"

"We'll be staying *here*. At Solitude."

She gazed around her in confusion. "But where?"

"In the barn."

He'd begun taking trunks of supplies from the wagon box when Marguerite realized he was serious.

"You intend for us to sleep in the barn?" She stared at the structure, the only edifice that still stood, but even that honor was less than comforting. The thing looked like a good puff of air would cause it to come crashing down at any moment.

"The barn?" she demanded again. "The *barn*." She marched toward him. "Now, see here, I'm not about to sleep in any barn. Especially not one that could collapse on my head."

He didn't even pause in his actions, but the stare he leveled her way burned with a controlled anger. One she sensed was directed not so much at her, as at the situation. When he spoke, his voice was low and harsh. "You will sleep where I tell you to sleep. The house and all of the outlying buildings will be repaired. In the meantime we will be living here, on the property, to discourage any more vandalism."

"Has Micah ordered you to do this?" she inquired. "Is that what he said in that telegram you received?"

Bram had told her that his brother had relocated in Ohio. In her opinion she thought it was asking too much to demand that Bram take care of it for him in his absence.

"Micah deeded the house and the property to me."

"What?" she breathed. The Micah St. Charles that she had known would never have abandoned his home. He lived for his family. For this place. "Why would he do such a thing?"

Bram's eyes narrowed. "You're very full of questions today."

"Just as you seem very reticent with the answers."

"I told you that Micah had fallen in love. He's remarried to a woman he met in Ohio. He is quite happy and content to stay where she is, so he has deeded Solitude to me."

She held a hand to her brow, trying to assimilate all she was being told. "Does Micah know about . . ." she waved a hand to the destruction.

"Yes. He was the first to discover it this way."

"Poor Micah," she said in genuine sorrow, knowing how finding Solitude so damaged must have hurt him deeply. "What about Jackson?"

Bram's lips tightened. "He hasn't returned home yet. We haven't . . . heard from him. There was a caretaker here for a while, but he's getting on in years and went to live with his daughter.

She sighed. "So much has changed—to your home, your family. It's difficult to believe that this isn't all some horrible nightmare."

111

"The nightmare is real," Bram retorted, eyeing her darkly. "A great deal happened to all of us while you were gone. If you had stayed here longer, you might have been of some help. This happened because Solitude was left alone—something that would not have occurred had you been here, since I would have hired a caretaker and guards to stay with you. As it was, the men we asked to take care of the place left to join the army."

Her lips pressed in a tight line. "Surely you don't intend to blame all of . . . *this* on me."

"Oh, but I do."

She started at the savagery that lay naked in his tone. "If you'd been here, the caretaker and guards would have stayed. The men who'd done this might have gone away as soon as they'd realized Solitude was occupied."

"Or I might have received the same despicable treatment!"

The look he gave her made Marguerite feel as if he wouldn't be averse to the idea.

"It appears to me that you should be blaming yourself," she said hotly. "After all, the Rebels who did this showed nothing but animal savagery."

"The Confederate Army had nothing to do with this mess. It was done by a fanatical group of soldiers headed by Ezra Bean."

"Bean?" she echoed weakly, vaguely recognizing the name.

"Micah's father-in-law." He yanked a trunk from the rack and strode to the barn. "You should have stayed, Marguerite. You should have stayed."

Marguerite squeezed her eyes shut as the sound of

his footsteps faded in the loose dust and ash, the nausea returning full force. At that instant she knew more than ever before that she had been right in leaving Bram and returning to France. Her darling Jeffrey could never have survived here so far from help and medical aid. And if she'd been alone . . .

She shivered, her resolve strengthened. Yes, she'd been right to return to France.

But how could she ever make *him* admit it was true?

It took some time to unload the supplies—especially once Casey and the other men arrived with the second wagon that held sacks of seed and building supplies.

Bram squinted into the dust as they drew to a halt beside him.

"Where will you be wanting this? The barn?"

He followed the line of Casey's gaze. Marguerite had disappeared inside the dilapidated structure not ten minutes before, a distinct look of distaste crossing her features at the idea that she would be forced to demean herself so much as to live in a barn. Bram hadn't bothered to reassure her that things would change. In a year or so, once the house was rebuilt. It was time she admitted that life was not without its sacrifices.

But even as he opened his mouth to give Casey the affirmative, he changed his mind. There might be problems that he and his wife needed to iron out, but that did not mean that he wanted her involved with this other business with Casey.

"Stack it next to the barn."

"Outside?"

"The weather's clear. It can wait there until a shed of sorts is built. All except the trunks that are in the wagon I brought," Bram said referring to the boxes of Union gold. "Those will need to go inside."

Casey shrugged. "Fine. I'll take care of the trunks."

"No," Bram said, but he should not have spoken at all. He should have allowed Casey to handle them, to toy with the contents, to incriminate himself if he were guilty. But suddenly he was feeling much too tired to deal with the consequences such an action might bring.

"No, Erickson and James can handle it. The others can unload this wagon and set up a tent for you to sleep in. I need you with me, Casey. We should head to Kalesboro and put out the word for laborers."

If Casey was irritated by the assignment, he gave no outward sign.

"Fine. I'll go saddle the horses."

During the time they spent together, Bram tried to determine if there was a difference in Casey's manner, but the man chatted about idle things—women, gambling, and horses—just as he always did.

Once in town, they went to several stores, saloons, and male boardinghouses, leaving notices about the jobs that would be available at Solitude.

"Sir?"

Bram was about to leave the railway office after leaving another handwritten announcement on the message board.

The man who walked toward him now was short and rotund, leaning heavily on a heavy crutch. "Mr. St. Charles, sir?"

The question was so hesitant, that Bram found

himself studying the gentleman more closely. "Lewis?"

The elderly man beamed. "Yes, sir. You hired me and my nephew Charlie to take care of Solitude during the war."

Bram gripped the man's hand. "It's good to see you."

Lewis shook his head. "Naw. I'm surprised you'd even talk to me after what happened at Solitude." His eyes glimmered with a suspicious moisture. "I'm so sorry, sir. So sorry. Charlie ran off, and I tried to stay at the place, but once those deserters came and razed it . . ." He cleared his throat. "I'm just thankful there wasn't anyone living there. It was awful. Awful."

Bram felt a niggling of discomfort. He'd insisted to Marguerite that Solitude might have been saved had she stayed. Now he was forced to see that she'd been safer in France.

Safer.

Before he could mull the thought over even more, Lewis held out a crumpled piece of folded paper.

"This came for you this morning. Came from someone from Ohio, it did."

Bram took the telegram, ripping it open and reading the simple missive.

> *Meet me at family graveyard.*
> *Tonight 7:00 P.M.*
> > > *Micah.*

"Is there a problem, Mr. St. Charles?"

Bram shook free his deep concentration. "No, Lewis. Thank you."

The rest of the afternoon, he saw to the task of finding skilled workers who could help to rebuild Solitude—but his mind was distracted by the telegram tucked deep in his pocket.

With the number of men looking for work, it took longer than Bram expected to complete his errand. By the time he had interviewed three builders and several dozen workmen, night was encroaching. He would have less than thirty minutes to make his way to the graveyard.

It pained him that his first sign that Solitude was near was the smell of ash and cinder.

"You have my sympathies about your home, Bram."

Casey's soft comment made Bram feel very small and mean. It was something a friend would say, not a traitor.

He didn't know how to respond other than, "It can be rebuilt."

"In time."

"Time well spent compared to what I've done the last few years. I'm tired of the lies, Casey. Tired of claiming to be a Confederate veteran when all the time I was employed with the Secret Service. If I'm to be known for whatever actions I've done, I want them to be the right ones."

Casey gave him a long, immeasurable gaze. "I know just what you mean." Then he reached into his pocket, withdrawing the stub of a cigar. After lighting it and inhaling deeply, he drew his horse to a halt, allowing his mount to catch its breath at the summit of the hill.

Bram followed suit, knowing that neither animal

was in condition for the traveling sustained over the last few days. The ravages of war had left the horses a bit gaunt and weakened even now.

"You know, I always wanted a place like this," Casey said, gesturing to the valley below him.

"What was your farm in Indiana like?"

"Small, cramped. Bordered by a creek on one side and too many neighbors on all the others."

"You could go back, you know," Bram said. "Once we've finished this last campaign for Sheffield." The nighttime shadows were too heavy for him to read his friend's expression, but he heard the nostalgia in his voice.

"Nah. It's no place for me now," Casey responded. "That's one thing the war taught me. That there's a world out there and twenty acres isn't near enough land for a man to live on."

"What will you do?"

Casey sniffed. "I'll bide here for a while, help you rebuild this place. Then I thought I might travel. Go west."

The words weren't those of a man who intended to reclaim a stash of gold he'd stolen once before. But Bram had long ago learned to distrust appearances.

"Let's head on in," Casey offered, clucking to his horse.

Bram accompanied Casey to the tent the other men had erected on the far side of the yard.

"Why don't you come in for a drink before you head up to the barn?" Casey suggested after they'd tied their animals with the others beneath a huge oak tree.

Bram glanced at the barn, thinking of his wife,

wondering what she'd done while he'd been gone, then accepted Casey's offer. Just for a minute. He'd surround himself in male companionship and remind himself that life didn't have to be complicated or radically changed. He could still spend time with the boys and pursue his own interests.

Slipping inside, he saw that the rest of his men had been waiting up for them. Casey immediately sat on one bunk, took a bundle of cleaning supplies from his trunk, and began rubbing the barrel of a rifle with an oiled rag. Erickson, Wilkins, and James had been playing cards on another cot, but it was obvious from the abandoned hands that they hadn't been paying much attention to the game.

"Well?" Bram asked, accepting the bottle Wilkins held out to him. Three inches of whiskey remained in the bottom, and he helped himself. "How did things go while we were gone?"

Erickson was the first to speak. "We unloaded the supplies like you asked." He shook his head. "Good Godfrey Moses, Bram! What is your wife carrying in those trunks of hers? They thumped and rattled like a half-empty son of a gun, but they weighed a couple of hundred pounds apiece."

Bram didn't even bother to answer. "Enough of that, we've got something more important to discuss, I'm afraid."

Erickson leaned his elbows on his knees, looking at Bram intently. "We were told Sheffield wanted one more mission before our release. Any word what it's to be?"

Bram hesitated, knowing quite well that the next stage of the plan was to heighten the stakes and force

Casey or any other would-be traitor to steal the gold. He was reluctant to put such plans into motion, but he didn't have much of a choice. A logical opening had been made, and he would do well to use it.

"Yes. As a matter of fact, I received our orders just before we left Baltimore." He withdrew a sheaf of papers from the inner pocket of his greatcoat. "But you're probably not going to like it much."

Wilkins swore under his breath. "Guard duty. Damn it all to hell, don't tell me it's guard duty!"

"It's—"

"Guard duty! I knew it was. Some uppity-up is planning a tour of the South, and we've been assigned to keep him safe!" Wilkins spat on the ground. "I just knew Sheffield would pull something like this as our last bit of service. I'm right, aren't I, sir?"

Bram nodded, all the while knowing that it was so much more than that. "A packet of wages and expense money for our mission will be delivered to the hotel in Kalesboro, suite five, by ten tomorrow morning. Wilkins, James, I want you to arrive an hour before that and post guard in the same room for the rest of the evening. When you go, you will be taking the trunks you so graciously carried into the barn for my wife. As you surmised, they aren't filled with feminine frippery, but with several thousand dollars' worth of gold."

"Good hell, Almighty," James breathed.

Wilkins offered a strangled, "Yes, sir."

Judging by their reactions, there was little doubt in Bram's mind that their surprise was genuine.

"Erickson, you'll spell them off at nine tomorrow evening. After that point, each of you—excepting

Casey—will rotate the guard duty in eight-hour shifts."

The men nodded.

There was a hesitation before Casey inquired, "And what am I to do?"

"You will be in charge of the arrangements for escorting our . . . guest into town. Then you will serve as his bodyguard for the remainder of his visit—along with whoever happens to be watching the room at the time, of course."

Casey shot a glance to each of his companions, then referred to Bram again. "Who exactly are we being asked to guard?"

Bram fixed him with a slow stare, trying to see if there was anything beyond curiosity in the man's gaze. He found nothing more than professional interest.

"Sheffield has been in touch with an ex-Confederate general who escaped to France midway through the war. This man is quite ill and wishes to come home to die—a fact made difficult since he has a price on his head for war crimes. He is petitioning for a pardon, twenty thousand dollars to begin a new life, a dozen rifles and ammunition, and foodstuffs for a month."

"Why would anyone take him seriously?" Erickson scoffed. "Twenty thousand dollars! For a dying man? Why even listen to such twaddle?"

"Because what the general offers in exchange appears to be worth the cost."

"And what's that?" James asked in the bored South Carolinian drawl, which had become his trademark.

Bram's eyes flicked from one man to the next, looking for any sign of concern, any sign of above-average interest. "The general will be bringing with him a list of fifty-two Union officers who supplied information to the Confederates during the war."

The silence became thick, electric, fraught with tension. Bram found himself scrutinizing them all even more. Erickson, with his frown of irritation, James with his brows lifting incredulously. Wilkins who sat with his mouth agape.

And Casey.

A heaviness sank into Bram's heart as he noted the way his friend became much too calm, too unconcerned, too bored. Gorge rose in his throat, and his fingers tightened around the butt of his revolver as the older man glanced at Bram, then looked away.

No. Not you, Jim. Not you.

But as he turned and walked blindly into the night, Bram feared that this time his prayer would go unanswered.

Because for a flashing instant, Jim Casey's eyes had displayed the look of a man about to be led to the gallows.

It took less than ten minutes for Bram to ride the winding road that led him past the main buildings to the knoll of trees that held the family plot. As he rode beneath the arching elms, between the stone posts that had long since lost their huge iron gates, he had to shake his head.

What in the world had possessed Micah to arrange a meeting here, of all places? Moreover, what was Micah doing in Virginia at all? The last time Bram had seen him, Micah had sworn he wouldn't be leaving Ohio for some time.

Above his head a hoot owl offered an eerie cry, and Bram cursed, glancing over his shoulder. But nothing was there. Not even his brother.

He tethered his horse to the limb of a withered lilac tree.

"Micah?"

The muted shout garnered nothing more than the flapping of wings—probably the owl he'd heard before. Cursing at his brother's warped sense of humor, Bram climbed a grassy hill and sank onto the ground. From here, he could see as much of the area as possible. It lay spread out before him in the glow left by the sinking sun, the dozen or more marble headstones gleaming like the ruins of some long-abandoned city.

Sitting with his back propped against the trunk of a gnarled oak, he stared out at the jumbled markers and beyond that to the crypt. To think that he'd been spared such a fate, such a final rest, was incredible to him after all he'd seen, all he'd experienced. But what was more incredible was the fact that not only had he survived, but he was also contemplating a future.

Future. There had been times when he'd thought he would never be able to consider such a thing. Now he discovered that it preyed on his mind—especially a future with his wife.

He leaned his head against the thick trunk. Folding his arms over his chest, he stared up at the stars. Marguerite was a spirited thing, that was for sure. More than she'd been when they'd first married. Her temper was even more fiery, more immediate. But she had not grown completely successful at hiding her feelings. Nearly everything she thought radiated from her face and those eyes. Those expressive deep blue eyes. She was angry, undoubtedly—defiant, to be sure. But there was more hidden deep where it was difficult to discern. Somewhere, in a tiny corner of her heart, she was afraid.

But of what? She must know that he would never physically hurt her, no matter what had passed between them. He might try to curb her spirit or bend her will to his own, but he would never break her. Had she forgotten all that? Had she forgotten everything they'd experienced together?

No. He refused to believe such a thing. When he'd held her, kissed her, she'd melted in his embrace. He had to keep believing that in time he would be able to tame her . . . perhaps even . . . forgive her.

"Such fierce thoughts."

The low voice melting out of the darkness caused Bram to start and reach for his revolver. It was unsheathed and aimed before he realized it was Micah who stood in front of him.

"Shit, Micah," Bram exploded, uncocking his revolver. "Don't sneak up on a man that way. I could have shot you!"

Micah—big, broad, wise-eyed Micah—grinned, taking a seat beside him. "I doubt it. I've been here nearly five minutes." Without a pause he asked, "So how's the little woman?"

"Difficult." Bram grimaced, then he stared at his brother with narrowed eyes. "But how do you know about her?"

"When you left Ohio several weeks ago, you said you were going to fetch her." He chuckled. "None of us thought you'd go about it this way."

Bram's eyes narrowed. "Don't tell me the news hit the papers in Ohio?"

Micah shrugged. "I wouldn't know, I haven't been there for some time." He poked Bram playfully in the arm. "Damn it all to hell, Bram. I've been trying to find you for the last week. If you weren't so secretive about your travel plans, I probably would have been able to locate you once I arrived in Baltimore—it sure would have saved me a hell of a lot of train travel. As it was, I finally figured out you were on your way to Solitude and took another train to Kalesboro. The whole way here, I had to listen to some biddy from Baltimore going on and on about the way the famous M. M. DuBois was kidnapped right out of her wedding ceremony. The woman was one of the guests, evidently, and had the whole car a-buzz. I think she would have fainted dead away if I'd told her I was related to the brute responsible."

"Brute?"

"Her words, not mine."

"Damn it! Why am I the only one who sees that I did what I had to do?"

Micah chuckled. "I think it would have been just as easy to knock on her door the morning before the wedding and announce yourself then."

"Maybe."

"But you wanted to make a scene. You wanted to make sure she couldn't go back."

Bram opened his mouth, but found he couldn't deny the statement.

Micah laughed, reclining on the verdant grass. "Do you still love her?"

Bram glared at his brother in annoyance.

"Come now, Bram. We all knew you adored her that summer she came to Solitude with her father," Micah said. "And she was smitten with you. It was all-but-embarrassing to be in the same room with you."

"Bullshit."

"Even Lili commented on it. She said she'd never seen a couple more in love."

"Marguerite didn't love me. She thought I had money."

"Well, you weren't exactly the pauper you've always insisted you would be."

"I was the second son—"

"Second son, hell. Father never planned to follow tradition. His will stated clearly that everything he'd worked for was to be divided equally among his sons. Even so, with the way you were always denying any claim to the St. Charles properties, why would you think Marguerite married you for money?"

"She all but told me so."

"And you believed her?"

"Yes."

"Was this before or after you swept her away from her wedding in Baltimore?"

"After," Bram said bitterly.

Micah shook his head. "Personally, I'd take anything she says with a grain of salt until you know the truth for sure. An angry woman will say a lot of things she doesn't mean."

"Why else would she have left me?"

Micah waited before saying, "Fear?"

Bram's lips tightened. "Fear of what?"

Micah began tugging at the grass. "War? Death?

Hell, man, her father was a member of the French government. Who knew what stories he told her?"

"That's ridiculous."

"Is it?" He tossed the blades he'd been shredding aside. "Don't you remember the way her father regaled us all with stories of what his own father endured during the revolution, all the gruesome, horrible details? Lili had nightmares from the second-hand events. Why couldn't Marguerite have been affected in the same way?"

No. The whole idea was preposterous. Marguerite had never said anything to him about being disturbed by her father's recollections.

"Think about it," Micah urged.

Bram sighed. "Enough of this. What about you, Micah? What are you doing here in Virginia of all places?"

Micah reached into his pocket, withdrawing a ring of keys. "I gave these to you once before. In Ohio. I'd hoped that you'd take the keys and the trunks they belong to home to Virginia, but in your haste to retrieve your wife, you forgot them."

Bram knew in an instant what Micah meant. "I won't take your money, Micah."

Micah looked genuinely affronted. *"My* money? That's the St. Charles treasure you're referring to, and to hear mother's stories of her never-ending labor giving birth to you, I'd say you were a St. Charles."

Bram's hands curled into fists. "It's to go to the eldest son."

Micah sighed. "According to legend, it was to be *hidden* by the eldest son, but used for any member of the family in need of assistance."

"Use it for you and your bride, then. And her brothers," he added, remembering the six young boys.

"We took our share, and it was more than enough for our needs. I divided it into four parts. One for you, me, Jackson, and the last to be hidden for the future just as the original Adam St. Charles decreed," he said, referring to the eighteenth-century ancestor who returned from a sea voyage to find his family destroyed by debt. Vowing such a tragedy would never occur again, he had amassed a fortune in gold, silver, and jewels, and hidden the treasure, keeping its existence a secret to be passed on to the eldest son of each succeeding generation. Now Micah was trying to give part of it to Bram.

"Take the keys, little brother. I've hidden the trunks in the family crypt." He looked around him at the dimly lit cemetery, his gaze resting at last on the pink marble crypt. The name *St. Charles* could be seen well enough even from this distance.

"Use the gold in whatever way you want," Micah urged. "Rebuild Solitude the way it should be done. Then use what is left to make a life with your bride."

Eyeing Micah, Bram felt an unaccountable envy. "Not all of us are married to adoring women, Micah."

Micah's eyes twinkled, as if he read Bram's weakening resolve.

"I have great faith in your ability to convince Marguerite to be whatever you would wish her to be."

Bram sat for several long, thoughtful minutes before holding out his hand. Chuckling, Micah put the keys in his palm.

"You'll find the treasure hidden in the cavern at the

southeast corner—as I recall, that hole was to be reserved for you and your heirs, so I think the location is fitting. Half of what you find there is Jackson's . . . once you hear from him."

Bram detected the thread of worry in Micah's voice, a concern he shared for the baby brother who had disappeared without a trace.

They both rose from the ground. Then Micah slapped him on the shoulder, tugging him close for a quick hug. "Take care, Bram," he said before turning and walking to his mount. "I've got to get home. I promised Lizzy I'd be back on the Sunday-night train. If I hadn't been so worried about the trunks, I would have sent them ahead, but now"—his lips twitched— "I'm glad I came after you. Maybe you'll think about what I've said. She loved you once, Bram. She'll love you again."

He paused once more to touch his brow in salute. Then he was gone, leaving Bram staring at the spot where he'd been, stunned.

Wondering what life would be like, *could* be like, if Marguerite learned to adore him just as Micah claimed she would.

It was much later when he rode into the main compound of Solitude again. When he did, it was to discover that Casey was waiting for him, leaning against a tree, whittling a lump of wood.

"Anything wrong?" Bram asked as he dismounted.

"You tell me," Casey said.

Bram immediately stiffened.

"You rode out of here like you were being chased."

Bram affected a casualness he did not feel. "I needed some air."

Casey didn't believe him. He knew that as surely as he knew his own name. But the older man didn't question him. He wiped the blade of its shavings on his pants and slid it into the scabbard at his waist.

"Good night, then, sir."

Chapter

8

Jim Casey had betrayed them all.

Bram sat quietly on the top of the hill overlooking Solitude, shredding the stem of a weed with his hands.

Trunks filled with gold, ammunition, and hardtack, and a fictitious general with a list of spies. It was the price his superiors had placed on a man's honor. On his dignity. On his anonymity. All Casey had to do was resist the temptation. If he did nothing to stop the supposed ex-patriot and his damning document, nothing to take the gold, Jim could not be convicted of his crimes. But would it all prove too much for him to resist?

Damn it all to hell. Why, *Jim?* he demanded

silently. Why would a man turn traitor? Especially after a twenty-year career in the army, campaigns to Mexico and the territories. Why, after working so hard in the Union's behalf, of volunteering for the Secret Service, of enduring the stigma of being recognized as a Reb soldier, of suffering the taunts by family and friends because he couldn't proclaim his true allegiance to the North? Why throw that away during the last few months of the war and the first few months of peace? It didn't make sense.

There was a rustling noise behind him. Bram automatically reached for the revolver tucked in his waistband and whirled, aiming the weapon at the unknown intruder. But it wasn't the enemy he found, Erickson or James, or even Casey. It was Marguerite.

She stood a few feet away, wearing that awful calico gown that he'd traded from the innkeeper's wife for a pound of sugar. But even with the harsh morning light spilling over her features and the wind tugging at her disheveled hair, she was beautiful. Not in the fragile porcelain way advocated by so many women of the day. No, there was something far more to Marguerite. Something heart-wrenching and painful to examine, yet so powerful in its appeal that he could not look anywhere else.

The wind was cool on his cheeks and must have been cooler on her own delicate skin, but she didn't shudder, didn't move for several long minutes. Then she stated, "I didn't know what had happened to you."

He wrenched his gaze away then, squinting into the rising sun. The view wasn't more appealing, but it was the safer choice.

"You didn't come back last night," she said when he remained quiet.

"Your concern about my welfare is touching." He hadn't meant to utter such a bitter retort, but the words tripped off his tongue in their haste to be free.

"*Your* welfare," she echoed. "Don't you mean my own? You've brought me to this cozy corner of hell and commanded me to stay. Is it any wonder that I should be a little panicked that something might happen to you and I would be marooned here?"

He sighed, throwing the weed to the ground. "Damn it, Marguerite." He rose to his feet, finally turning to face her, his hands planted on his hips. "When will you accept the fact that you won't be going anywhere? You are my wife. Your place is with me. Your home is at Solitude—and here you will stay until you take your place six feet under in the family plot."

Bram expected her to argue. He expected anything except the way she folded her arms beneath her breasts and squinted at him.

"Why have you done this, Bram? Why have you gone to so much trouble to claim me again when it is so patently obvious that any gentler feelings you might have had for me once are gone?"

The tone of her voice was so sad, so forlorn, that he felt a tiny portion of his heart begin to soften, but then he hardened himself against the sensation. She'd always been able to manipulate him, to bend him to her will. Before their hasty marriage, he would have walked over a bed of thorns barefoot if she'd but crooked her little finger his way.

She sighed when it became apparent that he wouldn't answer her. "Will you be gone the entire day again? Or will you bother to return at some point in time?"

She held up her hands, forestalling any response he might have made. "Never mind. I don't want to know. Anything you do, anywhere you choose to go, is no concern of mine."

Then she brushed past him and marched in the direction of the barn, little knowing that her words remained to haunt him.

She was right. It would have been easier to have let her marry Algernon Bolingbrook III. It would have been easier to have dissolved their marriage and begun a search for a new partner. So why had he claimed her? Why had he been compelled to bring her back here?

What was it about her that continued to obsess him?

For the rest of the afternoon, Marguerite wasn't quite sure what she was supposed to do with herself. Since Bram's men had relaxed their guard, she wandered over the property, examining the extent of the damage. But when she encountered what few signs of the gazebo remained—shards of wood burned blue-black left rotting where they lay—the sight soon depressed her so, that she went in search of signs of life.

By late in the day, all sorts of wagons had begun to arrive, filled with men carrying pickaxes and shovels. Wasting no time, the laborers swarmed over the area, gathering the wreckage of the house and hauling away debris in the same conveyances that had brought them.

Marguerite watched them for a time, but when it

became apparent that the laborers were staring at *her* with far more curiosity than the duties at hand, she sighed and returned to the shelter of the barn. Since she had no coat or wrap, the chill air of autumn was argument enough to close herself into the gloomy confines.

She stepped inside, noiselessly closing the door and heading down the central aisle to where an opening of sorts had been piled with trunks and furniture. When her slippers scraped against a rock, a shadow detached itself from the pile of trunks and she shrank back against one of the stalls.

The man stood, and she recognized Casey.

"What are you doing in here?"

"Bram sent me in to check on the trunks."

She glanced from him, to the trunks, which Bram had claimed held her "pretties." She'd tried only once to get an explanation from her husband as to their contents, but she'd been told in no uncertain terms that they were none of her concern.

"Why? Why would he want you to look at them?"

Her challenge seemed to catch him off guard.

"Ma'am?"

"Why would he have you check on them when they contain my things?" she inquired quite brazenly, hoping the man would call her bluff and expose the contents of the boxes. Early that morning, she'd tried to open one of them herself, just out of curiosity, but they'd been bound with chains held tight with iron padlocks.

Casey hesitated, his eyes narrowed and piercing. As the silence grew longer, she surmised that this man didn't believe they were filled with her things. He wanted to know the truth. Dear heaven, how he wanted to know the truth. It was there in the balling of his fists, the tension of his jaw.

"Why would he have you check them, Mr. Casey?" she demanded again.

This time he touched the brim of his hat, one that he hadn't bothered to remove in her presence. "I wouldn't know, ma'am," he said.

When he would have brushed past her, Marguerite surprised even herself by snagging his elbow and forcing him to stop. It was something that she never would have dared do years ago, but somehow, her modeling, the publicity, and Jeffrey's trials had made her see that there were times when it was better to challenge than submit.

"Mr. Casey, in the future I would appreciate it if you would not come into my home—"

"It's a barn, ma'am."

"But my temporary home, nonetheless. You will not invade it without my permission, regardless of what my husband has asked you to do."

"Yes, ma'am," he said again. Tightly. Sharply.

And as he yanked free and strode from the barn, she knew she had not made a friend with Jim Casey.

Emboldened by her own actions and her own claim that this was to be her temporary home, Marguerite worked until dusk to try to make some sort of livable conditions out of the barn. She raked the straw free to the bare earth and opened the huge door in an effort to allow the autumn air to purge it of the lingering smells. Then she took what little furniture Bram had brought with him, and made a keeping room of sorts from the bottom floor and two sleeping areas in the soft straw of the loft.

Through it all, she found herself wondering if this was where Jeffrey would live once he arrived. Surely not. A small boy who teetered on the brink of ill health, who caught every sniffle and cough and bout of influenza, needed a real home. One with proper walls and real beds, a stove for hot soups and fireplaces galore.

She paused in her efforts to hang a flour sack over the window in an effort to obtain some privacy. Staring sightlessly into the chill day, she wondered how long it would be before the docking of her son's ship? She knew Joliet and her family would take care of the details, that they would collect the boy as soon as he arrived and see to his needs. But it didn't ease the yearning she felt to take care of those things herself.

Closing her eyes, she leaned her forehead against the glass. This was the first time she had ever been separated from him for any real length of time. She did her best to shove all her thoughts and worries aside, knowing that those who cared for him loved him just as much as his own mother. But when things grew quiet and her mind's eye turned inward, she missed Jeffrey so much an ache formed in her heart.

An ache that could only be eased by working harder, making the barn as comfortable as possible, she thought with a sniff. If her son *did* arrive before other arrangements were made, she would need to make this place as livable as possible. Because she couldn't bear to be away from him a moment longer than necessary.

Her clothing soon clung to her body from the fine sheen of perspiration that covered her skin. Her back ached, her arms were on fire from raking and lifting, but at long last, the area could be considered habitable. By the time Bram stepped inside, she had even managed to collect a spray of autumn leaves for a centerpiece on the kitchen table and draped the rest of the empty flour sacks over the windows as draperies.

Bram paused just inside the threshold and surveyed her handiwork. She waited in tense expectation, trying to anticipate how she would react to his compliments. Should she remain coy and shy about it all? Or simply nod in acknowledgment of the favor she'd done for him?

"So this is how you spent your day."

In one statement it was clear he thought she'd wasted her time.

He surveyed the kitchen table, the bare dirt floors, the flour-sack drapes. "You should have saved yourself the trouble."

"Why?"

"This is a barn, Marguerite, not some hotel. There's no sense in prettying it up."

Her hands balled into fists. "I was only trying to make things appear homier."

"Why? We'll be out of here in a few months—by next autumn at the latest."

"Next . . . autumn?" She stared at him incredulously. "You don't actually think that I plan to spend a year living in this . . . in this . . . *barn*, do you?"

"Your place is with me."

"When you first suggested we stay here, I thought a week, maybe two," she continued without pause. "I wouldn't have even dreamed that you would propose something so absurd as to live here until the main house can be built."

"I told you we would be living at Solitude."

"Yes, but I thought you would erect some sort of temporary house or something."

His eyes narrowed. *"This* is our temporary house, and it's more than adequate. I've spent the last few years sleeping in tents and on the bare ground, so I see nothing wrong with staying here."

"And yet you would deny me the chance for a few tidy touches?"

He shrugged in obvious unconcern. "Do whatever you want, I don't really care. Just remember that this is a barn, Marguerite. Besides housing us, it will be used as a barn."

Finally, the sense of what he'd been trying to convey came through. "You wouldn't dare make me live in the same shelter as . . . as . . . livestock." She whirled on her toe and marched to the canvas rucksack she had used to house what was left of her wedding gown. Hoisting it into one hand, she strode back to the door, fully intent on making her way outside, and from there toward some point of civilization.

But Bram was too quick for her. He snagged her arm, causing her to face him.

"Where are you going?"

"Anywhere I can that is far away from you."

His hold became tight, nearly painful. "I believe I told you that you wouldn't be allowed to leave me again."

"That was before you informed me that I would be expected to bed with animals."

"We'll take the loft."

"That will make a fine lot of difference! I've told one of your men not to enter without my permission. I suppose they'll all be bedding down with us now."

Bram became immediately intent. "Man? What man?"

"That Casey fellow. He was snooping around the trunks. The ones you claimed held my 'pretties.' But we both knew that was a lie, didn't we?"

"I told you before. That is none of your concern."

"No more than living in the barn with animals, I suppose—of the two-legged *and* four-legged variety."

"My men are not animals."

"A point that could be argued considering how they look. And smell."

"I'm sure that such a point will be remedied now that they aren't forced to move from pillar to post at the slightest provocation. I'll speak to them about using the creek to bathe."

"What of the other beasts you mean to invite in here? I suppose that you'll command your stock not to smell or perform any bodily functions as well!"

"You're being unreasonable."

"Unreasonable! Tell me one other woman who would allow herself to be treated so rudely."

He opened his mouth, but she continued before he could respond.

"You can't, can you? Would you have asked your dearly departed mother to do such a thing?"

"We aren't talking about my moth—"

"Would you have asked Lili? Or Micah's new bride, whatever her name might be?"

"Lizzy."

"If my family had come with me, would you have

139

asked Aunt Aggie to share a stall with a cow? Or Nanny Edna to bed down with a pig?"

"Enough!" He took her other arm, shaking her until she grew silent. "Have you forgotten that *I* am the one in charge here?"

"Many dictators have been relieved of power when their requests became too extreme to tolerate."

He drew closer. "And just how do you propose to do that?"

In an instant she knew she'd said the wrong thing. It was entirely reckless to challenge him in his present mood—or rather the mood he'd been displaying for days.

"I didn't mean . . ."

"I think you did. Tell me, Marguerite. Just how do you propose to . . . limit my power over you?" He took another step closer, then another, until his legs pressed against her skirts and the heat of his body seeped into her skin.

"I—"

"Will you try to tease me from my views, hmm? Or will you pamper me and baby me?" His tone deepened, grew dark and rough. "Or will you tempt me with the pleasures to be found with your body?"

She felt as if the air had been sucked from her lungs, robbing her of the breath to protest or even deny his claims.

His hand cupped her cheek, making her look at him.

Seeing the extent of his emotions carved on his face, Marguerite felt an inexplicable wave of sadness. When had he grown so bitter? So hard? This wasn't the same man she'd loved all those years before.

"What happened to you, Bram? Surely you can't have become so petty as to deny me a few amenities if I'm to live here?" She didn't know that she'd said the words aloud until they escaped from her lips.

"Do whatever you like. I don't care."

She started as if he'd slapped her. *I don't care.* The words had been said with such vehemence.

"What's made you so angry about life, Bram?"

"You mean other than the destruction of my home, the abandonment of my wife, and the upheaval of my plans for the future?"

She remained silent. There was no safe answer to such a question.

He stood for long minutes in silence, before answering her question with one of his own. "Have you ever wanted something so badly that it obsessed you, that it filled your every waking moment, that you could taste its essence in your mouth and feel its warmth? Have you ever had something you wanted linger just outside of your reach so that every night you dreamed of it?"

Marguerite found herself dumbstruck by the vehemence of his tone and the strength of his stare.

"Do you know what it's like to be denied the thing you want most, time and time again, until you begin to wonder if you're sane to even think of it at all?"

"Yes," the whispered response broke from her lips.

"Ahh." One of his brows lifted. "What did you wish for, Marguerite?"

She tried to push him away, but she couldn't even cause him to budge.

"What did you want, Marguerite?"

She swallowed against the tightness closing around her throat. "I don't think it's any of your concern."

"But it is. I want to know. I want to know if you've really experienced what I've talked about."

"We were speaking in regards to *you.*"

"Then we'll swap. One of my secrets in exchange for one of yours."

Chapter

9

"You go first, Marguerite."

"I don't think that's quite fair."

"Why not?"

"If I go first, you might refuse to reveal anything at all."

His lips quirked. "Do you trust me so little?"

"Yes."

"So blunt."

"Just honest. What did you expect me to say after all I've been through in the last few days?"

"I've never lied to you. From the beginning, I've been nothing but honest."

Painfully honest in some respects, she could have added, but held her tongue.

"You first," she said stubbornly.

He walked outside, and she fell into step as he followed a path of sorts that she suspected had once been worn deep into the ground, but was now only a depression covered with a thin layer of grass. Climbing up the hill to the same spot where the wagon had once paused to give Marguerite her first glimpse of Solitude, he finally turned, holding her shoulders and forcing her to look.

"This, Marguerite. This filled every waking moment."

"Solitude?" she asked in confusion, sure that he couldn't possibly mean the desolation so prevalent everywhere she looked.

Bram sighed as if he pitied her. "Look harder, Marguerite. Or have you become so jaded that you can't see it?"

She strained to comprehend what he meant, noting the fiery burst of autumn color that lingered in the trees around them, the withered grass, the hills, his home. The smells of wood smoke hung in the air along with the crisp, unidentifiable scents of crushed foliage that could only belong to fall. But what else? What had possessed this man so fiercely that he had changed so much in such a short passage of time?

"Life, Marguerite," he said fiercely in her ear when it became evident that she wouldn't guess his secret. *"My* life. *My* future. For the past few years, it has been the only thing to drive me on, one more day, one more hour. I saw the Confederacy beaten into the dust and the Union forced to unknown cruelties to defeat them. I saw all that was good and noble in mankind as a whole be blasted away. I saw men abuse and debase one another and everything they held dear, all for one simple concept. To survive."

His fingers tightened, biting into her skin. "You keep saying I've changed, and it's true. I'm no longer content to allow fate or men's vanity to determine the course of my future. I have lived through this war simply because I willed myself to do so. And I'll be damned before I let another person take that away in the name of politics or patriotism." He turned her to face him. "Not even you, Marguerite."

She didn't have time to respond. His head bowed, his lips crushing against her own. His hands swept around her waist, lifting her to him until she was forced to wrap her arms around his neck in some sort of support.

He became hungry, almost desperate, breaking away to kiss her eyes, her jaw, her neck, and Marguerite nearly swooned from the intensity of it all. It was as if this place, this tiny corner of earth, held some sort of power over her in regards to this man. She was inundated with a thousand memories that she had locked away in her heart. For the first time, his embrace was too familiar, too overwhelming to resist. Somehow, the younger Bram, the boy who had stolen her heart, melded with this older, fiercer being, becoming a man altogether too difficult to resist.

When he began to lower her, bit by bit, she didn't say nay. When he collapsed to the cool earth, pressing her into a bed of autumn leaves, releasing their heady fragrance, she didn't complain. And when he kissed her, ardently, insistently, then made love with her, fiercely, completely, she returned each embrace full measure, knowing that she would never be able to free herself from this man as she had the day of her wedding to him. Something was happening between them, an emotional storm of sorts that refused to be ignored. They must either deal with the repercussions or be lost.

When his passion had been spent, his body sated, Bram lifted his head, forcing her to look at him. "Do you understand, Marguerite? Do you understand me now?"

Her own body was trembling, aching, so close to the moment of its own release. But she wouldn't beg him to stay. Not now. Not like this.

"Do you *understand*, Marguerite?"

She wanted to shake her head, she wanted to claim ignorance, but she couldn't. Bram St. Charles had lived in a hell of his own making for years. She could only pray that he could move on, repair his life, and find a niche for himself. For them both.

But most of all, she prayed that she could find a way to tell him that she, too, had prayed for life, just as fervently, just as feverishly. Not for herself.

But their son.

Marguerite did not return to the barn. Bram had left her almost immediately. Mumbling something about chores to do, he'd briefly helped her repair her clothing, then with one more glance in her direction, as if he'd expected her to say something, he turned and strode down the hill into the gathering darkness.

She could have followed, she supposed. She could have marched after him and forced some sort of confrontation, but she didn't have the energy. She was completely drained of the will to fight him. Too much had happened in the last few days. Too much had happened in the last few years.

What was she going to do? a small voice cried deep in her soul. She had come with Bram, fully expecting to hate him, to battle him, to make his life a living hell until he let her go. But now, she discovered that she didn't have the will to do such a thing—not because she'd changed her mind about staying. No. She couldn't do that. She wouldn't do that. But she was beginning to see that he had already been punished. Not so much by her leaving, but by all that had happened in the interim.

The scars.

They flashed into her mind's eye, the healed and half-healed welts that crisscrossed his chest and back. She was beginning to believe that the outward marks received in countless battles she knew nothing about were minor compared to the inner wounds.

What had happened to this man? He'd offered her an explanation of sorts, but it wasn't enough. She wanted to know the specifics. She wanted to know what had caused each of those gashes on his skin. She wanted to know what had made him distrust humanity so much, what had caused him to hate.

She wanted to know why he had fought for the wrong side.

Bram had been so adamant about fighting for the Union cause. At times she could have shaken him for the way he'd gone on and on about God and justice and freeing the slaves. Being raised in France, she'd had no real understanding of the American issues at that time—nor had she made an effort to try. But she couldn't deny that his furor on the topic had enthralled her even as she'd been frightened by his passion for war.

So what had gone wrong? Was it for money as Casey had claimed? The whole idea was preposterous. She couldn't believe that her own defection could cause such a change in his ideals. Something terrible must have happened to make him fight for the South. But what? *What?*

Her brain scrambled for some sort of logical explanation, but try as she might, she couldn't fathom anything that could have forced such a radical change in the man she'd once known. Once loved.

And what of it? Hardening her soul to all the questions that pummeled her brain, she stood and brushed the leaves from her skirt. She wouldn't think about any of it. It was no concern of hers anymore. Her time with Bram was limited. She would leave him again. She must.

But this time, *he* would have to be the one to tell her to go.

"Are you all right, Mrs. St. Charles?"

She jumped slightly, whirling to see that Casey stood a few yards away, propping a hand against an old oak tree. Marguerite felt a tide of embarrassment, wondering how long he'd been there. Watching.

When she didn't answer, he straightened and moved toward her. The heat of her cheeks intensified as she realized that even if he'd only been there for a minute or two, the crushed grasses around her spoke eloquently enough. Although it was nearly dark now, it wasn't dark enough to hide that point.

"I'm fine, Mr. Casey," she hastened to reassure him, hoping that he would politely leave. But he seemed in no rush and, in fact, ruffled the mashed grass with the toe of his boot.

When he looked at her again, there was a hard glitter to his eyes. "Those paintings don't do you justice, do you know that?

Marguerite remained silent, deciding then and there that she didn't like this man any more than she'd liked his accusations about Bram's fighting for the Confederacy as some sort of way to earn money. He might be Bram's friend, but she wouldn't trust him an inch.

"Tell me, Mr. Casey," she said, deciding it was time to assert her own will a bit, just as she had in the barn. "You spoke once of fighting the Rebel cause for money. Yet, I see no evidence of your having money at all. Indeed, you seem to be living off my husband's goodwill." The jibe must have hit some sort of nerve because his lips momentarily thinned. "Where, pray tell, is this so-called profit you earned?"

If she had thought to anger him, she was mistaken. Other than the way his lips twitched in a slight smile, he appeared bored by her query.

"So you *have* been giving my words some thought?"

"Not so much that they kept me up nights."

"But you still wondered."

"I think that's exactly why you told me what you did, isn't it, Mr. Casey?"

This time he smiled openly. "I do believe I've underestimated you, Mrs. St. Charles. But even *you* could not be so naive as to ignore the evidence of your own eyes."

She refused to be baited and did not respond.

"Can't you see that your husband is using some of his funds?"

She shook her head.

"What of the men he's hired?"

"They could be trading labor for . . . a plot of land or the wild hay that grows in the meadows or future profits."

"Perhaps." He gestured to the wreckage around him. "But I think that all this will prove to be far too much of a temptation for your husband to resist, I'm afraid. He will no doubt want Solitude restored to its former glory." He took a step closer, crowding her with his very presence even though a good three feet separated them. "For that, he will need a great deal of money. Where do you think he will find such a thing, hmm?"

She refused to answer.

"I believe I told you once of the gathering of . . . souvenirs. For a profit."

"Yes." The word was a mere whisper.

"What did you think I meant by such a statement?"

She shrugged. "Ammunition, arms?"

He chuckled as if her answer truly delighted him. "That is the stuff of amateurs, Mrs. St. Charles."

"Then what?" she asked, tipping her head to a proud angle, wondering if this man were simply toying with her through some unknown goal for personal amusement.

He slid his revolver from his holster, and she jumped, thinking he meant to point it at her, but he merely rubbed at the barrel with one finger, the action almost loving in its intensity.

"Do you know how much an officer costs? A major? A colonel? A general?"

Her brows furrowed in confusion, and he laughed out loud.

"What's the matter, Mrs. St. Charles? Surely even you know that every war has its mercenaries, its assassins. I'm told that it's an honorable enough occupation as long as one does not extend such practices to peacetime."

When the meaning of his words hit home, she felt her heart clench. "You're lying," she whispered.

His brows dropped and his eyes gleamed, all trace of amusement fading from his features. "Am I? Then ask your husband about those trunks. Both of us know that you have no personal belongings to claim. Bram has seen to that himself. So ask him what's inside. Ask him how much gold he's amassed. Then ask him just how he got it."

Marguerite stood stunned, motionless, the very ideas this man had raised causing her to quiver.

"You believe me, don't you?" Casey murmured, beginning to back away. "What else could explain how much he's changed from the kind of man we both know he was at the beginning of the war?"

Then he left her. Alone.

With far more disturbing questions than those she'd had before Casey had come.

Chapter

10

Marguerite blinked and roused, rolling slightly in the soft bed of straw and hugging a pillow more tightly under her chin.

She could tell by the indentation beside her and the evidence of bedding that had not been there the night before, that Bram hadn't heeded her none-too-subtle hint to sleep on his own side of the loft and had joined her, but she had no memory of the event. After waiting for him until past midnight, she'd dragged herself up the steps and gone to bed, knowing that it would be foolish to attempt any sort of confrontation in her current state of mind.

Lying quietly, she listened for any noise that might reveal her husband's whereabouts, but she heard nothing. If not for the extra blankets beside her, she might have believed that he'd never come home at all.

Home. That was an odd way to refer to a barn. A barn that she was sure would prove to be nothing but temporary living quarters for them both. She would not spend the winter here. And she would *not* share her quarters with animals—two-legged or otherwise.

Filled with a sudden purpose, she pushed the blanket away and scrambled to her feet. Donning the ivory slippers she'd put in the straw by the staircase, she rushed down to the bottom floor.

Bram was gone. Good. It would give her a chance to clean up a bit before she met him again. She'd been forced to sleep in the calico gown he'd given her, corset and all, but she would not greet the day without at least combing her hair and washing.

Lifting a metal pail from the hook on one of the stall's beams, she hurried outside. But one step into the sunshine, she paused, frozen by the tableau she encountered.

Bram stood at the pump, a bucket of water beneath the spout, his hands plunging deep into the liquid then splashing it over his face, his chest, his arms.

She halted where she was, transfixed by the way the autumn sunshine gleamed on his wet skin, enhancing the shape of each muscle, each sinew, each ridge of bone. The droplets sparkled like diamond chips, holding her entranced.

Marguerite's breathing came faster, a fact that she damned as being an overt sign of weakness. She wasn't some child, some adolescent, to be held captive by the first sight of a man's bare torso. After all, she had seen this man without his shirt on at least a dozen occasions.

But it was different. At this moment in time, after so many years, she could not look away.

Setting the bucket noiselessly on the ground, she leaned against the doorjamb, trying to hide from view as much as possible should he look her way, yet provided enough of a view to give her the opportunity to stare. She watched in fascination as he thrust his head under the rushing water. Then he rose and shook the excess moisture from his hair and slicked back the dark strands with his hands. Strong hands. Sensitive hands. Next, he proceeded to soap his chest and arms, rinse them again and dry them with a rough towel, all the while affording her with a clear view of his broad back, the scars, the rippling musculature.

Drat it all, the entire process made her tremble, more than it ever should have done. A liquid heat pooled deep in her loins, and she shuddered beneath its effect. Gripping the rough wooden supports, she closed her eyes, trying to push away the effects of her spying, but she couldn't—and what frightened her more than anything else was the fact that she found she didn't want the sensations to abandon her. This was the only man who had ever been able to make her feel this way. After leaving him, returning to France, and bearing a child, she'd thought that the sensations were an aberration, that she'd imagined them to be more than they were. But here she stood, her knees weak, confronted with the inescapable conclusion that the fiery passion she'd felt at sixteen had not died. It had merely smoldered, deep inside her, waiting for the spark to be fanned into a flame again.

She leaned back against the threshold, trying to draw deep breaths into her lungs. A mixture of panic and exhilaration continued to thrum through her veins.

"Marguerite! It's time you were up!"

The sudden shout caused her to jump. The deep male voice pierced her very soul. Automatically, she scurried to pick up the bucket and hurry toward him as if nothing had occurred, as if the very foundation of her emotions had not been shaken to the core. But she feared that her cheeks were tinted a telltale pink and that her eyes were bright and feverish.

When she appeared so quickly after his call, Bram regarded her with a bit of surprise, then shrugged into his shirt as if he were somewhat self-conscious of the fact that in clear daylight, his scars were even more garish, more horrible. The fact that he might be embarrassed by her seeing them so clearly made her feel light-headed, as if in the armor of pride and bitterness he'd fashioned, she'd found the tiniest of chinks.

"Good morning," she murmured, softly, awkwardly.

He began to button his shirt, causing her to believe that her assumptions had been correct.

"I thought you were sleeping."

"No."

The verbal exchange was trivial, relaying nothing of substance, but beneath the innocent words lingered meanings of another deeper kind. The awareness that he *had* slept next to her, that their routines had entwined, become casually intimate, passionately explosive.

Seeing Marguerite's bucket, Bram took it from her and filled it to the rim, then handed it back to her.

"You'll want to wash in the barn." He gestured to the tent a few yards away where his men had slept the past few nights.

She nodded, realizing that if they weren't up and about, they would soon be rousing.

"Thank you."

Turning, she made her way back to the barn. It wasn't until she began to close the door that she discovered Bram had followed her.

This time it was her turn to be self-conscious. She set the pail on the table on the far side of the barn, then turned, wiping her hands down the folds of her skirts. Bram was watching her intently, too intently. She wished she could read his mind, but his expression remained quite blank, his eyes dark.

"You must have made a wonderful soldier." The words slipped from her mouth before she could stop them.

"Why is that?"

"You never give anything away," she admitted after a slight hesitation. "I never know what you're thinking or feeling."

"And you want to know?" he asked, his voice like a knife through velvet.

"Yes." If not for the fact that her will had become slightly weakened over the last few minutes, torture couldn't have dragged such an admission from her mouth. But the need to get inside this man's head, to understand him more fully, was overpowering.

Had he killed for money as Casey had claimed? Had he hoarded trunks of gold earned by shedding another man's blood?

"How many men have you killed?" The question burst from her lips before she could retrieve it.

Bram frowned. "I was at war, Marguerite."

"How many?"

"I didn't count the corpses." His scowl deepened. "Holy damnation, woman, what kind of a ghoul do you think I am?"

She shook her head, holding out a placating hand. "I'm sorry . . . I just."

He grabbed her elbows forcing her to look at him. "You're as pale as death. What's got into you this morning?"

Marguerite hesitated, then decided she might not have another chance at such a line of questioning. "Where did you get those scars, Bram?" she asked, hoping to ease into the accounting of his victims if there were any.

"In battle." The words were forced through clenched teeth.

"Hand-to-hand combat?"

"A few. The rest are from gunshots or mortar fire."

Her eyes squeezed closed, and she felt suddenly weak as the sense of what he was saying sank into her head. Raw metal had plunged into his body, ripped it, savaged it.

Unable to help herself, she gripped at his shirt. "Why, Bram? Why did you feel it necessary to fight?"

"Honor."

His one-word answer struck her as oddly ironic considering the fact that he'd fought for the South, but judging by the ring of sincerity it carried, Bram did not suffer from any such qualms.

"And were you honorable? Did you adhere to the ethics of war?"

He clasped a handful of her hair, forcing her to look at him. "How can war have any ethics of its own?"

"Did you fight for something you believed worth dying for?"

"Yes."

"Did you remain true to your ideals?"

"I tried."

Her mouth grew so dry, she feared she would not be able to form the words. "And did you ever take money for another person's death?"

It was obvious he disapproved of her line of questioning, but he answered her nonetheless. "No."

She wilted with relief, forcing Bram to take a portion of her weight.

"What's got into you, Marguerite? What's made you think such things, let alone ask the questions?"

"I . . ." But what could she say? That Casey had been toying with her, feeding her lies and innuendo as fact? That he'd been making a fool of her to get to her husband?

"Nothing," she said, wriggling free. "Just bad dreams."

"You've been dreaming of me?" The thought seemed to please him. "Well, then. Perhaps my plans for today will prove more enjoyable than I had first imagined."

"Plans?"

"I thought we would go into Kalesboro." He took a few quiet, catlike steps toward her. "I was thinking that it was time we got you a change of clothing."

Her lips pressed together in annoyance. A critique of her attire had been the last thing she had expected him to give.

"The color of that dress doesn't suit you."

"It wouldn't suit anyone," she mumbled.

Bram's lips twitched and the unexpected hint of

amusement tugged at her heart in such a manner she never would have expected. She found herself staring at him, willing him to smile, really smile. Just once for her.

"I suppose we'll have to take you shopping."

"We haven't any money. What little you had left after the war destroyed Solitude must be spent by now."

"I would have thought you'd be a wealthy woman yourself by now, what with all your modeling for Joliet."

"A less than lucrative occupation. Despite the facade of the social circles I've been introduced to in the process, the wages I receive are less than a schoolmarm's." What she didn't add was that what few coins she earned were spent to house and feed her family and to pay for a private nurse and the specialized care Jeffrey required.

"The elaborate wedding you planned must have cost you a fortune."

"Not my fortune. Algy's. I would have been happy with a quiet ceremony in a judge's office, but Algy wanted to make a show of it all."

Once again, Bram's lips lifted in a near-smile. "I believe he got more of a show than he'd bargained for."

She couldn't prevent her own humor from surfacing. "Yes, I suppose he did. I can only imagine how he and the rest of the Bolingbrooks have spent the interim."

"Aurelia and four of her sisters have left for a tour of the continent—their own way of avoiding the shame. Camellia has approached a convent for added schooling. And your husband-to-be, Algy Bolingbrook, has shut himself in the country estate with a case of brandy and refuses to come out."

"Poor Algy," she murmured.

"Rumor also has it that he sent for Claudette Schiffler, his longtime dance tutor, to ease his heartache."

Marguerite stared at him openmouthed, first because of the news that she had been so quickly offered, then in disbelief of Bram's having such knowledge at all.

"You're lying."

"I'm not. I assure you."

"How could you possibly know what has happened when you've been with me this whole time?"

He moved forward, cupping her cheek in his palm. "That was my job during the war. Gathering information. Things haven't changed so much since then."

Her brow creased. "You were a scout?"

"Of sorts."

It wasn't the answer she wanted, but after he'd revealed this much of himself, she didn't dare push him any farther than she had, considering her earlier line of questioning.

"Why did you fight for the South?" she finally whispered. The fact plagued her now more than ever. Bram's brother Micah had gone to West Point to study engineering, and she'd had to listen time and time again to Bram's lamentations that only one of the St. Charles sons would benefit from the military academy. He'd wanted to learn, wanted to serve his government. What had happened to those views? Had he been tempted by money as Casey had claimed?

Bram sighed, and she knew by his closed expression that she may have asked one too many questions. But to her surprise, he did respond. "Someday, perhaps I will be able to find a way to help you understand. Maybe I'll find an easy way to tell you everything. But not today." Holding her, he bent to place a soft kiss on her lips. The gesture was so gentle, so tender, it brought tears to her eyes. "Today we are going to buy you a dress. I'll go hitch up the team."

When he walked away, she stared at him in disbelief. "But we haven't any money!"

He glanced at her over his shoulder. "Maybe you don't. But I do."

Marguerite was quite sure that the statement was meant to reassure her.

It only managed to intensify her worries.

Bram took her into the heart of Kalesboro, a city of nearly one thousand people that was located in the northwest portion of the state. Having lived in some of the largest metropolises of the world, Marguerite hadn't bothered to expect much in the way of its shops and services, but she was pleasantly surprised.

At first she trailed reluctantly after Bram, embarrassed by the state of her clothing and hair. It occurred to her that she should be angry. If the man wasn't as strapped for funds as she had at first supposed, then why had he dressed her like a refugee? Was it part of his efforts to humble her?

But as soon as the thoughts seeped into her brain, they were pushed away again. All it took to drive them from her head was for Bram to usher her into the first dressmaker's shop he came to. In an instant she was inundated with the rich scents of sachet and powder, expensive fabrics and brewing tea. Her surroundings became immediately feminine. Tiny gilt chairs padded in pink brocade, scraps of lace and satin and wisps of silk. There were mirrors draped with ribbon samples, hangers carrying bodices and jackets in all stages of completion, tables laden with tiny reticules and gloves and bonnets.

"How is this possible?" she whispered, gesturing to the well-stocked shelves.

"The proprietress is well connected in Europe. As soon as the blockade lifted, she was able to receive the shipments of supplies she'd ordered long before the conflict—about the only place in the South that has been able to stock such luxuries so far."

A tall, statuesque woman came forward to greet them. Upon recognizing Bram, she held her hands wide, issuing a torrent of greetings in Italian. Bram allowed himself to be hugged, kissed on either cheek, then studied up and down. Marguerite was able to interpret the woman's remarks enough to know that she inquired about his brothers' health, and Solitude's reconstruction all without waiting for an answer. Then she clasped Marguerite's hand, pulling her into the light and studying her up and down.

"Who is this charming creature, Bram?"

"My wife."

Her eyebrows shot up to her hairline, and she nudged him under the chin with one finger. "You are a devil. No one knew. No one guessed."

Marguerite was left to wonder what had happened here in Virginia after their hasty elopement, what rumors had surfaced, but came to the conclusion that word of the nuptials had not leaked back to Kalesboro.

"You'll be wanting a complete wardrobe for her, yes?"

"Yes. She'll need gowns, underwear, foundations, and hosiery, Sophia."

Marguerite's cheeks burned at having a man speak so plainly about her needs for undergarments. It didn't matter that he was her husband or that he planned to pay for such things. She had a brain of her own, a tongue of her own, and if her peers were to be believed, some sense of taste. There was no need for him to order her dresses as if she were a child.

"She'll need something right away," he continued before Marguerite could object.

"Of course." Sophia made a clucking sound with her tongue. "The war. It took so much from us women, don't you agree?"

For the first time she addressed Marguerite, but once again, she didn't wait for an answer.

"You will give me the afternoon for this project."

Bram frowned, but she shooed him away. "Trust me in this as your dearly departed mother trusted me with her own designs. To ask for an afternoon to complete such a task is not too much, I assure you. Go take care of whatever business you have. Visit a barber, buy new clothes, sit at a hotel and read something, I do not care. But do not return until six."

Bram took his time considering the order, then complied, settling his hat on his head and backing to the door. "Behave yourself," he warned, shaking a finger at Marguerite as he left the building.

Marguerite could have cheerfully strangled him. Her cheeks burned at the way he'd treated her in so cavalier a fashion in front of Sophia.

But the woman merely shrugged and waved a dismissing hand. "Men. They are such beasts at times, yes?"

"Yes," Marguerite answered heartily. "They are indeed."

"Well, now," Sophia sighed in pleasure after looking her up and down. "Shall we begin?"

Marguerite touched the woman's wrist when she would have walked past in order to collect her things.

"I cannot pay you for—"

"But your husband will be paying."

"I suppose, but—"

Sophia patted her cheek as if she were an elderly aunt and Marguerite just a child. "Do not worry, *cara*. If Bram orders this expense, it is because he wishes it and can afford it." She clucked her tongue in delight, rubbing her thumb and forefinger together. "Of all the St. Charles men, that one is the most . . . tight."

"Tight?"

"Frugal. He would not spend a penny unless he had a dollar to spare."

He would not spend a penny unless he had a dollar to spare.

The words continued to haunt Marguerite through her fitting. Money. Where in the world had Bram earned enough money to rebuild Solitude, let alone the expenses he would incur today? His family's wealth came from land and horses. All that was gone now.

Damn Casey. Damn that man to hell and back for putting such doubts in her head. If not for him, she could have been enjoying this day, this experience. Instead, she was overcome with worry.

But hadn't Bram told her himself that he'd never killed for money? an inner voice whispered, causing Marguerite to grow still beneath Sophia's tape. She

164

remembered the surprise he'd shown at such a question—in fact, he'd appeared almost insulted.

So why would Casey say such a thing if it weren't true?

But even as the thought sprang into her head, she pushed it away. Bram had never lied to her. Never in all the time she'd known him. Indeed, if he had any faults on that account, it was that he was too honest. She would have to trust him in this matter.

Trust.

Dear heaven above, after all that had occurred, did she continue to trust him?

Yes. As amazing as it seemed, she *did* trust him. Quite completely. She might be angry for what he'd done, irritated, frustrated, and peeved. But she knew through it all that he was not the sort of man to kill for money. He was . . .

Honorable.

After sweeping whatever misgivings remained aside, the next few hours passed swiftly for Marguerite. As soon as Sophia discovered that Marguerite had spent most of her life in France, she dropped her attempts at English and spoke in fluent French, grilling Marguerite for updates in fashion and style since many of the design books she used as her guides were delayed months—sometimes years—as the effects of the war were repaired and shipments became more regular.

As she took measurements and fitted and pinned, she related the hardships of being a dressmaker during the last few years, the shortage of cloth, of pins, of needles, of thread. She spoke in a quavering voice of the women's suffering she had seen, the loneliness, the desolation, the fear. She mentioned her clients, some of whom currently worked for her instead of ordering creations of their own.

Now and again, a woman would stop in Sophia's shop. Sometimes they did nothing more than look at Sophia's work. A few bought a ribbon or a yard of lace. Several delivered embroidery and beadwork. Each time Sophia would introduce them to Marguerite—"This is Amanda Farquahr of the South Carolinian Farquahrs" or "This is Emily Tate of the steel mill Tates"—making it apparent from the beginning of any changes in her customers' social prominence, since the war held little significance to her. These were her dear and loving friends, and she was more than willing to include Marguerite in the same ranks.

At noon, they paused briefly in their endeavors and dined on the soup, bread, and cheese brought by one of her workers. All talk of clothing soon disappeared beneath a wealth of inconsequential gossip and giggling. Then, at four, they paused again for tea and tiny sandwiches, a habit Sophia admitted to acquiring from a British woman who did her cutting.

An hour before Bram's expected arrival, Sophia turned the shop over to her assistant and escorted Marguerite upstairs to her own private apartments. There, despite Marguerite's protests, she insisted on preparing a bath for her so she could feel clean and fresh in her new clothes. Then Sophia sat on the other side of an elaborate eighteenth-century privacy screen, sewing on one of the sleeves that would soon grace an afternoon dress for Marguerite.

"Tell me, *cara,* how did you and Bram meet?"

Hidden from the woman's view in her tiny cocoon of solitude, Marguerite froze, wondering what she should say. Was there some special story that Bram wanted her to use? Was she supposed to avoid any sorts of personal questions?

Not sure how she should respond, but knowing instinctively that Sophia knew when discretion was demanded of her, she said honestly, "We met before the war."

"Ahhh."

Marguerite didn't know what that response meant, since she couldn't see Sophia's face.

"Love at first sight, I suppose?" the woman inquired.

"Yes. Yes it was." It had been a long time since Marguerite had allowed herself to even consider that point.

"Then you must be the young Frenchwoman I heard tales about just before the war. I remember I was making ball gowns when first I heard of you. Wasn't there such a ball you were invited to attend?"

"Yes," Marguerite responded in surprise. "Yes, there was."

"All the women were, how you say—atwitter?—when they came for their fittings. They had heard so much about your beauty, your fashions, that they didn't want to be overshadowed that night." She sighed happily. "Such gowns I made! Each more beautiful than the last. I hired a half dozen women to keep up with the demands."

"I'm sorry," Marguerite responded, squeezing a sponge in reflex as if it had been her fault that the woman was at one time overworked.

Sophia laughed. "No need to apologize, *cara mia*. The earnings from that season alone gave me what I needed to get through the hard times that followed."

She hummed. There was the snip of scissors. "He must have loved you dearly to send for you to come home from Europe so soon after the war."

If only that had been the case. If only that had been the sequence of events. "I suppose."

This time the heavy silence came from Sophia. "You mean you do not know?"

"I—"

Sophia chuckled. "He adores you. This I know."

"Why . . . why would you say that?" Marguerite inquired as casually as she could.

"Ahh, all brides need to be reassured, no? How many times have I been in this position of relaying what should be obvious?" The chair squeaked, and Sophia's face soon appeared at the top of the screen. "In my career as a dressmaker, I have been forced to lie to many a young woman being fitted for a trousseau. But, in this instance, I can say with all honesty that the man cares for you, cares deeply, perhaps even more than he has admitted to himself."

She pointed a finger in Marguerite's direction. "His mother was one of my finest clients. Beautiful? Oh!" She kissed the tips of her fingers. "It was a tragedy she died when Bram was but sixteen or seventeen. She adored her sons, they were all she talked about. I watched them grow from boyhood to manhood, and know each of them as well as I would know my own blood."

Her voice dropped to a conspiratorial whisper. "That Bram has always been a stubborn one. Frugal to the point of indecency. Single-minded. Hard. A man happiest with his own company." She threw her hands up as if the rest should be self-explanatory. "To see him this way, afraid to leave you alone, spending money on *you* when Solitude is in ruins, should be enough to reassure you. But the eyes"—she pointed to her own—"they cannot lie. They follow you wherever you go. Especially when you aren't looking, they are filled with a burning . . . with *amore.*"

Marguerite shook her head, knowing that the woman was wrong. That there were other, harsher reasons for such reactions. Reasons meant to humble and punish her.

"You do not believe me?" Sophia asked, shaking her finger at her again. "Then, you wait. You wait and see for yourself."

Chapter

11

By the time Bram was expected to return, the woman who sat waiting for him on one of the tiny brocade chairs held no resemblance at all to the one he'd left there that morning. Her hair had been combed and drawn to the back of her head, held in place with beaded hairpins, one long sausage roll resting on her left shoulder.

She wore a simple dark blue suit trimmed in black velvet, one that had been altered from a prewar order that had never been claimed. She had a matching lace and velvet reticule, sensible black boots, and cotton hose. The effect was elegant, yet maintained a sense of purposefulness, as if it were known from the beginning that Marguerite would need the ensemble for more than a walk through a rose garden.

Her breath caught when she saw Bram heading in her direction. It was obvious that she hadn't been the only one to use her time effectively. His hair had been trimmed, and—although on the longish side—looked clean and healthy and neatly combed back from his face. His jaw was bare of the shadow of beard that usually lingered there in the evening. The dusty, sun-bleached uniform had been replaced with a startlingly white linen shirt, fitted brown-black trousers, a black jacket, and new shiny boots.

"He could persuade an angel to fall from grace, yes?" Sophia murmured next to her.

Yes, Marguerite agreed silently, he could.

He stepped into the dressmaker's shop as if he owned it, his eyes falling on Marguerite. She found herself automatically standing and growing still under his careful scrutiny. When he gestured for her to turn, she complied, all the while wondering if Sophia was right. Did he stare at her when she wasn't aware of his actions? Did he watch her every move with some emotion that could be misinterpreted as adoration?

"Thank you, Sophia," he said in a rich, dark voice.

"You are more than welcome. I will send the rest of her things as they become ready."

"Good. You've included some items for her in the meantime?"

"Of course. I've some boxes over there with a few day gowns, some skirts and blouses for work, good, heavy gloves, aprons, and stockings. I chose practical items, since I knew you would have her help you with Solitude." Her eyes twinkled. "One of my girls has agreed to deliver them on her way home tonight. I will send you a bill."

He nodded decisively, taking Marguerite's elbow and ushering her from the building without any more ceremony. He said nothing to her, merely strode down the boardwalk.

"Well?" Marguerite finally asked when she could bear the suspense no more.

"Well what?"

"What do you think of Sophia's work?"

She damned herself for wanting to hear the words, of forcing some sort of grudging compliment, but she couldn't help herself.

"It will do."

It will do. The words echoed in her brain. It will *do?* Damn his hide, she'd spent the entire afternoon being poked and prodded to look her best and all he could say was that it would do!

She stopped, yanking free, glaring at him. "You know, you could have saved yourself a good deal of time and money if you'd simply sent for my trousseau. You didn't have to take me to Sophia's."

He backtracked to stand right in front of her, so close she could feel the heat of his body and smell the musky scent of bayberry on his skin. "I won't have you wearing clothes that another man has bought for you."

For some reason, her heart made an odd little leap in her breast at the degree of possessiveness she heard in his voice. "Why should it matter?"

He lowered his head so that when he spoke, she could not escape the seriousness of his gaze. "Because you are *my* wife, *my* responsibility."

"Is that all?"

His eyes flared briefly when she refused to let the matter rest. "What more could it be?"

She thought of what Sophia had said and the fact that the woman believed he cared for her. Truly cared. In some small way. Marguerite discovered that she'd never wanted anything more.

But she would not beg for his affections.

Ignoring Bram's question, she said instead, "I suppose we'd best be starting for home. It will be dark soon, don't you think?"

He didn't move, but looked at her with an intensity that made her skin prickle with awareness. "Don't play games with me, Marguerite."

"Games?" she echoed weakly when his tone emerged with a razor's edge.

"Those feminine wiles that women use to turn a man inside out, batting their eyes, acting coy, pretending an innocence of worldly issues that they don't have." He bent closer, closer. The traffic of the street around them faded away. "These questions you've been asking, these demands for attention, all have their own secret purposes."

"What?"

"You think to bend me to your will, to make me admit that I find you beautiful, intelligent, and overwhelmingly desirable. You want to whittle away my resolve and leave me a mass of putty in your hands. Well, it won't work. I refuse to fall victim to such machinations."

With that parting shot, he turned and strode away, simply assuming that she would follow.

She did. Not because he wanted her to. But because in the midst of his tirade, he'd offered her the compliment she'd wished to hear.

Bram St. Charles found her overwhelmingly desirable.

Intelligent.

And for the first time since leaving him so long ago, she actually felt that way. Inside. Where it counted most.

It was late evening by the time they returned to Solitude. The place appeared even more desolate, more ravaged in the moonlight. The silvery sheen that trickled from the intermittent cloud cover showed a ground riddled with ash and rubble. The skeletal remains of the rose garden and what had once been an orchard gave Marguerite a macabre shiver, as if she were looking out over a graveyard.

"We will rebuild it all, Marguerite," Bram said, once again reading her thoughts with a stunning accuracy.

"How?" She gazed at him then, her eyes pleading. "You might have the proper funds for clothing and food and supplies"—she waved a hand at the valley below—"but it would take a fortune to put all this to rights."

The shadows cloaked his expression so that she could not tell if she'd offended him by her remark.

"What if I were to tell you that I had a fortune?"

She felt a flood of dread, but refused to allow the doubts she'd felt earlier to assail her again.

"What's the matter, Marguerite? Didn't you tell me that you intended to marry Algy for his money? Does it disturb you that you were already married to a wealthy man?"

"But the war . . ."

"Took a great deal, but I have managed to scrape a little together."

She felt another twinge of fear deep in her belly. Casey had been right. Bram had somehow earned a profit fighting for the South. "What have you done, Bram?" She gripped his arm. "What crimes have you committed?"

"Crimes?"

"Were you a thief? A profiteer?"

A cold silence met her demands. Then his fingers wrapped around hers, forcibly removing them from his arm.

"You don't have much of an opinion of me, do you?"

She continued as if he hadn't spoken. "We've got to find a lawyer, someone who will protect you, someone who will keep the authorities from coming for you. You can claim temporary madness, pressures induced by the war. We could see that whoever you've harmed is repaid, and—"

"Hush." He laid a finger over her lips. This time, there was a curious tenderness to his tone that she couldn't understand. "Marguerite, I haven't stolen anything."

"But, the money . . ."

"Is mine. My family's. We were able to hide chests of valuables before the conflict began. A treasure, really. Most of it gold and jewels handed down for generations through my family. The treasure has been divided among the three St. Charles brothers. As it is, with the price of gold going through the roof, there is more than enough in the family coffers to satisfy our needs."

"Oh." The soft puff of bewilderment spoke volumes.

He cupped her cheeks, tipping her head into a patch of moonlight. "You were worried about me, Marguerite?"

She tried to yank away, damning herself for revealing so much with her outburst, but he held her fast.

"The money garnered from the St. Charles treasure will never be put in your hands. You know that, don't you?"

The remark hurt, more than it had a right to do. "I don't care about the damned treasure."

"But you were ready to marry Algy for money."

"I was willing to marry to provide a means to survive."

"Some would consider your motives a bit mercenary."

"No," she insisted. "Just practical."

"In time your modeling might have provided the same results. You've become quite famous. Why didn't you just wait instead of jumping into matrimony?"

She made a soft snort of disbelief. "Joliet pays me what he can, but most of his profits are eaten up by gallery owners, suppliers, and his own living expenses. What fame I've gathered is transitory at best. I never could have made enough for my family to live in any sort of comfort."

"You could have worked for other artists."

"Joliet is the only man I would ever allow to paint me."

"Why?"

"I trust him."

Bram's hold tightened, digging into her skin. "Is he your lover?"

She couldn't help the quick laugh that bubbled from her throat. "Joliet? Surely you've seen pictures of him, a stooped, wizard-looking old man with a snow-white goatee and spectacles."

"Was he your lover?" Bram demanded again.

"No!" She pushed his hands away exclaiming angrily, "No man has *ever* touched me that way but you!"

The words echoed in the night, but Marguerite was not sorry that she'd said them. Not when she saw the way Bram's eyes flared and a bit of the hardness eased from his features. Then he lay the backs of his knuckles beneath her jaw, skimming across the soft skin.

"No man will ever touch you that way but me," he vowed. Lifting the reins, he urged the horse down the hill.

They were met in the barnyard by two of Bram's men. No words were spoken. As if they'd performed the chore a hundred times before, the men automatically took charge of the horse and wagon and began unloading the supplies Bram had bought in town.

It was not until Bram began leading her to the barn that Marguerite was confronted with the fact that nothing had changed. She might have been given new clothes, she might have spent the day away from this place, sipping tea and gossiping and laughing. But reality had returned and with it all the petty problems she had so briefly escaped.

"Will the animals be joining us for the evening?" Marguerite inquired under her breath. He'd had a whole day to think about things. She wouldn't have been too surprised to find that he'd moved a dozen pigs into the structure while she'd been gone.

"No." His hand slid around her waist to guide her through the gloom.

"What about your men? Will they be sharing the loft?"

"They prefer to stay in the tent where they don't need to mind their manners so much."

"Just what does that mean?"

His palm at the base of her spine was warm, insistent. "They've been without the gentler influence of a woman for some time. They prefer to speak . . . plainly, without guarding their tongues—although you will note that they've all bathed and shaved."

"Oh."

"Besides which, this is to be where we will stay. Alone."

Bram opened the door for Marguerite. Once inside he bade her to stay there until he could light a lamp. The rasp of a match on a board caused a flare of light that flickered and intensified when touched to the wick of a lantern. Bit by bit the glow intensified, spilling into the empty corners and causing Marguerite to gasp at what she saw.

The space had been transformed. Marguerite had decorated the barn with what few things Bram had brought with them that first day. But now the area had been transformed into a palace of sorts. Thick Aubusson carpets covered the dirt floor, gleaming brass lamps hung from the beams, the "rooms" were filled with sturdy chairs and graceful ottomans, and every convenience imaginable had been included. One of the stalls now sported fresh pine-board walls, a stove, and a pie safe. Another held a pitcher and basin, a tub, and a drying rack. In the main portion, where hay and grain had once been stored, there was a settee and rocker, two chairs, a swooning couch, and three marble-topped tables complete with crocheted doilies and vases of fresh marigolds.

"Bram?" she dared breathe his name, so stunned was she by the transformation. She was afraid to blink for fear that it would all disappear.

Bram's brows creased in a scowl of warning. "Don't read too much into what you see, Marguerite. None of this was done solely for your benefit. After your meager attempts at decorating the place, I got a taste of what it was like to live more normally. Today, walking through town, seeing Sophia, getting myself some clothes and such, I admitted to myself how much I missed some of the creature comforts. My men and I worked most of the day, then I came back for you."

"Of course." She was too bemused by it all to make much more than that weak reply. Only the day before, he'd been so adamant that they "make do" with what they had.

He walked to a sideboard that had been placed against a far wall. A collection of crystal bottles and glasses lay on a delicate-tatted runner. He filled two tiny thimble-shaped glasses with an amber liquid, giving her one.

"Sherry?"

She took it, not so much because she wanted it, but because he had offered it to her. Because his eyes had lost some of their hardness. The entire situation struck her as being strange. The transformed barn, the wine, the two of them together this way.

"The color of your suit is very becoming. Have I told you that yet?"

She shook her head.

"It makes your eyes sparkle. Your skin seem so pale." He caressed her cheek with his knuckle, sighing her name. "This was the way I imagined I would see you."

"In a barn?"

Again, the twitch of his lips almost developed into a crooked smile. How she wished that would happen. From the depths of her soul, she wished it would happen.

"No. But it will have to do, won't it?" He touched her hair, nudging at the beaded hairpins. "Are you hungry?" he asked. The tone of his voice was so soft, so deep, so rich, she found herself wondering if he were inquiring about more than food. The thought alone caused her to tremble.

"Not really."

"Good. Neither am I. Nor am I thirsty." He took the glass from her, setting both hers and his aside. Then he took her hands, drawing her backward into the "parlor" portion of their new home.

Marguerite knew what would happen next. She'd known it from the second he'd placed his hand at her waist to usher her inside, and earlier, when he'd come to Sophia's and his eyes had begun to burn with a familiar, seductive heat.

When he framed her face with his hands, she didn't resist. She leaned into the caress, not too proud to admit that she wanted this, needed this.

"I want to make love with you, Marguerite."

"Yes."

"With you, Marguerite."

There was only one answer she could give.

"Yes."

Even as she spoke, she knew she was agreeing to far more than his touch. She was agreeing to give their future a chance.

Chapter

12

The embers that had burned deep in his eyes flared to life. His head bent and he kissed her, lightly, sweetly, making her heart ache with the tenderness she saw.

Unaccustomed tears gathered at her closed lashes. How she had missed this in her life! Not just the caresses, the kisses, but the tacit reverence, the elemental adoration, the need. It had been so long since anyone had come to her for something more than a means for food, shelter, friendship, or advice. To be held this way, caressed this way, made her more aware that she was a woman, and it had been a long time since she'd truly felt like one.

"Touch me, Marguerite," he said against her, into her.

It was all the encouragement she needed. Her hands rose to his chest, to touch, explore, to reacquaint herself with the hard planes, the line of his ribs, the rich dusting of hair down the center.

He swept her into his arms, pulling her against his body, making her conscious of each valley, each ridge. Her arms wrapped around his neck, and she held him as if he were a lifeline—which indeed he was. He was the anchor in this storm of sensation. Her rescuer from a dull life she might have spent with Algy Bolingbrook.

Their kisses became greedy and intense. When he carried her to the swooning couch, she did not resist. Nor did she resist when, after setting her down, he began to work impatiently at the buttons of her jacket. She tried to help him, but even she seemed to have lost some of her coordination. With a grumbled apology, Bram yanked at the edges, causing buttons to pop and scatter all over the floor.

"Help me," he rasped against her lips, then backed away to grapple with his own clothing.

She stripped as fast as she could, paying no heed to her own disrobing as she stared at Bram. With each garment that fell to the floor, she became more desperate to touch him. He was so beautiful, so leanly muscled, so tall, so strong. She wanted to be in those arms, flesh to flesh.

The instant she stepped from her pantalets, the last and final barrier, her silent plea was answered. Bram scooped her close, and she gasped when their naked bodies met, breast to thigh. She squeezed her eyes shut beneath the immediate burst of passion that exploded in her body and the heated fullness that settled in her loins.

He kissed her frantically on her lips, her neck, her shoulder, and she returned each endearment in kind, delighting in the tastes, the textures she encountered.

When he lifted her and lay her on the swooning couch, she responded by pulling him onto her, needing to feel his weight, his length. With her hands, her mouth, the arching of her lips, she told him all the things she could not put into words. That she wanted him to love her, to satisfy her needs.

The moment Bram reached low to test her, she whispered, "Yes, yes." His gaze was hot and full of passion as he nudged intimately against her, so hot, so warm, so insistent. Then he was positioning himself above her, sliding into her in one smooth thrust, causing her to close her eyes and grip the tasseled pillows beneath her head at the sheer pleasure of it.

Her whole body, her whole mind, centered around that point of joining, feeling each nuance of sensation, each blinding thrust. An exquisite pleasure was drawing taut in her body, causing her to whimper and grind closer, raking her fingers down his shoulders. It had been so long since she'd experienced such bliss. So very long. Her entire body tensed in anticipation. And when her release came, it was so blindingly sweet, so overpowering, that she couldn't prevent the cry that rent from her very soul.

That response seemed to be what Bram was waiting for, because his own pleasure came swiftly on the heels of hers, the primitive moan he uttered squeezing her heart with its complete abandonment.

When he collapsed on top of her, she ran her hands through the hair at his nape, her eyes closed, absorbing all that had happened between them—far more than just a physical act. As much as either of them might damn the fact in the future, a change had occurred in their relationship. They could no longer claim to be strangers, intimate or otherwise. Too many confidences had been shared, too many defenses had been shattered. Their lovemaking was only an outward reflection of other, deeper emotions that were beginning to boil beneath the surface.

Marguerite blinked, looking up in time to see that Bram was watching her in just the manner Sophia had claimed. Heatedly. Thoroughly. Rather than reassuring her, Marguerite felt a frisson of fear. There were so many things that stood between them and any sort of ease together. So many secrets.

"You look so solemn," Bram murmured.

She shook her head.

"Regrets?"

She considered her answer before saying, "No. Not since I looked up to find you striding up the aisle of St. Jude's."

His gaze glittered with surprise and more, so much more. Pride, pleasure, wariness.

"And before? Do you regret anything that occurred before?"

She closed her eyes. The truth would be the hardest thing to admit. "Yes."

He did not ask her to explain, and for that she was glad. She had bared too much of herself, more than she had ever planned on doing. To tell him more, to admit more of her own private anguish would be too much.

Bram settled at her side, drawing her into the hollow of his shoulder, caressing her back, tickling her nape. The actions were soothing, releasing the last bit of tension that lingered in her body. Soon she found one arm draped over his chest, her legs tangled with his own.

"Marguerite?" he whispered some time later when she was all but asleep.

"Mmm?" she barely scraped together the energy necessary for the response.

"You were telling me the truth when you said there were no other lovers?"

"Yes."

"Good." She felt him kiss her hair. "Good."

Marguerite woke late the following morning to discover that Bram had once again left before she'd awakened. She dressed in one of the pretty cotton day dresses that Sophia had sent, covering it with a voluminous mother hubbard apron. With her hair combed and plaited and her hands protected by gloves, she took a battered wooden bucket once used to feed stock and made her way outside.

Bram was there, shouting instructions to the dozen or so men who had come to begin rebuilding the house. Her cheeks pinkened slightly when she realized the hour was quite late for rising. She'd been sleeping so deeply, she hadn't even heard the laborers arrive.

She had nearly made her way to the wreckage of the house when Bram caught sight of her. He tugged a pair of leather gloves from his hands, swiped an arm across his sweaty brow, then sauntered toward her. The sinuous grace of his movements, the unmitigated power of his form, caused an immediate reaction in her own body, making her remember the way he'd

loved her the night before—on the swooning couch,
then later on the iron bedstead that had been assem-
bled in the loft.

"Good morning." His voice was liquid smoke,
flowing over her, into her, making her warm even
more.

He took the bucket from her hands, cocking one
eyebrow in silent inquiry.

"What's all this for?" he asked, gesturing to the
gloves, the apron, the sensible leather boots.

"I thought I would do some work in your mother's
rose garden if you could find me a spade and a pair of
shears."

He frowned. "The flowers are dead."

She shook her head. "Not all of them. The new
growth is proof of that. The plants might be stunted
and struggling, but the roots are very much alive. A
little pruning, some care and mulch, and they may
even bloom next summer."

The fact that she had shown some interest in
Solitude, especially his mother's rose garden, seemed
to please him. Did he remember the way she did, how
they had stood one day, on an afternoon much like
this, a few weeks before Thanksgiving? Did he recall
the way she'd gripped the marble terrace railing and
looked out over the last hardy blooms of the year?
She'd made a wish then, to see the blooms in spring.

It was then, with the threat of her father taking her
back in a few-weeks time that she'd begged Bram to
marry her, to help her stay in America. With him.
She'd already known that she carried his child. But
that hadn't been her main reason for asking. She'd
wanted to stay with him. She'd wanted to be his bride.

She'd wanted to live in this fairy-tale land with its green fields and rolling mountains, away from the squalor and gloom of Paris's twisting streets. She'd wanted peace and room to breathe.

How young she'd been, how naive. She'd thought that all she had to do was imagine something in all its perfection and those images would come true. She hadn't even bothered to listen to the grumbles of political discontent. They couldn't affect her, wouldn't affect either of them.

She'd been so wrong.

Not for the first time, Marguerite wondered how things would have been different if she'd stayed. But as the thought took shape, she knew that, despite the price of her actions, remaining in America would have been far more dear. Little Jeffrey would never have survived the threat of conflict, the lack of medical supplies, the tension, the worry. He never would have been able to thrive and grow and learn as he had with his special tutors.

No. She'd made the right decision in returning to France. Her son might not have been born perfect. His spine might be twisted, his body frail, but she loved him with a desperation that consumed her entire soul. There was nothing she wouldn't do, nothing she wouldn't give. Even if it meant losing all hope of her own happiness. She could only pray that somehow, some way, she could find a way to encourage the same sort of bond between Jeffrey and his father.

A pang of longing caught her breath. She'd tried to keep all thoughts of Jeffrey from crowding close and making the wait that much more interminable. But she couldn't deny her eagerness to see him, hold him, talk to him. How many more days until he arrived?

How much longer before she was forced to divulge all her secrets?

"You've grown solemn."

She started, having been so deep in her thoughts that she'd forgotten Bram stood near.

"Just imagining." When he waited for some sort of elaboration, she said, "Imagining what Solitude will look like by the time these flowers bloom. You'll have the house nearly constructed by then."

Bram squinted, gazing out over his land as if he could see the finished result. "We'll need to be buying breeding stock. I intend to continue my father's work with Thoroughbreds." He squinted at the remains of the house. "But that will have to wait until next year."

"What then? Once you have your house, your livelihood, and your horses, what will you do?"

He smiled. "Live out my life, with my wife and a family of our own. Other than that, I don't intend to plan too much of a schedule. I intend to live one day at a time."

With that parting remark, he backed away, turning to begin issuing more instructions to his men.

He had no idea that he'd left her feeling incredibly anxious. Her fingers clenched in front of her to still their trembling.

A family.

Family.

It wouldn't be long before Jeffrey and his nurse would dock in Baltimore. With each hour that passed, marking his imminent arrival, Marguerite wished to see him with all her heart. But his presence would bring untold conflicts. She knew that she wouldn't be able to hide the fact that he was Bram's son—and she didn't want to try. But she also knew that to tell Bram about why she had kept the boy's identity a secret for so long would be one of the hardest things she would do.

Would Bram ever be able to forgive her for not informing him about the boy until now? Would he be able to understand why she was so protective of their son? Besides his obvious ailments, Jeffrey had always been so sensitive, so keen to other people's feelings that she had always tried to shield him from the world's harsher realities. Would Bram ever accept that she'd done what she'd thought was best?

But most of all, what would Bram do that first instant he met the boy? As soon as they met, it would be obvious that Jeffrey would never be the sort of heir he would have wished to have. He would never go galloping over these hills, hell-bent-for-leather as Bram and his brothers had done. He would never slide down banisters or break little girls' hearts. Would the mere fact of his deformities cause Bram to shrink back in horror? To send them both away?

Or could he somehow find a way to accept the boy?

Her eyes closed in a brief heartfelt prayer.

Please. Please, let it be so.

In the next week, Marguerite felt that she and Bram had settled into a tenuous sort of truce. It was as if Bram's overtures to make the barn a more comfortable setting and the efforts she had extended toward regrooming his mother's rose garden had eased the tension between them for a time. With each day that passed, the idea of a future together became less nebulous. Not that Marguerite was anticipating any "happily ever afters"; she was just beginning to believe that Bram had been telling the truth when he had said he would never let her go.

She was his. The thought was not always comforting. Sometimes, she wondered if his possessiveness was the same that he might extend toward a horse or a rifle. Something that bordered more on feelings of ownership than those of concern. He desired her. Their nights together were filled with lovemaking. But for some reason she didn't understand, the passion wasn't enough. She was beginning to crave a relationship based on more than mere physicality. She wanted to know that the fragile overtures of trust and compassion she was willing to extend to him would be returned.

"The garden is actually taking shape beneath your care, Marguerite." The low voice startled her, but only for a moment. Then the same slow sizzling heat she experienced whenever Bram was near began to seep through her veins.

She leaned back on her heels, shading her eyes with her hands so that she could stare up at the towering wall of muscle and bone that was her husband. Marguerite would never fully comprehend how the mere sight of him could cause her pulse to quicken, over and over again, with the least provocation.

"Do you think any progress has been made?"

Bram stared out over the gravel paths that had been raked into place and smoothed, the rich beds that had been neatened and freed from weeds. It had been an arduous task, but one made easier by the boy Bram had assigned to help her for a few hours a day. There was so much to be done, planting and pruning and grafting, which couldn't be accomplished until spring, but she wanted to think that there was some tangible sign of her efforts.

"You've done wonders. Even if the bushes don't bloom, it's good to see some order on the grounds."

"They'll bloom," she said decisively, and rose to her feet. She stumbled slightly as her shoe caught her skirts, and he reached to steady her. A flurry of sparks coursed through her body, beginning at that tiny point of contact. Looking at Bram, she wondered if he knew how easily he affected her, how easily he made her forget that she should guard her emotions and do everything in her power to keep her heart from flip-flopping whenever he was near.

"The house appears to be coming along as well," she said in an effort to return her thoughts to a safer plane. She pointed to the wreckage that had been hauled away and the rock foundations that were being formed.

"Yes. The architecture won't be the same style as it was before the war, but it will be as beautiful. It was a promise I made to Micah."

"Have you heard from him?" she inquired, aware that Bram sent regular reports of Solitude's progress even though Micah had long since signed over its responsibility to him.

Bram became curiously evasive. "Not since his telegram. But I'm sure he's busy. He had a good deal of rebuilding to do on his wife's behalf. Once Solitude is finished, I'd like to convince them all to come here for a visit, a real family party. Next summer, I think." He glanced at her. "When the roses you are so sure will grow are in full bloom."

She felt a warmth seep into her cheeks at his careful regard. She wasn't quite sure when it had happened, but Bram's anger had eased a little in the past few days as well, allowing glimpses of the old Bram she'd known to show through.

"What about Jackson?"

Bram's jaw hardened, and she feared she'd unintentionally offended him. But she soon realized his frustration was directed toward other sources.

"Still no word."

She didn't dare ask the question that immediately sprang to mind. *Is Jackson even alive?* Instead, she inquired, "Where was he last stationed? Maybe he hasn't been released from the army yet." There were garrisons of Union soldiers in the South serving as provisional government officials until other more permanent arrangements could be made. Jackson could have been part of those forces.

Bram shook his head. "The last record of him through official sources was made the fall of sixty-four when he was listed as wounded during some sort of assassination attempt on General Waterton—the man he served under."

She heard the worry in his voice as well as the unspoken dread. Jackson had been listed as wounded. Not missing, not dead. But if no one had heard or seen him since then, it was not a good sign.

Disturbed by the way some of the tension had returned to her husband's features, Marguerite touched his arm. "Don't worry about him, Bram. He'll be fine. He always was a bit of a scrapper, but Jackson never failed to come out on top." Even as she offered the cliché, she knew it was a hollow assurance.

Bram visibly shook off the melancholy mood, throwing a wry smile in her direction. The action caused her to hold her breath and stare. A smile. A slight, but very real smile. She had been anticipating this moment for so long that now it had come, she didn't quite know how to react. She was frozen in her tracks, dumbfounded, feeling very much like a young girl who had caught her first wink across a crowded ballroom.

"Sophia delivered a new trunk of things for you to wear."

"Oh, really?" She had been so absorbed in her work, she hadn't heard anyone approach. Of course, the sound of the workmen could have drowned out the arrival of a regiment.

"I wondered if you would care to join me tonight for dinner. I thought we might dine in town."

She opened her mouth to offer a quick, automatic agreement, then hesitated, wondering if the outing was such a good idea. She was sure that part of the reason for their getting along of late lay in the fact that they spent most of their time concentrating on their own tasks with minimal bouts of conversation. At night they turned to passion as a means to avoid arguing. To go into town would mean a long buggy ride and at least an hour or two over dinner.

"Well?" he prompted.

"I think I'd like that very much." The words rushed from her lips before she had time to reconsider them.

"Good. We'll leave here about six. Dress warmly."

Then he turned to go back to his duties, leaving her staring at his broad shoulders, narrow hips, and leanly muscled thighs.

A thick sense of foreboding seeped into her limbs. She would be in the man's company for several hours without a bed to solve any awkward silences that might crop up. She would have to do her best to control the thrust of their verbal exchanges. She would have to ensure that they had a comfortable evening, spoke of the weather and Solitude and horses. Or she could take matters into her own hands, gird her courage . . .

And somehow find a way to tell him about Jeffrey.

Chapter

13

In honor of the occasion of actually being *invited* to go somewhere with her husband, Marguerite wore a garnet-colored gown. A border of black jet beads encrusted the low neckline and the ends of her sleeves and hung in wide bands across the front of her underskirt. Black hairpin lace—so delicate it could have been fashioned by fairy-tale spiders—fell in a deep swathe from her waistline and had been gathered in back over a padded horsehair bustle. Her hair was swept over one ear and pinned there by an elaborate ebony comb edged with more jet beads.

Except for the black lace mitts that ended above her elbow, her arms were bare, the rounded décolletage of her gown exposing a good deal of her throat and bosom. Over it all, the bustle, the poufs of fabric, the ruching, she wore a thick padded cape of black sateen with a stiff collar spilling with more intricate lace.

She hesitated before rounding the privacy screen, glancing (unseeingly) at the beam overhead where Bram had driven nails to hang her gowns. Her palms were slightly moist, but not through fear. No, it was more a sense of anticipation, of exhilaration, as if this night held something for them both. Something that could be special if she could only say and do the right things.

Taking a deep breath, she held it, her ribs pushing against the constraint of her corset and making her feel as if her bosom might spring from her daring bodice. But as she kept her head high and stepped into the keeping room of sorts, there was no denying that the dress had been able to handle the strain.

When he heard the rustle of her skirts against the dirt floor, Bram put down the glass of liqueur he'd been sipping. His eyes became darker, sultry, filled with meaning, informing her without a word that he'd been waiting for her. Watching.

A cool shiver of delight coursed her spine when she realized he must have been able to see her silhouette etched against the canvas insets of the screen.

"Spying, Bram?" she inquired, her voice huskier than she would have liked.

He didn't even bother to deny it. "Yes."

"So bold a course of action."

"Not really. Considering the tempting view that greeted me when I looked up, it was the only thing I could do."

The sensual banter caused her skin to tingle, breaking out in gooseflesh as she absorbed the way his gaze ran intimately from head to toe.

For several minutes neither of them moved, allowing Marguerite a chance for her own inspection. Sweet saints alive! Did he know what he did to her? Did he know that he stole her breath, standing so tall, so lean, clad in dark gray trousers, a black coat, and patterned vest, with a gleaming white shirt. If not for the way she was able to clutch the support post beside her, she would have literally swayed in reaction. Such civilized attire blatantly juxtaposed against the almost pagan waves of hair that flowed unrestrainedly to a spot well past his shoulders was too much for her to credit.

Despite the new clothes and all the changes made at Solitude, he hadn't taken the time to tame the brown-black waves with pomander, as was the style. Or maybe it wasn't a matter of time, but one of defiance. As if he weren't quite willing to surrender the darker, harsher side of himself that had been fostered the past few years.

"Those colors become you." It was Bram who broke the silence.

"Some might consider them to be the colors of demi-mourning. Garnet and black. It might even be argued that the choice is rather severe."

"Perhaps. There are those who look pale and washed-away by such intense shades. On these women mourning becomes especially harsh, an added tragedy."

"Does this mean that because you find it becoming on me, I should wear mourning as a matter of choice? That I should suffer some sort of loss?"

He moved closer and cupped her cheek. "That's not

at all what I meant. On you, black does little to signify grief. It becomes vibrant and incredibly alluring. What was it Byron said? 'She walks in beauty like the night . . .'"

Poetry. He was quoting poetry to her. The effect was incredibly arousing. The huskiness of his tone crept into her body, wrapping its way around her heart, making her wish, inexplicably, that the gown she wore beneath her cape were completely black as well.

"Come," he said, crooking his elbow for her to take. "We'd better go now. Otherwise, we won't be going at all."

The words alone had the power to set her on fire, but combined with the open passion she found in his gaze, it was an even headier experience, robbing her of the will to resist him.

Taking his proffered arm, she followed him into the cool night air. There was a bit of a breeze, making her glad that she'd worn a cape. Yet she could not deny that part of the cause of the reaction she felt lay in the fact that once they reached town, she would be forced to take it off—and then the revealing nature of her bodice would be open to his gaze.

"Sorry you came?"

"No. Not at all."

His lips lifted ever so slightly in amusement. "So you're beginning to resign yourself to my company?"

"Your company has . . ."

"Become more pleasant?"

"And a bit less . . . threatening."

He frowned. "I never would have hurt you, Marguerite."

"Not physically. But sometimes the words can wound just as easily."

He took a breath, holding it for an instant, then exhaling. "We've both said things in the heat of the moment which—"

She interrupted him with a hand on his arm. "Which are better left forgotten this evening."

"Yes," he said, his brow furrowed in such a way that she knew her reaction had startled him. The old Marguerite would have pouted and bullied and railed at him.

"I intend to enjoy myself this evening, Bram."

"Then I will do everything in my power to make it possible."

They dined in a small, elegant café situated just a block off Main Street. Marguerite was entranced the minute she walked inside. The tables were covered with lace-edged linens and adorned with huge golden chrysanthemums floating in bowls of colored water. The china was delicately rimmed with gold filigree, as were the goblets. A discreet string quartet played a selection of Brahms from one corner, while the guests in attendance were jeweled and bedecked in splendor.

"Do you think they recognize me?" Marguerite whispered as they entered.

"Undoubtedly." He tucked her arm a little more securely against his waist. "How could they fail to notice such a beautiful woman?"

Her steps faltered. "You've made it difficult for me to melt into your world, Bram."

"Something I never wanted you to do. You are famous for your lovely face and form, I see no need to hide that you have an equally feminine talent for handling adversity."

She would have uttered a pithy remark, but she could feel a tide of interest following them into the room. Luckily, she and Bram were ushered to a table in the near corner, one that was all but hidden from the rest of the diners by a trellis of clematis. A window on the opposite side afforded them a view of a tiny outdoor garden twinkling with tea candles.

The signs of war were there—the linen carefully darned, the silver dented and scratched in places, but Marguerite was entranced rather than repelled. Everywhere she went, she saw efforts of rebirth. Much like the roses she'd been tending at Solitude. Given care and time, something bigger and better was imminent.

Bram helped her remove her cape, his hands lingering on the bare skin of her shoulders. "Such a beautiful gown, Marguerite," he whispered next to her ear.

"Thank you."

"Let it be known I revise my position on your wearing black. You may wear any color you wish providing I am allowed to be the man at your side."

The words pooled deep in her body, making her wish that they weren't in such a public place so that she could turn to him then, wrap her arms around his neck and—

"Madame?"

She flushed as a waiter held out a chair.

As soon as they were both seated, the maître d' handed them huge leather-bound menus, Marguerite's discreetly missing its prices. She was delighted to see that the menu was French and on Bram's request, ordered for them both—although it was Bram who chose a rich red wine to accompany their meal.

Once the waiter had left, they were pooled in a warm, velvet quiet—one that was not as uncomfortable as Marguerite had imagined it would be.

"I feel guilty," she said, gazing around her, peeking through the foliage at the other distinguished-looking diners.

"Why?"

"Such extravagances."

"You think I can't afford them? Even after I told you where the money originates?"

"I don't know what to think anymore."

His eyes became intent, hooded, his fingers toying with the stem of his glass. "Tell me, Marguerite—the truth. Did you marry me all those years ago thinking that you would gain some sort of fortune?"

She could not lie. "No. I had no illusions. You were the second son. Solitude would eventually be willed to Micah. I didn't care."

"Then, why?"

She tried to shrug casually. "I fancied myself in love."

"And were you?"

The questions were causing her heart to slow to a heavy, deliberate beat. One that made her body tremble.

Afraid of prying eyes, she leaned forward to whisper, "Must we get into all this now? The past is gone, over. We both made mistakes. Must we ruin the evening to resurrect them all again?"

She waited tensely for his response, knowing that she wouldn't tell him about Jeffrey. Not here. Not with others about.

When the line of his shoulders relaxed ever so slightly, she was able to relax.

"You're right. For now we will enjoy the evening. But first, answer one more thing. If I let you leave tonight . . . Would you go?"

The question came without warning, and like a gunshot, pierced her wall of reserve.

"What?"

"If I told you that you could go, that I would give you your annulment and that we would never see one another again, would you go?"

Why was he asking such a thing? Now. When the answer was no longer so simple. Mere days ago, she would have responded in the affirmative without hesitation, but after wriggling into his life, his routine, his confidence, her response was shrouded with all the repercussions it would bring.

Could she prove a coward? Could she leave him now, avoid the inevitable questions and explanations? Could she walk away as if these weeks had never happened and she hadn't been drawn back into his arms? His overpowering passion?

"Your answer, Marguerite."

"Yes." The word was wrenched from her heart. Not because it was the answer she wanted to give, but because it would be the wiser course.

"Then, I believe I can safely assume that you aren't staying with me for my money now."

When she realized the thrust of his questioning, her eyes filled with unexpected tears. "You mean you thought that I had . . . stayed with you . . . for *money?*"

"The thought occurred to me. After all, you have not complained about your new wardrobe or the changes to the barn."

She balled her napkin in her fist and threw it on the

table. But when she would have stood, he grasped her wrist.

"You cannot fault me for asking, Marguerite."

"You bastard."

The curse only made him grin.

"And now the question has been asked, it will not be brought up again."

She remained perched on the edge of her chair.

"Nor will I ever give you the opportunity to leave me or this marriage."

She didn't know whether she should be relieved or terrified.

"You are mine, Marguerite. Now and for all times."

"Why?" She could barely force the word from her lips. "If you hate me so much . . ."

"I don't hate you, Marguerite," he said slowly, as if surprised by the fact. "You can be maddening at times, quite irritating, in fact, but it isn't hate I feel for you."

"You did at one time."

"Yes. But I find my mood being swayed by something else."

"Oh?" His thumb unconsciously stroked her wrist, wreaking havoc on her senses and plundering her will to resist.

But even as she willed him to reveal his feelings, he said instead, "You are more beautiful than ever, Marguerite."

"It's the dress."

He shook his head. "It's the woman you've become. Not just on the outside." His brow creased, and he scrutinized her even more. "You're not so unsettled, so . . . flighty."

"Well, thank *you* very much." She tried to snatch her hand back, but he held her fast.

"I meant it as a compliment. You're more reserved, more introspective—without losing any of your fire. It's as if you've found a . . . purpose in living."

She grew quiet.

"What secrets of happiness have you discovered, Marguerite? While I was at war, you had an opportunity to see another side of life. What did you do during the years you were gone to help you find contentment?"

She responded with a question of her own. "Is your existence so awful, you've found none of your own, Bram?"

He paused before responding. "Until now."

His answer caused a subtle heat to spread through her veins, but when she would have responded, the waiter interrupted with a muffled, *"Pardon."*

The moment shattered, but not the lingering feelings. The languor, the sense of well-being, the desire.

As if sensing her thoughts, Bram met her eye. "Later," he said lowly. "We will discuss this when we are home."

Despite the renewed glow of a truce that coursed through her body, Marguerite knew it was a none-too-subtle warning of things to come.

"I thought we might take in a show," Bram said later as they walked into the cool night air.

"Theater?" she could barely summon the word.

"Of sorts."

His hand was firm at her elbow, leading her irretrievably down the street to where a blaze of gas lamps illuminated the high facade of Wilton's Imperial Theater. Once inside, Bram handed the gilt-tipped tickets to one of the black-clad employees, then leaned close to murmur a set of instructions in the man's ear. The elderly gentleman nodded, bowing slightly in Marguerite's direction. Then snapping his fingers, the man gestured for a young boy to take her wrap. He ripped the tickets in half before giving them to Bram again. Bram, in turn, handed them to her.

"Here. I know how women like to keep tangibles of such events."

"And men?" she asked. "What do they keep?"

His smile was the barest tilt of his lips. "The intangibles."

She cocked one brow in silent query. "And what are they?"

"Mental records of how things looked, and smelled"—again the slight smile—"and tasted."

Her knees began to tremble, so much so that she feared she wouldn't be able to walk properly. She could only be grateful that he took her arm, tucking it securely at his side, and led her to the sweeping staircase to the right.

He ushered her inside a private box, and she sighed in pleasure. From her vantage point she could see the set quite easily, note the detailing, the colors, the rich patina-like shades caused by the gas lanterns.

"What will we be seeing?" she asked as Bram held her chair, then reached to touch her shoulders, her arms. Her voice quivered ever so slightly in reaction.

"A melodrama."

"Melodrama?" she echoed in delight. How enchanting. Not some stuffy ballet or opera, but something distinctly American. Something fun and frothy.

He handed her one of the programs that had been left on the marble railing surrounding the enclosure. Eagerly, she read the title; *"The Malicious Matchmaker*. Oooo, how delightful!"

"I'm told that the acting is quite good."

But even as the comment was made, Bram's voice became almost . . . distracted. Marguerite glanced his way to see that he was not studying the program, but the audience. Odd. Almost as if he were looking for someone.

But who?

Bram waited until it was nearly time for intermission before excusing himself. "I think I'll check on a few things."

Marguerite, chuckling from the antics on the stage, glanced up at him, her eyes bright, her face wreathed in happiness. It was the first time he'd seen such an expression from her before. It made him realize how somber she'd become, how reserved—especially when compared to the flirtatious girl she'd been once.

"What things?" she asked, a hint of a frown clouding her brow.

He leaned close to kiss her forehead, to ease away the lines. "I arranged for light refreshments to be brought to our box. I thought I'd check and see if everything was on schedule."

Before she could question him further, he slipped out the narrow door and into the passageway, making his way down the darkened corridor to another door that opened into a private staircase reserved for theater personnel. Once inside, there was a curved set of iron steps and a single dim lantern.

Walking silently and taking care not to make any

sounds on the metal treads, he made his way down three flights, below stage level, to a prop storage room beneath. There, wending his way among the trunks, he headed for the tiny sliver of light bleeding beneath another rough door.

Sheffield waited for him there, seated on an absurdly huge carved chair that must have been used at some time for a throne.

He smiled when Bram entered. "So punctual. I've always liked that about you, St. Charles."

Bram didn't bother to respond. He would have been more than happy to deck the man in his present mood. He resented the fact that business had interrupted a night with his wife.

"Let's get it over with, Sheffield."

If the man was annoyed by Bram's hostile attitude, he gave no sign.

"I'd like to introduce you to someone." He crooked his finger, and a figure stepped from behind a steamer trunk laden with hats. "This is Roger Cornby, our actor. He will be playing the part of General Patterson. Quite an amazing resemblance, don't you think?"

It was. If Bram hadn't known the man who faced him was an actor, he would have been forced to take another look. The florid features and paunchy build were an exact duplicate of the Confederate general Horace Patterson. Any discrepancies could be attributed to the fact that a man's face inevitably grew harsher during war, more angular and filled with bitterness. Combined with rumors of illness, there would be no reason to question the slight differences he noted.

"He'll do."

Sheffield gave him a mocking glance. "So glad you approve." His tone softened ever so slightly. "You must realize by now that Casey is responsible. Am I wrong?"

Bram didn't bother to answer but asked a question of Cornby instead. "Have you been briefed?"

"Yes, sir."

"Good. Then I'll expect to see you at Solitude, in two day's time. See to it that a message is sent via my men, not by me. Until then keep out of sight and for hell's sake, don't do any talking."

Without waiting for a response, Bram turned and strode from the room.

But even though his business for the evening was finished, he couldn't quite banish the bad taste that lingered on his tongue.

The ride home was completed without conversation, without explanation. Marguerite sat tensely on her side of the buggy seat, wondering what had gone wrong. There had been a few minutes of upset in the café, true, but they had quickly recovered from that, and the evening had become almost magical again.

Until Bram had gone to check on things during intermission.

Did he know that she'd stood to follow him? That she'd poked her head out of the doorway only to see him slipping through one of the actors' entrances? Was that what had bothered him? That she'd followed him?

No. She was sure he hadn't seen her. He'd been so intent, his face so steely and determined that she hadn't dared to go any farther. He couldn't possibly know that she burned with curiosity as to what he'd been doing—because one thing was obvious. When the theater staff appeared a few minutes later with a bottle of champagne and a selection of pastries, they had not met him on their way up. In fact, they'd been quite puzzled when she'd asked how much longer he would be. And when he'd returned, so distracted, so . . . so *angry,* she hadn't had the heart to question him.

Was it because of her? Had *she* done something to annoy him? Her skin suddenly grew as cold as ice. He'd once told her that he was an expert at gleaning information. Had he somehow discovered the secrets she'd withheld? Or worse yet, had Bram discovered the secret she'd kept from him? That he had a son? Did he mean to confront her with the fact?

Her heart beat so loudly in her own ears that she feared even Bram could hear it.

"Is something wrong?" she blurted, unable to help herself.

He looked at her then, strangely, as if he'd forgotten she sat beside him. "No. Why?"

"You're so quiet."

"That displeases you?"

"No, but I thought perhaps I had done something to displease *you.*"

He took her hand. "Not at all. I enjoyed having you with me tonight."

"Because of the stir we created?"

His brows rose questioningly.

"That's why Algy intended to marry me. To become his showpiece of sorts."

"And you think I'm of the same ilk as Algy?"

"No, not at all."

"I know, Marguerite. I'm sorry." He sighed and

touched her cheek. "After all we've been through are we destined to hurt each other even more?"

The comment was made more to himself than to her, but it caused her heart to make an odd little leap nonetheless.

"There are things I haven't told you, Marguerite. Such as what I've been doing—"

She put a finger to his lips, her hand trembling so badly, she feared she would give herself away. "No. Not yet. When we get back. When it's quiet, and we are in no danger of interruption."

He apparently agreed with her suggestion, because nothing more was said between them until the buggy stopped in front of the barn.

To Marguerite's ultimate displeasure, they were met by Casey.

"A package came for you while you were gone. It's from a man named Joliet."

"For me?" Marguerite asked breathlessly, praying it was not some sort of telegram or letter saying Jeffrey had arrived. As much as she wanted to be reunited with her son, she needed this night—and she needed all her wits about her to tell Bram the truth. After that she would deal with whatever repercussions might come.

"No. It's for Bram."

This time it was Bram's turn to frown. "What is it?"

"A crate. A painting. We saw enough of those sorts of boxes being packed up during the war to know what it was. I took a quick peek inside to make sure." He looked at Marguerite then. "You make a very lovely subject, Mrs. St. Charles. Such beautiful . . . skin."

The comment caused Bram's expression to grow even darker.

LISA BINGHAM

Marguerite couldn't move. She knew the exact painting that Joliet had sent. The portrait of mother and son. Marguerite and Jeffrey. And judging by the gleam to Casey's eyes, he'd already made his own assumptions.

"Where is it?" Bram asked.

Casey was still watching Marguerite, but answered nonetheless. "The boys carried it into the loft for you."

Bram nodded, putting a hand to Marguerite's waist. "Will you see to the horse, Casey?"

"Of course."

"Thank you. Good night."

They stepped into the barn, a barn that was beginning to seem something more like a real house with each day that passed. He helped her with her wrap, draped it over a chair, then knelt in front of the iron stove to light a fire to help ward off the chill.

"Aren't you going to look at it?" Marguerite demanded. He was angry. She could feel it. But not at her. At Casey. At whatever intimate details he supposed the painting had revealed to his subordinate. She was sure he thought Casey had seen her in dishabille.

"At what?"

"The painting."

He shook his head. "I want nothing from that man. Not even a glimpse of *you* through his eyes."

"I see." She waited for several minutes, noting the way he didn't hurry over the task at hand, but took great care in arranging the kindling and stouter branches.

"I think I'll change," she finally said.

He barely glanced at her. "Fine." But she'd taken

212

more than three steps before he asked, "Why, Marguerite?"

"Why?" she echoed weakly.

He stood, brushing his hands on his slacks. Then in calm measured treads he crossed the room, taking her just above the elbow and holding her there. She felt the way he eyed each angle of her profile, probably wondering how it compared to the painting in the crate.

"Why would you expose yourself that way with that man—with the public?"

"I was more than adequately clothed. You'd see that if you looked at the portrait."

"I've seen the man's work, and that's not entirely what I'm talking about. Regardless of what you were —or weren't—wearing, why would you allow anyone to see such raw emotion? Especially knowing that it would be sold for a profit? That it would hang in drawing rooms and dining rooms for all the world to gawk at?"

"Does it matter?"

"Yes. Very much."

She hesitated only a second before saying, "I needed the money."

"There were other ways you could have earned it."

"How? Prostitution?"

"Damn it!" He shook her slightly. "You know I never intimated that you'd consider such a thing!"

No. He hadn't. Although a few weeks ago, before coming to Solitude, she knew he would have been more than ready to accuse her of such indecency. It was a sign of how much he'd changed. How much they'd *both* changed since being together.

She finally relented. "I tried to find other work. But

I needed something which could be done in my own house."

"Your father made you work?"

She hesitated before saying, "No. I was no longer living with him at the time."

"So why not get work in some sort of shop or school?"

"I was needed at home."

"Why?"

It was obvious that he couldn't comprehend what she was trying so hard to tell him, but she needed just a little longer. A minute or two to bolster her courage.

To prepare herself for his scorn.

"I tried piece work at first," she said as if he hadn't spoken. "Nightgowns, I believe. I did a little bead-work, too—that's why Sophia and I got on so well. Even though I didn't tell her that I'd once done such work before, I was impressed with the way she treated her own employees. My experience was not nearly so pleasant."

"How long did you work at it?"

"A few months—most of one winter, in fact. But I couldn't finish things fast enough to pay the expenses piling up. There were so many bills."

"You were alone?"

"No, I was with Aunt Aggie and Uncle Wilson by then. And Nanny Edna."

"Surely your aunt and uncle and Edna didn't expect you to provide for them as well?"

She shook her head. "No. It wasn't that. They were helping in their own ways. Nanny Edna with her husband's pension, Uncle Wilson and Aunt Aggie with their yarn business. But I couldn't ask them to pay for the . . . medical expenses which I incurred."

Bram became still, very still. "Medical expenses?"

"C-can I change first?" she asked, hesitant about revealing all so soon. She wanted to ease into this, bring the mood back to the one they'd shared before he'd been confronted with the painting.

"Please?" she uttered when he didn't respond.

His response was to release her, nod, and turn to the liqueur table. "Five minutes."

"Of course."

She stepped into the changing cubicle and drew the curtain over the opening. Thankfully, Sophia had seen to it that her clothes were made with front hooks and fastenings—although whether it was because she sensed that Marguerite would be hesitant to ask for help or because Sophia obviously valued a woman's independence, she didn't know and didn't care. Bit by bit, layer by layer, she stripped to the skin. Then, needing every womanly bit of advantage she could muster, she dressed in a delicate batten-burg wrapper lined with pale blue silk, tied the ribbon around her waist, and stepped into the other room.

Chapter

14

The parlor was quiet, filled with a thousand shadows and even more regret. So much had happened. So much that had to be resolved. But Marguerite shored her own courage by focusing on the fact that the first threads of a future had been laid, and like the filament of a spider's web, there was a surprising strength to the fragile foundation. Marguerite could only pray they would prove strong enough to endure the next few days, the truths that would have to be uttered, the secrets revealed.

"Bram?" She began softly, moving into the room to where he sat in the darkness, staring into the fire seen through the bars of the stove grate.

He did not speak, but held out a hand to her,

waiting for her to come to his side before pulling her close. She curled her hands over his shoulder, absorbing the nearness, the fact that for now, there was a stillness between them. A waiting. An expectancy.

"I'm so tired, Marguerite."

His sudden admission of weakness struck her to the very core. It was something he'd never done before.

"I want to make love with you," Bram whispered. "I don't care what you have to say. It can wait until tomorrow. Or the next day."

The words he spoke eased into the silence. But when he would have moved, would have stood and drawn her into his arms, she stopped him with a slight pressure against his shoulder.

"Not yet." It was a bare whisper of sound.

She felt the slow tensing of his muscles, as if he sensed that she must speak her mind first and what she had to say would not be easy.

"Please, Bram. I have one or two things that I should have told you. Long before now. I would like to say them swiftly. Before I lose my courage yet again."

His grip grew tighter, as if he feared what she had to reveal.

Feared? Could it be possible? Could the strong, indomitable Abraham St. Charles actually feel enough for her that he could *fear* what she might say?

Her thumb rubbed against the soft linen of his shirt in an uncontrollable caress, a reassurance. But she did not feel reassured herself. In the next few minutes, she could be responsible for undermining all that had been built between them in the last few weeks.

"You asked once why I married you years ago."

"Tonight you said it was because you . . . fancied you loved me."

"Yes. In part."

The silence of the room pressed into them both, then she continued. "But I didn't tell you the whole truth."

Marguerite felt his expectancy, his tension.

"It was true that I found you amusing, loving, the consummate companion. All of those amounted to the beginnings of an infatuation such as I had never experienced before." She shook her head. "But that was only a small part of what I felt for you. From that very first instant—when I stepped from my father's carriage and saw you—I knew that my life would never be the same. I was struck to the core, as if a surge of lightning had pierced my soul. To discover that you had similar feelings was . . . heady to the extreme. Sometimes, I felt as if I could barely breathe when you were near. I wanted you so."

"Then, why—"

"Why did I leave you?" She gently eased her hand away, knowing that she could not touch him. Not now when she needed all her wits about her. "Some of what I told you was true. I *was* young. I didn't realize the seriousness of my actions." She walked to the small window that was covered with its flour sack. She stared out the milky glass, not seeing what lay in the yard beyond.

"Subconsciously, I think that I believed you would ultimately follow me if I left. That you wouldn't be able to live without me." She shrugged self-deprecatingly. "Such utter conceit can only belong to the young."

Taking a quick breath, she continued. "Some of what I told you was true. I was morbidly afraid of your war. When I was a little girl, my father used to tell battle stories over and over and over again. He must have thought he was relaying a sense of patriotism and loyalty, but all he managed to do was scare me. I knew, deep in my soul, that I wouldn't have the strength to survive such a conflict myself."

"You sold yourself short."

"Perhaps." She looked at him then. "But one thing I did know for certain: I could not stay and watch you die." Again, she shrugged. "It was hard enough living away from you, knowing that the possibility was there without seeing the actual evidence of war. When I saw your name on that list"—she closed her eyes at the horrible memory of that day—"I became physically ill. I had to be carried from the consulate. For weeks I was nauseous and weak at the mere thought that you were . . . dead. It was inconceivable that such a life force, someone so active, so vibrant, could be . . . gone."

"I was never really gone," he said with regret and understanding.

"But I didn't know that." She laced her fingers together, knowing that the time had come to tell him the rest. "Even so, I must confess that my fear of war was not my only reason for abandoning you."

He had grown inestimably quiet.

"My visit to you began in mid-August."

She knew by the expression on his face that this was not something he had forgotten.

"We married the first week in December."

He raised his brows, as if the importance of her statement had escaped him.

"When I left you, I was several weeks pregnant."

The absolute silence was shattering in its intensity. "Pregnant? But . . ."

"Even you remarked once on the frequency of our lovemaking. I thought surely that at some point you would realize that our . . . activities had never been . . . interrupted." She could feel the heat seeping into her cheeks at the intimacy and frankness of her speech.

Bram was staring at her, as if she'd punched him in the stomach and he was struggling to recover.

"Pregnant?"

"I tried to tell you. Over and over I tried to tell you. But I didn't think it would matter all that much. We were in love. We wanted to marry. We could worry about a baby after all of that had been taken care of. But then, not minutes after our wedding, you informed me that you would be joining the Union Army. That it was your moral obligation to be part of a war that was sure to occur within the year."

Her hands lifted in frustration. "That news, combined with my father's growing suspicions of my conduct, the thought of a baby, and rumors of battle were enough to terrify me. I didn't know what to do. I didn't know where to turn for help. I only knew that I had to go somewhere safe . . . home . . . France. Anywhere I could think. Anyplace, where there might be a chance of luring you away from your war."

He looked away, staring into the dark corner beyond her shoulder.

"A baby."

"I thought to tell you once I returned, before it had been born, but by then, I found it difficult to find you. The letters addressed to Solitude came back unopened. My inquiries to the Union Headquarters—I thought—were ignored. It was not until later that I discovered you had enlisted in the Confederate ranks."

"No."

She started slightly at his response, wondering what the denial meant.

"No, I did *not* enlist in the Confederate Army." His eyes opened then, glowing with some fierce emotion. "I served as a spy for the Union Army. First as an advance scout for General Meade, then later, under the command of Pinkerton in the new Secret Service."

This time it was Marguerite who was stunned.

"A *spy?*" The word emerged as an incredulous whisper. Even saying it out loud made the whole concept seem surreal, impossible. But she had no doubts that he was telling her the truth. It was there in his eyes, in his careful posture.

Suddenly, it was all so clear. The appearance of his defecting to the wrong side, the apparent lack of conscience. All the while he had been working for the causes he believed in, but in his own way. Quietly. Intently. Without the pomp and glory he could have earned as an overt Union officer.

"That's why you were listed as dead?"

"No. That truly was a clerical error. By that time I had worked my way into a position of command. An overzealous clerk thought that the horrible saber wounds I'd received at Bull Run would prove mortal."

"The scars," she whispered.

He nodded. "A few came from other campaigns, but the majority were inflicted at Bull Run. They proved to be an asset of sorts. Reaffirming my loyalty to the South," he said dryly. "After that, it was quite easy to advance in the ranks."

Marguerite covered her face with her hands, feeling the way it began to crumple. She would not let him see her cry. She would not.

But there was no need for such measures. He took her in his arms, having moved across the room without her knowing that he'd even risen from his chair. She didn't bother to think of the consequences of her actions, but threw her arms around his neck, clinging to his warmth, his strength.

They had made mistakes, both of them, but a confession of sorts had been made. Marguerite was honest enough to admit it hadn't solved things, it hadn't made their relationship any easier—and perhaps had complicated things even more. But at least the most pressing questions had been answered.

She grew motionless.

Had *almost* been answered.

As if their thoughts were in tune, he drew back.

"The baby?" The query was barely audible, as if he feared the response she might give. "What happened to the baby?"

It was obvious from the guarded light of his eyes, from the fingers that dug into her skin in mute denial, that he thought the boy was dead. Marguerite could only pray that he would not consider the truth to be even worse to bear.

"Come with me." She drew him from the room to the narrow staircase. One by one she took the treads, her heart beating a little more forcefully, more painfully, with each step she took.

It was clear that Bram didn't understand why she

felt it necessary to change the venue of their discussion. Once, he opened his mouth as if to question her, but when she refused to meet his eye, he grew quiet again, as if sensing the explanations would not be easy for her.

She took him into their bedchamber. Into that simple loft with its iron bed and its steamer trunk for a wardrobe.

Leaving him in the middle of the room, she walked to the box—one whose shape was so familiar. That crate and its canvas followed her wherever she went, whatever travels she made. It was Joliet's none-too-subtle hint that she must make peace with her husband.

Jeffrey's father.

Sliding the latch free, she lifted the lid on its hinges and drew the frame free. It had been swathed in muslin, kept cool and dry during its sea voyage. Along with the original wedding ring Bram had given her, it had always been one of Marguerite's most prized possessions.

"It was cheeky of Joliet to give you something that belonged to me," she stated quietly. "But I suppose it was his way of telling me to get on with things."

As if she were taking the swaddling from an infant, she drew the covering away, standing slightly in front of the portrait so that her body blocked it from Bram's view.

Wanting to be the first to see it, she dropped the last piece of cloth and stared at the picture that had become so much a part of her world. For years, it had been the first thing she looked at each morning, the final thing she peered at each night. The ritual had never been altered. Until the last few weeks. Until Bram had reentered her life and interrupted her plans to marry for money.

"Marguerite?"

Even with his gentle prodding, she remained where she was. Staring. It wasn't her own face that she looked at, or the way she stood silhouetted against a guillotine window swathed in lace.

No, it was the child in her arms. Little Jeffrey. As he'd been at barely a year. How like his father he looked, even then. Dark hair, dark disturbingly hazel eyes, thick lashes, and the face of an angel. But even as Joliet had managed to capture the sweetness of his expression to perfection, the man had shown no gentleness, no guile in portraying the rest of his body. The withered arm, the twisted legs, his utter fragility. Deformities that would obviously never be outgrown.

Wordlessly, she stepped aside, confronting her husband with the truth. That her son—*their* son—was what most would consider to be hideously deformed.

"This is Jeffrey Abraham St. Charles," she said softly. "Your son."

For long agonizing seconds, Bram didn't move, didn't speak. His gaze had become carefully set, guarded, revealing nothing of his thoughts in that way she had seen so many times before and hated all the same.

A desperation began to build inside her. She wanted to cry out, Give him a chance! He has a mind, a quick wit! He may never straddle a horse or attend West Point, but he has other qualities which are just as endearing, just as important!

But the words were lodged in her throat.

"Where . . . is he?" he asked after some time.

She considered hedging, disguising the truth of Jeffrey's arrival, but there had been too many secrets between them.

"He may arrive in the United States any day."

She saw the first spark of something in Bram's eyes when he looked at her.

"What?"

"Jeffrey and his nurse are on their way from Paris. They will reach Baltimore by steamer some time within the fortnight, depending on the difficulty of the crossing."

Bram sank on the edge of the bed. It was the first reaction that she had been able to interpret to any degree since he'd seen the portrait.

"He's . . . beautiful."

She frowned, wondering if Bram had been drawn to the face and had not caught the significance of Jeffrey's body yet.

"He is . . . crippled. Born with twisted legs and a stunted arm—a pitifully crooked spine."

Bram waved those comments away as if they were of no consequence. The very action, the casualness of it, caused a tightness to grip her throat. He didn't appear to mind.

He didn't mind.

"How old is he? Where was he born?"

"He was born in May. The fifteenth. In a little village near Dijon."

Bram was staring at the picture again, but he flicked a short glance her way. "Not with your father?"

"Jeffrey—not my modeling—is why my father disowned me."

An ember of anger kindled deep in his eyes.

"When it became apparent that I had conceived long before my marriage to you, my father first insisted that I contact you—that was about a month after I arrived in France. It was all the excuse I needed, but as I said before, my letters to Solitude returned unopened. My father took this to mean that you no longer wanted me or the child. He even went so far as to claim that perhaps you weren't . . . the father. So he disowned me mere months after I'd left America, sent me out onto the streets. Luckily, Aunt Aggie and Uncle Wilson were willing to take me in for a time. Being Mama's kin instead of Papa's, they were aghast at what had happened. Especially considering my . . . condition. But they did their best to provide for us all. It was only after Jeffrey was born that the bills became so numerous that I was forced to look for some sort of employment myself.

"That was where Joliet found me, going door-to-door asking if anyone needed a house servant. At first, when he suggested I model for him, I was horrified at such a proposition. My mother would never have considered such a thing proper. But Aunt Aggie agreed to serve as my chaperon during the sessions, and as Jeffrey's needs increased I felt I couldn't refuse."

Her lips tipped in a faint smile as she regarded the painting. "It was the right thing to do. Joliet became my friend as well as my employer. He helped to find doctors for Jeffrey and arranged for the delivery of medicines." She looked back at Bram. "It was he who convinced me that it was time I made my peace with you and told you of your son."

Bram stood, walking toward her. "Remind me to thank him. To thank them all."

When he reached for her, drew her close, she couldn't prevent asking, "You aren't . . . disgusted by the boy, then?"

He frowned. "Disgusted?"

"That he isn't perfect."

He brushed the hair from her forehead. "None of us is perfect, Marguerite. And I have seen enough of war and shattered limbs and pain to know that it's character that makes a man." He grinned. "Or in this case, a little boy. My son."

It was nearly dawn when Bram jerked awake, not knowing what had disturbed him, but sensing instinctively that something was wrong.

He remained as he was, barely breathing, one arm held protectively around the woman who cuddled against his side. He could not forget the lovemaking they had shared only hours before. Never in his life had he experienced such infinite passion rounded out by such gentle sweetness. Because there were no more secrets. No more wondering what went wrong, or why, or when. They'd simply been two people—two very young people—who were unprepared for the way the world and its politics could interrupt their own plans for a future.

But their future had finally caught up to them. They had the time and the resources to do whatever they wanted. And Bram intended to do everything in his power to see to it that their dreams came true. One way or another. All that remained was to get through the next few days.

Slowly, praying he wouldn't disturb Marguerite, he slipped from the bed, taking the revolver that he invariably hid under his corner of the mattress. Tiptoeing to the hay door, he eased it open, his eyes scanning the darkness, looking for the slightest sign that something was out of place.

It didn't take long. Seconds later, there was the flare of a match, then the glow of a cigar. In that brief flutter of light, Bram knew who watched the barn with an almost predatory stillness.

Casey.

Damn it, why hadn't the man made his move? Why hadn't he gone for the gold that was now kept in a hotel suite with a minimum guard? It would be a simple enough matter to send Wilkins or Erickson or James away for a few hours under the guise of a meal. He couldn't possibly know that the other rooms in the same wing had been commandeered by six of Sheffield's men.

Or could he?

With each day that passed, Bram grew more and more uncomfortable with the situation. He had this nagging feeling that somehow Casey was ahead of them each step of the way.

"Bram? What is it?"

When Marguerite spoke, her voice husky with sleep, he quietly closed the door.

"Nothing." He returned to bed, refusing to embroil his wife any further in this sordid affair. Come morning, he would take precautions to see her safely removed from the area, hire his own private guard to watch over her if necessary. Then, once Casey had been caught, she would never need to know how much he'd worried about her safety.

"If nothing is wrong, then why the need for a gun?"

"Old habits die hard."

He slipped back beneath the covers, leaving the revolver on an upturned crate beside the bed.

She appeared about ready to question him again, then succumbed to her own weariness, resting her head on his shoulder. "I wouldn't think you'd be able to pry your eyes open," she murmured, running her hand over his chest, twining her fingers in the hair she found there.

Bram didn't speak, he merely cupped the back of her head, forcing her to look at him. The time had come for her to know the one part of himself that he had held back until now.

"I love you, Marguerite."

The words were simple and heartfelt, but even as they slipped from his lips, he wished that he had a talent for something more flowery and poetic.

But she didn't seem to mind.

"And I love you, Abraham St. Charles. So very, very much."

Then, without another word, she slid to straddle him, taking his head in her hands and kissing him, the embrace filled with such hunger, such longing, such passion, that he could scarcely believe it was directed at him. As her lips caressed him, loved him, adored him, he wondered how in the world he had ever lived without this? Moreover, how had he ever found the means to hate this woman?

"Marguerite?" he whispered when she broke free.

Her hair tangled about them just as it had so many times in the past. In his dreams.

"Shh." She touched his lips. "There's no more need

for words, Bram. Don't you see? We've found each other at last; we've laid the past to rest. That's all that matters."

Yes. That was all that mattered.

As long as Jim Casey was not given the opportunity to sabotage such plans.

Chapter

15

From that night on, everything changed for Marguerite. With the promise of Jeffrey's imminent arrival, it became clear that—although Bram might make *her* live in a barn—the same would not be true of his son.

He made several trips into town, attempting to obtain some other form of living arrangements for the winter, but met with little success. Due to damage during the war, and people forced to shelter relatives and friends in whatever form of housing remained, there were few alternatives better than the barn where they stayed.

With each day that passed, Bram grew a little more intense, a little more brooding. But Marguerite noted such emotions were never directed toward her. In fact, if anything, Bram became overly solicitous about her welfare, almost to the point of smothering her. She was not allowed to leave the barn without either Bram accompanying her, or one of his men—Casey being excluded from the chore to her immense delight.

The way Bram secured a house for them proved surprising to Marguerite. She was hauling a bucket of water to the rose garden when she stopped short in her tracks.

It was late evening and the workmen had gone, leaving only Bram, Casey, and the young man, Wilkins, in the yard. The three weren't conversing. Indeed, there was a bit of a strained silence between them as they surveyed the stone foundation. The tableau was so quiet, so unassuming, but in an instant it changed. From the end of the drive came a clop, a squeak.

They whirled, Casey and Wilkins aiming revolvers, Bram bending to scoop a rifle from the ground. Both men sighted down the barrels, aiming at the unlikely, dandified pair who drove toward them in a gleaming black buggy.

Marguerite backed into the shadows of the barn's overhang, hoping she wouldn't be seen, partly because her apron was dusty from working in the garden, her hair windblown and untidy, and partly because Bram had once again grown so stiff, so wary, so . . . hard.

The buggy came to a slow stop, and the two men, obvious businessmen judging by their natty attire, tipped their hats in Bram's direction.

"Gentlemen, you are on St. Charles land," Bram proclaimed softly.

"Yes, sir," one of them responded, a portly, be-whiskered gentleman with a florid face. "We hav-come here to speak to you specifically, Mr. St. Charles. If you *are* Mr. St. Charles." His glance skidded to Casey.

"*I* am Abraham St. Charles."

The men returned their attention to him, but Bram's rifle didn't lower.

The taller man—who wore a pasty-faced expression in direct contrast to his companion—hastened to add, "We were sent to talk to you, sir. About the nature of your taxes."

"My taxes have been paid."

"Yes, we know that!" the chubby one exclaimed.

"You were paid in gold—a very sizable amount, too."

Bram didn't respond, but Marguerite felt a tickling of unease. He may not have noticed the reaction, but Casey's aim had faltered.

She felt a quiver of suspicion. On each interchange he'd had with the man, Casey brought up some mention of gold—a stash of gold that Bram had supposedly earned through less than honest means. Although she'd had her doubts about her husband's wartime ethics, she now knew the truth behind Bram's career in the Confederacy.

But what about Casey? The man was obsessed with the gold he thought Bram had. So much so that he had planted vicious rumors with his friend's wife.

Was that why Casey had taunted her with stories about Bram's serving as a mercenary? Had the man somehow discovered the existence of the St. Charles treasure? Were his motives for staying at Solitude linked to this knowledge? Was he trying to find some way to steal it?

No. It couldn't be. Bram trusted him. Bram considered the man to be his friend.

But the doubts could not be pushed away so easily. Especially when she saw the way the gazes of the men in the buggy gleamed with an evident greed. Would Casey's echo the same expression?

Setting her bucket on the ground, she eased forward, walking as quietly as she could to the line of trees just a few yards away. From this vantage point, she was able to see things more clearly. See Bram's irritation. And Casey's . . .

Anticipation? Hunger? What? His features were completely shuttered and blank. Far more than they had a need to be.

"Sir, if we could speak with you," the corpulent visitor began. "I'm Mr. Rutger, and this is Mr. Reed. We've heard of your recent inquiries into available property in the area, and we have a business proposition that we would like to discuss with you."

"Go on."

"Our dear, aged aunt recently passed on, and we find ourselves the joint owners of a house nearby," Mr. Reed hurriedly explained. "We would be willing to sell the property to you . . . in exchange for cash."

"I own property, gentlemen. I'm merely looking for a temporary residence."

"Exactly!" Mr. Rutger explained. "But wouldn't it be wiser to *buy* some sort of property rather than rent?"

"My funds are tied up in the restoration process."

"But surely, sir, the rumors can't be entirely false. If, as they say, you had the means to pay the taxes on such an estate such as this, in gold, no less"—Reed waved his hand—"then surely there is a little left over . . . for . . . other needs?"

Marguerite edged closer. Sudden gusts of an intermittent wind caused the conversation to grow indis-
tinct at times, and she felt an urgency within her to
hear everything that was being said. She could see the
way that Casey had grown even more quiet, more
intent. If she could only round the bushes a little more
and . . .

Thunk.

Her eyes squeezed closed in disbelief when the pail
she'd left behind was caught by a burst of wind and
knocked against the barn wall. Drat it all! Why hadn't
she been more careful? Why hadn't she—

"Marguerite?"

She unwillingly opened her lashes to confront her
husband's furious gaze. It was obvious to all that she'd
been eavesdropping.

"Go into the barn, please."

"But—"

"Now."

Deciding that now was not the time or the place to
assert her will, she rushed inside, slamming the door
behind her. She hurried up the steps to the loft, intent
on the hay door, which might provide her with some
view of what was happening below. But even after
carefully pushing it open and holding her breath
against the squeaking hinges, she discovered that she
was too far above them to hear anything of value. She
could sense the tones of their voices and see something of Bram's movements, but that was all. When he
sensed her presence, he threw her a potent look of
warning.

Marguerite ducked away, damning herself for getting caught once again. Brushing her skirts off, she

went back down the steps, knowing that when Bram finished with his conversation, she would have her answers.

But he was gone much longer than she had originally thought he might be. First, she stood glaring at the door, her toe tapping. Then she began to pace, then fret, then worry. Had something happened to him? Had the two businessmen been somehow threatening? Or Casey? Had he knocked Bram into the dust and demanded to know the whereabouts of the treasure without her knowing that something had happened?

Even as the thought occurred, she tried to push it away, but it returned with even more force. Gathering her courage about her, she stormed outside.

But he was gone. They were all gone. Even the presence of an ever-present guard that she had grown accustomed to finding underfoot was mysteriously missing.

That fact alone was enough to cause a rash of gooseflesh to pepper her skin. Glancing at the tree where Bram usually tied his horse, she sensed that he'd ridden away without so much as a word to her.

She was inundated by a wave of concern. After all his pampering, his worrying, his smothering, what would have caused him to leave without even a warning? Belatedly, she wished that she had thought to check under the mattress to see if the revolver he kept there at night was there. Here, alone, she felt suddenly defenseless and ill equipped.

Making her way to the roped-off corral behind the barn, she tried to convince herself that Bram hadn't gone. That he was still here. Somewhere.

She held her hand up to her eyes to shield herself from the setting sun. There was one horse there, meaning that one of Bram's men remained on the premises. Probably the one assigned to be her guard —Wilkins, no doubt. The thought gave her a slight sense of relief, but if the boy *was* nearby, why hadn't the man shown himself?

"Your husband has gone to look at some property."

She froze when Casey spoke just behind her. Turning, she offered him a withering glance.

"I don't believe you. Bram wouldn't leave me here—"

"Without your guard?" Casey laughed, slipping a knife from the scabbard at his waist and using the tip to clean beneath his fingernails. "He did leave a man." His eyes suddenly gleamed. "But he's gone now."

"Gone?" she whispered.

Casey did not respond for some time, then said, "I sent him away on an errand."

Marguerite shifted nervously. She was sure that Bram would be furious with Wilkins once he learned that the boy had left her alone with Casey. In the meantime she did not relish the fact that she was apparently alone at Solitude with this man. When he put the knife away and took a step toward her, she blurted, "Kindly keep your distance from me, sir."

His brows lifted. "Whatever for?"

"Because I do not wish to consort with your type."

"My type?" he echoed with a chuckle.

"Liars."

"What makes you think I've lied?"

"I've spoken to my husband. He's told me the truth about his funds. You have no need to intimate that he earned his money through nefarious deeds."

"Are you *sure* what he's told you is the truth?"

"Yes," she forced out between clenched teeth,

marching past him, intent on returning to the barn to wait.

"You have a great deal of trust in a man that only weeks ago you hated so intensely," Casey remarked.

She didn't pause, didn't turn.

"Tell me, Mrs. St. Charles. Is that trust worth your life? How about the life of your son?"

That question caused her to stop and glare at him over her shoulder.

"We know about the boy, you know. Bram told all of us about him. Just as he joked with us about how he'd fooled you, how he'd convinced you of his innocence."

When she didn't speak, couldn't speak, he laughed again. *"Now* who's telling you the truth?" When she refused to be goaded into speaking, he said, "Ask him what he's doing here—the real reason. You may not feel so smug and safe if he tells you."

Mockingly touching the brim of his hat, he sauntered in the opposite direction, whistling under his breath.

And as he retreated, Marguerite damned the fact that once again he'd made her doubt.

What was she going to do?

She loved Bram. Loved him more than life itself. But if what Casey had said was true and Bram was involved in something dangerous, she could not risk involving her son however indirectly.

She wouldn't.

"Planning a trip?"

Bram's mocking query slid through the air like a blade through silk.

Marguerite squeezed her eyes closed. She'd been

caught in the act of packing a few of her belongings into the one satchel she'd managed to find.

"I can't stay here," she whispered through a throat grown tight with tension. "I thought I would go to Baltimore to see if Jeffrey has arrived yet."

Immediately, she sensed the silent accusations that flowed toward her from her husband. The pain.

"I don't believe I ever gave you a choice."

"You aren't my master!"

"No, I'm your husband. I thought we established that fact, and you'd resigned yourself to live with it—even enjoy it. Or were your confessions of adoration all part of some elaborate ruse?"

She took a deep breath. "No. No, I still love you."

"But you're ready to leave me. Forgive me if that doesn't appear like love." He took a step toward her.

"I told you all of that . . . before . . ."

"Before what?" he demanded curtly.

The calico gown she'd grown to detest crumpled beneath her fingers. It was the only item of clothing she felt she had the right to take.

"Before I discovered that you haven't told me everything."

He grew quite tense, making her believe her assumption had been correct. "What exactly is it that you think I haven't told you?"

"Why you're really here? What you're doing at Solitude?" She looked up then, eyeing him intently. "You haven't been released from the Secret Service, have you? You're working for them right now, aren't you?" She glared at him. "And somehow *I've* been involved in your little plots."

He remained absolutely motionless. "What makes you think that?"

"The small details I've gathered. The way you came for me in such a public way. The way you kept me by your side even as you seemed to hate me." She uttered a short bitter laugh. "But I would have remained unaware, completely ignorant, if not for the last few days, the way Casey baited me, the way you've kept me under guard night and day. You're using me as some sort of screen for your covert activities."

"Covert activi—"

"Damn it, Bram! Don't lie to me! Not now." She tried to calm herself. "Too much is at stake here. Not just for me, but for our son."

"At least you acknowledge that he is partially mine."

"I never denied it. I may have kept his identity a secret, but I always knew he was part of you as much as he was part of me."

"So why leave? Why leave now?"

"Because I think you are continuing to mislead me. I think something is happening here, something that could prove dangerous." Her chin trembled unwillingly, and she clenched her jaw.

He touched her neck, his fingers curling around the delicate column. "I believe that we established that I am your husband, that my intentions have been honorable. What more needs to be said?"

"Stop it, Bram! I'm not the same naive fool you once knew. I won't give you blind obedience without its being earned. I won't be your slave."

"I didn't ask you to be."

"Then, what do you want? What role do you want me to play? Your housekeeper? Your partner? Your concubine? You certainly haven't trusted me enough to allow me to be more."

He pushed away from her, heading to the stairs. "I don't have time for this nonsense."

"So you *are* involved with the Secret Service. Right now. Here at Solitude."

"I won't answer that."

"Why not?" She threw her hands into the air. "I don't think I'm being unreasonable in demanding the truth. After all, I'm a woman with my own set of needs, Bram." When his brows cocked in a smug manner, she stamped her foot in the dust. "I am not referring to your lovemaking, and you know it!"

"Do I?"

"Yes, damn you. I am referring to the fact that I must protect a little boy who cannot protect himself. I will not endanger his well-being, and I will not be separated from him again once he arrives. No matter how much I love you. No matter how much leaving you again will . . . wrench out my heart," she said unsteadily. "I have to be in control of the facts."

"Do you want to know the answers to the questions you're asking, Marguerite?"

The words throbbed in the air, and Marguerite pressed her lips together to keep from crying, Yes, yes! Show me you really care!

But before she could utter the words aloud, it was Bram who said, "I have one more mission to complete for the Secret Service. Then I will retire and become the gentleman farmer I've so far claimed to be."

The breath escaped from her lungs in a *whoosh,* astounding her at how much she'd wanted this confidence.

"Does it involve Jim Casey?" she asked softly.

Bram stiffened. "Don't ask, Marguerite. I can't tell you."

It was clear that he thought she would press for answers, but there was no need. In that one unguarded instant, she'd been given the information she required.

"Very well. I'll stay. But I don't wish to live in the same area as Mr. Casey. He and I do not . . . get along."

Bram's eyes narrowed. "Has he done anything to you?"

"Other than idle taunting, no."

"Taunting?"

When his face clouded with anger, she shook her head. "It isn't important. It became apparent today that he is only trying to make things difficult between us."

Bram held her shoulders, forcing her to look at him.

"What has he done?"

"He continues to claim that your wealth was obtained by less than honorable means—but of course, I didn't believe him."

"You didn't?"

"As if I would. You've always been a man of honor, Bram."

He blinked at her, as if the words were completely unexpected.

Marguerite touched his cheek. "That's why I was so confused that you could have fought for the South. I should have realized. I should have guessed."

His grip became firmer, almost painful. "I don't want you near Casey again, do you hear?"

"I wouldn't have been near him at all, if the other gentleman serving as my guard hadn't disappeared."

"What?"

"Wilkins left—at least, I assume he did. I haven't seen him all day. Casey said something about sending him on an errand."

Bram paled. "Good hell Almighty. You were alone with him for nearly an hour."

He hauled her close, crushing her against him. "I'm going to give you a gun, do you understand? I want you to keep it with you at all times."

"But—"

"Just do as I say," he ordered vehemently. "I don't know what Casey is up to—I don't even know the extent of his past deeds. But I no longer trust him. Neither should you."

He drew back, willing her with his eyes to admit the serious nature of his warning. When she nodded, he kissed her. Then, crossing to the bed, he felt beneath the mattress, offering her the revolver. "Keep this with you, do you understand."

"Yes."

"Good." With one last squeeze of her shoulders, he brushed past her on his way to the steps.

"Bram? Where are you going?"

"To send for Wilkins. He and I need to have a talk. Then I'm going to send James into town to hire you a permanent set of bodyguards."

"Bodyguards!"

He pointed a fierce finger her way. "You will not argue about this point, Marguerite."

"Fine. But in exchange, I am also quite serious when I say that I will not stay at Solitude if Casey is on the property."

"There's no need to press the issue. I've made arrangements for you to transfer to another house."

Marguerite stared at him. "A house?" Her eyes narrowed. "Was that what Mr. Rutger and Mr. Reed wanted?"

He nodded. "They were willing to part with a parcel of property which adjoins Solitude—for an astronomical price, I might add." He cast a dismissing glance over the trunks and things that had been so carefully arranged in the barn days before to give it a certain sense of comfort. "After what you've said, we'll be heading there right away. Gather everything together that you càn. Come nightfall, we'll be moving on."

"Where?"

"To a place bordering Solitude to the south. Willow Brook."

Upon leaving the barn, Bram stood with his hands on his hips, staring at the group of men waiting for him a few yards away. Erickson was taking his turn guarding the suite at the hotel—and supposedly guarding the gold. "Wilkins!"

The boy detached himself from his comrades and loped toward him.

"You left my wife alone this afternoon."

"Casey sent me into town."

Bram opened his mouth to utter a scathing reply to that remark, then swallowed it. Sometimes he forgot that the other men didn't know that Casey was under suspicion. To obey one of Casey's orders would not have been out of line for the boy.

"Fine. But right now, I want yóu to help my wife with some packing," Bram instructed.

"Packing, sir?"

"Do whatever she asks, but do *not* let her leave the

barn and do *not* let anyone but me enter, understand?"

"No one, sir?" he asked, obviously confused.

"No one. Not Erickson, not Casey, not even the blessed Ladies' League if they arrive. I'll be back in an hour."

"Y-yes, sir." He saluted. "Oh, and, sir. These were given to me in town to deliver to you."

Bram was handed two telegrams. The first was from Sheffield stating that tonight he would arrive at midnight with General Patterson.

The second was addressed to Marguerite from Francois Joliet, but he opened it anyway.

Jeffrey had arrived.

Bram felt the paper crumple in his grip.

"Anything wrong, sir?"

"No." He clapped the man on the back and strode numbly toward his horse. Tonight. The whole affair would have to be settled with Casey tonight. Before Jeffrey could come. Before his family could be put in even more danger. Because if things did not go well, he would have to make arrangements to send them away somewhere safe. Somewhere away from him.

"James! Front and center. We've got a job to do," he called.

But what he did not tell the man was that Bram intended to return within the hour, bringing his own private army of sorts.

Chapter

16

Willow Brook.

Marguerite remembered the place well. She remembered that day five years ago when she and Bram had taken a buggy ride one afternoon. The air had been crisp and delightful. It had taken only a few minutes to dodge his brothers, who served as chaperones, and begin a slow leisurely gait that had allowed them to cuddle beneath the light linen lap throw.

They'd made plans for the future that day. Bram had wanted six children, she'd wanted five. He'd wanted a house of stone, she'd wanted one of brick. It had been nearly a month before they'd married. Too soon for her to begin panicking about being with child, but far too late to stop the cascade of events that would follow.

When they'd passed Willow Brook—a simple three-story frame affair painted a sparkling white with green shutters and wrap-around terraces on each level—they'd stopped, right there at the first sight of the building, and decided that someday they would live in that very house.

Someday.

So why did Marguerite feel an increased unease at the fulfillment of a dream? It wasn't because of the years she and Bram had spent apart, their arguments, or the tension of the last few weeks. She and Bram had resolved all that.

No, it centered more on Willow Brook itself and the sudden change of living quarters. Bram had told her of Jeffrey's arrival, but there was more to the move than that. Bram meant to get her away from Casey— and although she heartily approved of the idea, she felt that there was something about the whole situation that she was missing. Something obviously wrong.

Sighing, she refused to think about it any longer. Her head ached with the effort—just as her jaws ached from being clenched shut to prevent herself from questioning Bram further. She refused to do so. Not after he'd trusted her and had told her more than he'd ever meant to do. She wouldn't ask why he'd been gone for nearly an hour only to return in a shiny new buggy. She wouldn't ask why James and Wilkins had been dismissed early to join Erickson in town, or why Casey had been sent on some errand mere minutes before a pair of brooding new guards had arrived to accompany them to Willow Brook. It was all so puzzling, so odd.

Marguerite saw the house long before they reached the front drive—a fact caused by dozens of candles and lamps blazing from every window. She wondered at the extravagance when candles must be a precious commodity so soon after a war. But the fact didn't appear to concern Bram a whit. He stopped the buggy in front of the cool marble steps and walked around the front to help her alight.

Marguerite felt underdressed. A home such as this, even one in need of a touch of paint and a shine to the windows, was not a place to be seen in the faded calico. Because of the precipitous packing, she'd worn work clothes and her hair was mussed and wind-blown. Willow Brook might be a simple dwelling compared to some of the other plantation houses, but it radiated an understated elegance that demanded attention. She should have taken the time to change into one of her new dresses.

The door opened, a bar of light slipping down the steps. A stout woman with hair the color of old pewter waited, her wrinkled features creasing even further in a welcoming smile.

"They're here, Burt. They're here!" she shouted to some unknown occupant in the house. Fairly bubbling with impatience, she waited for Bram and Marguerite to join her. Marguerite idly noted the way one of the guards took a place on the end of the porch and the other circled to the back.

The old woman who had greeted them closed the door, causing an echo of the *thump* to resound throughout the nearly empty foyer. "Mrs. St. Charles, how nice to meet you! I'm Willa Mae Eddington, Bram's old nurse."

Marguerite shot Bram a quick look. "I thought you told me once that I was too old for nurses," she murmured under her breath. "Does this mean *you* are not?"

He grinned, allowing Willa Mae to enfold him in a bosomy embrace. "She is not here to take care of me, Marguerite. She's here for Jeffrey."

"Where is the little boy?" Willa exclaimed, drawing back. "When will he be coming?"

"Soon," Bram answered vaguely. "Did you prepare the Rambler Room for us as I asked?"

"Of course. Burt hauled an armload of wood up there, and I saw to it that there were fresh linens on the bed and a small supper laid out by the fire. We'll do the rest come morning."

"Thank you, Mrs. Eddington. I think we'll head on up to bed."

She giggled, obviously thinking that there was much more than rest on her old charge's mind. "Burt and I will be in the kitchen unpacking dishes. If you need us, just tug on the bellpull." She offered Marguerite a waggle of her fingers, then toddled off down the hall, calling something to the unseen Burt.

"Her husband," Bram explained close to her ear. "The poor man hasn't been able to fit a word in edgewise in years."

"Then he and Uncle Wilson should get along fine."

With a hand at her back, Bram led Marguerite up the staircase to the master suite. An intimate drawing room opened up to two adjoining bedrooms—as was considered genteel—as well as masculine and feminine dressing rooms.

"Will this suffice?"

"Oh, yes," she breathed.

In contrast to most of the plantation houses in the area, the rooms were small and intimate—especially the drawing room. An oval table with six chairs had been arranged by the fireplace, a sideboard and bookcase lining either wall.

"You will sit here, Marguerite."

Bram pulled a chair away from the table. Not at the opposite end as was the usual custom, but just to the left of his own.

After she'd been seated, he took his place.

"I hope you'll approve of the menu. There wasn't a great deal of time for Willa to prepare something for this evening, but she promised something special."

"I see," she said blankly, somewhat confused by this precipitous change of events. Before she could begin to question him more, a tall elderly gentleman entered to begin serving the meal.

"This is Burt."

"Mwhmf," the man responded, making her smile when his response reminded her of Uncle Wilson.

She was about to ask Bram when he would be sending for her relatives, but she soon lost all interest in such questions. Burt had begun to lift the silver covers from the chafing dishes, revealing one of the most marvelous meals she had seen since leaving America for France.

There was soup and fresh bread, pasties and roast lamb, sweet tender carrots and peas, sliced turnips and pickled peppers, preserves and candied fruit. She truly could have eaten no better at many of the fine restaurants in Paris—and the fact that it had been prepared by Willa and her husband made it even more special to her than the restaurant where she and Bram had dined in Kalesboro.

Burt quietly withdrew, leaving them alone, but when Marguerite would have reached for the spoon to the gingered peaches, she hesitated. It was all so wonderful, so perfect, it didn't seem that such wonders could be real.

Bram lay his hand over hers. "Don't worry, Marguerite. Just give me until tomorrow. By evening tide at the most, all your questions will be answered, and I'll be free to determine my own destiny. Can you wait that long? Can you trust me that long?"

She could wait. She *would* wait. Because she loved this man so much, body and soul, that only an act of God could convince her to leave him again.

Bram waited until his wife was sleeping, until she was hugging a pillow to her chest, her hair spilling about her naked shoulders, before he eased from the bed, dressed, and left Willow Brook.

He didn't want to go. Actually, the need for such measures grated on him now more than ever before. But there was also a sense of urgency behind each move he made. He wanted out of the Secret Service—and the best way to do that was to finish what he'd come here to do. So he'd sent a message to Sheffield, to the men staying in town, and to Casey at Solitude. By midnight, everything would be set into motion. Within two days—maybe less—it would all be over. Then, like any other soldier who had fought in the war between the states, he could go home a free man.

The house was quiet as he slipped through the shadows, tiptoeing down the stairs. But the silence was far from brooding. It had a curious quality to it.

As if the rooms were waiting. Waiting for the laughter of a young boy. Within the week such noises might become commonplace.

The mere fact that he had a son was astounding to Bram. He kept thinking that somehow he should have known. He felt that when Jeffrey had taken his first breath, there should have been some corresponding reaction deep in Bram's soul. To acknowledge that the child had been on this earth for so many years without Bram's being conscious of him was incredible. He fairly brimmed with impatience for the day when he would finally meet his son, his heir.

He had no illusions that there wouldn't be an instant of shock, perhaps even a few days of growing used to dealing with him. Joliet's painting had been graphic enough in its detail to forewarn Bram that his son had very special needs. But he didn't care. For so long, there had been a part of him that had wanted a child. Not just someone to receive all the St. Charles family had to offer in tradition and influence, but a part of him he could teach to fish in the old swimming hole, or relay the stories of the original blackguard St. Charles who had amassed the same fortune Bram would use to rebuild Solitude.

Soon.

So soon.

Rushing outside, Bram waved briefly to the guard who stood in the shadows of the porch. Moving swiftly, he saddled his horse, urged into an even quicker pace by all the things he wanted to do. Tomorrow he would see about preparing Jeffrey's room. One with tin soldiers and books and games. There were doctors to contact in order to ensure his medical care was continued, there were . . .

So many things!

Things only a father knew were important to a boy.

Marguerite jerked awake, automatically fighting against the hand that was pressed over her lips.

"Stop it! Lie still."

She forced herself to grow quiet, not recognizing the harsh whisper. But as her eyes focused to the darkness, she saw Casey looming above her, his eyes cruel and glittering.

"You're going to get up. Now. But no noise, do you hear me? If I hear a peep out of you, you'll be dead before you can finish."

Marguerite had no reason to doubt him. Not when the revolver he carried gleamed in the moonlight streaming through the bedroom window.

Rising, she shrugged into a wrapper, wondering if she dared to dodge for the revolver she'd hidden under her pillow.

But Casey was dragging her to one side. "Shoes. Get yourself some shoes."

She did as she was ordered, slipping into the battered ivory slippers that she had worn from the day she'd been retrieved at the church until her trip to Sophia's.

"Where are you taking me?"

"Outside" was his only gruff response.

"C-can I take my wrap?" she asked, hoping to stall for time so that she could think. *Think!* There was no sign of Bram—no sign that he'd been there at all when this man had broken into their room. She could only hope that he was somewhere close. Somewhere where he could hear her.

"No use, screaming. He's not here," Casey said, reading her thoughts. "He's gone to Solitude."

"Solitude?"

"Yes. Even as we speak, he's waiting for me in the graveyard. Let's not disappoint him by being late."

Jerking the revolver, he motioned for her to precede him out the door. She complied, shuffling toward the archway in what she hoped would be noisy enough steps to awaken the Eddingtons or alert her body-guards. But Casey caught on within a moment, pushing her violently toward the door and causing her to bump into the dressing table there.

"None of that! Nice and quiet and easy. Your guards were knocked unconscious hours ago and dragged into the woods." He grinned. "I was waiting ever so quietly on the porch steps when your husband ran into the darkness. I even saluted." He leaned close. "That was his mistake, you know. Hiring private guards. As soon as he did it, I knew that tonight was the night."

"The night?"

"For the exchange."

When she continued to stare at him blankly he offered, "Hasn't he told you? Tonight they intend to exchange my gold, *mine,* to some lily-livered ex-Confederate general and his list of spies. Well, I'm not going to let it happen. I intend to take the gold *and* the list." He grinned. "Imagine what a treasure trove that will be. A big long list of all those fine, upstanding citizens who will pay plenty in order to keep me quiet."

"Blackmail?" she breathed.

"A gentleman's occupation, I assure you." He

jerked on her elbow. "Now, get going. And don't do anything to attract the attention of the other occupants of this house. I couldn't get to them to silence them myself, not with that blunderbuss of a gun the old man keeps by his side, but I will be taking you with me. If you make a sound, it *will* cause me to ensure that they don't tell tales. Permanently."

Nodding, Marguerite made a show of bracing herself against the dressing table, while at the same time, she scooped a hat pin from the half-emptied bandbox on her dressing table. She hid it in the voluminous fabric of her sleeve, praying that Casey wouldn't see it. As weapons went, it was not the most fearsome object, but it was her only choice.

Casey took her elbow, all but dragging her down the hall and out the front door. Marguerite could only close her eyes in regret when she saw the light at the back of the house and heard Willa Mae and Burt's murmured conversation.

But they did not hear her.

They would have no idea at all what had happened to her.

The ride to the rendezvous point passed much more swiftly than Bram had expected. His mind was filled with a thousand details of future activities as well as dozens of questions he needed to ask Marguerite about Jeffrey.

It was when he rounded the trees that bordered the family plot that he managed to push everything from his mind but business. All the plans in the world would do him no good until Casey had been proven to be a traitor. Only then would Bram be free.

A pale band of moonlight stretched down the center of the road, but other than that tiny ribbon of grayish glow, the rest of the area was blanketed in darkness.

Drawing on his reins, Bram rode cautiously past the stone posts to the cemetery. Automatically, he surveyed the neat crosses of distant relatives and family servants who had asked to be buried in this quiet corner of the property. Beyond that, pale and serene and quiet was the marble archway to the family crypt, a huge carved angel with its wings outstretched hovering motionless over the entrance. Only Micah would have dreamed of hiding the St. Charles treasure in there. As a boy, he'd fostered a morbid fascination about his ancestors. He would linger in the shadows, luring Bram closer and closer. Then Jackson would leap out of the bushes and scream.

"Bram?"

At the soft voice, Bram jumped, his revolver aimed and ready. But it was Wilkins and James who emerged from the trees. Behind them, a pair of mules waited with a wagon, Erickson tending the reins.

The two soldiers chuckled as Bram slowly replaced his weapon. He damned the way his heart beat too forcefully in his chest.

"Good hell Almighty, I thought you were my little brother."

"Or a ghost?" James drawled.

"No. Not a ghost." Bram's jaw tightened. "Jackson will never be a ghost; not until *I'm* good and buried."

There was an awkward silence, and Bram knew he'd revealed too much of himself to his men, something he'd never been comfortable doing, so he became professional.

"You've brought the trunks from the hotel?"

"Yes, sir."

"Good. And word was sent to Casey to join us here for General Patterson's arrival?"

Wilkins squinted into the gloom. "He should be here by now. We sent a runner to him nearly twenty minutes ago."

As if on cue, there was the galloping of hooves. A single horseman approached from the rear of the graveyard, his posture, his outline so familiar that no one bothered to draw their weapons as Casey skidded to a halt beside them.

"Any sign of the general?"

"No. Not yet." It was Casey who answered. "But the note I received from Sheffield said they would meet us here at midnight."

Bram regarded his onetime friend, wondering how things could have progressed this far. Why hadn't Casey merely taken the gold in the mismarked trunks and attempted his escape? If he had, there would have been no need for the continued ruse. The fact that he knew what the trunks contained would be admission enough of his guilt. But even though Bram had left the cases unguarded time and time again, Casey had never tried to steal them.

From far in the distance there was the muted sound of horses, the jingling of traces.

"There's Sheffield, Bram," Wilkins noted.

Bram squinted, peering into the darkness and recognizing his superior upon a bay mare. With him was a magnificent carriage drawn by four gray steeds.

The muscles of his jaw tightened, his hands clenching around the reins.

"Look alive, men." He could not prevent the way his glance flicked to Casey.

Casey was watching *him*.

"Just like old times, isn't it, Bram?" he said.

Bram wasn't sure how he was supposed to respond.

The carriage thundered closer and closer, pulling off the road onto a grassy knoll before coming to a stop. No one moved, no one breathed. Then Sheffield leaned down to murmur something through the window of the carriage. From deep inside a shadow moved, but did not emerge. Then Sheffield straightened and rode toward Bram and his men. A careless wave in the direction of the brim of his hat was the closest he came to a salute.

"Evening, men."

"Colonel."

"Sorry to have pulled you all out of bed. But we've a list of traitors to obtain."

"Is that the man, Colonel?" Wilkins asked— looking even more boyish when he scowled, as if about to confront some sort of snake.

"Yes. Yes, it is." Sheffield turned his attention to Bram. "You've brought the gold?"

"Yes, sir."

What Bram didn't say was that he'd held some back, replacing the bars with iron substitutes. He wanted something to use as bait should tonight fail to capture their traitor.

"Very good." Sheffield nodded in agreement. "All right, men. Take that wagon closer to the carriage for the general's inspection."

Bram scarcely noted the ensuing activity, staring hard at Casey, trying to gauge his reaction. It was not until that instant that a series of irrefutable facts wriggled into his brain.

Fact one: near the war's end, a Union supply train

had been ambushed, all of the accompanying soldiers except Jim Casey killed. The gold had then been stolen and hidden. Fact two: Bram had unknowingly stumbled over that gold and turned it over to Sheffield. Fact three: an elaborate game of cat and mouse had been organized, and the trap was about to spring shut—with the only witnesses to the gold's existence situated here, in one place, in the dead of night.

The only witnesses.

Damn it all to hell, that was why Casey had delayed. He'd believed the ruse. He'd believed the fact that General Patterson was about to appear with a list of traitors. So Casey had stayed and played a dance with the devil, hoping for this night. Because in an instant, he thought he could have it all: the gold, the list, and the death of his witnesses.

Immediately, he became conscious of each man's placement. James and Wilkins had returned to the wagon, jumping up into the seat while Erickson urged the mules to approach the carriage.

Sheffield reined his horse to follow, but Casey held back, stopping his mount on the outskirts of the group. The perfect spot for an ambush.

"We're ready, General."

There was a rustling from inside the carriage. Then the door to the conveyance opened, and a figure hesitated, half in, half out.

Bram straightened in his own saddle, identifying the man who emerged. The careful application of greasepaint may have altered his features and subtle padding given his shoulders a bit of a stoop, but there was no denying this was the actor Bram had met at the theater. The "supposed" General Patterson stepped to the ground, resting his weight on a black and silver cane just as a near-invalid would be expected to do. He appeared suitably unsure of the soldiers' reaction to his presence, then took the first steps toward the group.

Bram had to quell the urge to whirl and knock Casey to the ground, to bash his head against the ground and force him to confess while a few feet away, Patterson clicked his heels together and bowed. "I believe you are the men who have been assigned as my guardians?"

Sheffield was talking, from some point far away.

"Yes, sir. Major Abraham St. Charles and his men will be at your service."

Bram watched in seemingly slow motion as Patterson's lips twitched. "How polite you are to an old man and an ex-soldier. I didn't expect that." He took a pair of spectacles from his pocket and peered at the other shapes in the darkness.

"May I know their names?"

When Sheffield glanced questioningly at Bram, he hurried to act completely at ease. "Of course. These are my assistants. Jim Casey, Elijah James, Delbert Erickson, and Henry Wilkins."

Patterson nodded to each in turn while Bram inwardly cursed. *Expose yourself, Casey. Expose yourself now before anyone is hurt.*

"I trust that all my . . . requests have been arranged in regards to payment for my . . . information?"

"Yes, sir," Sheffield barked.

With a crook of his finger, Bram motioned for Casey to come forward, hoping that the sight of the gold would cause him to tip his hand. "Show him what's inside the top trunk, Casey."

It was the first time that Casey showed any rea

reaction. His lips tightened, but he slid from his horse and strode to the wagon. Swinging into the back, he used the key left in the padlock to unlock it, then lifted the lid. Hefting a single bar out, he held it up to the moonlight so that there was no mistaking that it was gold.

Patterson nodded in acknowledgment, and Casey put the bar back in its place, closed the lid, and dropped from the wagon.

Damn it! Why hadn't he reacted more? Why hadn't he given some sign that *he* had been the original man to steal the gold? That he had ambushed several trusted Union soldiers to obtain it, only to have it slip through his grasp and show up here? Now?

It was not until Patterson tried to step toward the wagon to take a closer look that Casey showed any real interest in the events as they were unfolding. He jumped to the ground and caught the man's arm, causing him to pause. "I believe there was some documentation that you were supposed to bring with you?"

"Casey!" Wilkins barked in obvious affront at the break in procedure.

"Well, hell, boys. Shouldn't we be checking to make sure he's willing to hold up his end of the bargain? Unless . . ."

He whipped his revolver from his waistband, pulling Patterson in front of him as a shield. "Unless there's nothing to lose. At least not on my part."

Before Bram could react, an explosion rocked the night, another, another. Sheffield fell from his horse, a blossom of red appearing at his neck. James was next, thrown from the wagon when he tried to stand and shoot, taking a bullet to the stomach. Then Erickson in the chest, and Wilkins, the blond, fuzz-faced boy, right between the eyes.

"Don't," Casey ordered lowly when Bram lifted his own weapon. "Drop it."

Bram did as he was told, holding his hands out to the side, not wanting to antagonize the man who faced him.

Casey's lips lifted ever so slightly in approval. "At last we understand one another." He shook his head. "You underestimated me, you know. From the moment you claimed those trunks held your wife's possessions, I knew it was a trap. There wasn't even any need to do such a poor job of re-stenciling them. As soon as I saw the other boys struggling to lift them, I knew what they contained. I was so *maddened* by how they could have disappeared from my original hiding place, but as soon as they showed up under your protection . . . why the explanation was obvious. You'd always been so honorable, so above corruption. I knew you would only keep them through official means—which meant somehow you knew I was involved."

"Why, Casey?" Bram asked, on the one hand wanting to know the man's motives, while at the same time needing to distract him from the hostage he held in front of him.

"Why, what? Why did I ambush those men for the gold all those years ago?" He shrugged. "I wanted the money." He grinned. "Or perhaps your question is more immediate. Why did I ambush *these* men?" The smile disappeared beneath a bitter twist of his lips. " wanted the money."

His gaze briefly flicked around him, but not enough to provide Bram with an opportunity to move. "You see, I didn't come from a background like this. My home was a rocky little plot in Indiana. My family was nothing but trash, more than willing to accept the blood money given to them by the owner of the neighboring ironworks. They didn't even ask if I wanted to fight for that yellow-bellied bastard. They just took the money and shoved me out the door."

Casey had been forced to fight? Had been *paid* to fight by a neighbor? Why had he never told Bram?

"Thirty dollars. That's what he paid my parents to have me enlist in his place. Thirty dollars. I was nearly forty years old, but my parents had the gall to claim the ultimate say in the matter.

"Of course, after a while, I was glad to go. Glad to be gone. I soon saw that there was more to life than rocks and dirt and sweat. And the money . . . holy heaven, it was sweeter than anything I'd ever imagined."

"Our pay wasn't—"

"Who's talking about pay?" Casey laughed. "That wasn't anything but spit in a bucket. I soon found other ways to . . . augment my earnings."

Bram felt a slow wave of horror, one that was quickly confirmed.

"What I told your wife was true. I soon found ways to charge a nice, tidy fee for souvenirs. Judges. Colonels." He grinned. "And generals! I killed them all. For a price."

Before Bram could react, he shoved Patterson ahead of him, gunning him in the back, then turning his revolver on Bram again.

"Consider that one a free sample." He made a gesture with his revolver. "Now, I suppose, it's your turn, although majors have never been entirely profitable. But I can't have the witnesses, you see. That's why I waited until tonight before making my move. I even brought myself a little insurance—call to him, Marguerite!"

Bram stiffened, inundated with an icy horror.

"Prove to him I mean what I say!"

There was a long silence before he heard a soft, "Bram?"

Casey chortled in delight. "You didn't think I could do it, did you? You didn't think I could steal her away from your hired guns. Well, I did. After years of hunting men like I used to hunt rabbits, it was easy. All I had to do was pop her guards over the head and drag them into the woods. Then she was mine for the taking."

"It won't work, Casey. They'll be after you."

"Who? Who will be after me? Don't you see? Anyone who ever knew about the gold will be gone. Sure, Sheffield might have told one or two of his superiors about me, but I doubt it. He always was a cocky bastard. Felt he had a right to control everything. I wouldn't have put it past him to have engineered this whole plot."

He held the revolver in both hands. "Now, I want you to get down off your horse and come find the general's list. Otherwise, I'll blast you to kingdom come and have your wife help me." His brows suddenly furrowed. "Damn. The list was a sham, wasn't it? This whole setup was a sham."

"No."

Casey gave a genuine guffaw of amusement. "Don' try to lie to a liar, Bram! We've been together too long completed too many campaigns together. I am genu inely sorry that I will have to kill you now—and tha pretty little wife of yours. But you see . . . there can be no witnesses. None whatsoever. Then, when your bodies are found charred in a mysterious fire in the barn, anyone who comes to question what happened will cluck their tongues and pity the accident." He pressed his lips together. "I'm just sorry you didn't wait on moving one more day. It would have made matters so much easier. But"—he shrugged—"I won't be here to worry about the gossip, will I?"

Casey held the revolver higher, aimed. "Good-bye, Bram."

Then he pulled the trigger.

Chapter

17

Bram felt the bullet strike his shoulder even as he dived from his horse and rolled beneath the wagon. His eyes squeezed closed beneath the pain, one that he thought he would never experience again once the war had ended.

He heard Casey swear, heard him prowling around the wagon, and he lay motionless, hoping that the man would not be able to see him in the shadows.

"It's no use, Bram. You might as well come out. I *will* kill you."

Bram didn't dare breathe, didn't dare twitch. At one point, he was sure that Casey was staring straight at him, studying him. He could imagine the scowl on his face. The one Bram had seen countless times when something didn't go his way.

"You'll have to come out sometime, you know. After all . . . I've got your wife."

There was the scrape of Casey's boots in the dirt as he began to walk backward, leaning one by one over each of the corpses and relieving them of their weapons while all the while steadily making his way toward the graveyard and the direction of Marguerite's earlier call.

No, damn it. No! Bram would not let him do this. He would not let Casey harm her.

He rolled to his stomach and began to belly-crawl from beneath the wagon. If he could only get close enough to reach inside the trunks. At least one of the bars could provide some sort of makeshift weapon.

Never in all his life had Bram felt the icy breath of fear breathing so closely against his neck. Inch by inch he rose from his knees, stood, and slid a hand over the wagon box. Blindly, he felt for the top of the unlocked trunk, silently swearing when the wooden lid mashed his fingers in his effort to get inside. But he was able to grab one of the bars and lift it free.

As soon as he'd returned to the cover of the wagon's side again, he moved to the back, waiting for his eyes to adjust to the deeper blackness beneath the graveyard pines.

At long last, he saw Casey, holding a wriggling Marguerite directly beneath the wings of the outstretched marble angel.

"Heaven help us both," he whispered, then half crouching, half running, began to make his way around the side of the cemetery.

"Come on out, Bram!" Casey called. "I have your beloved right here. In my arms. Don't you think you'd better come fetch her?"

"No, Bram!"

Marguerite's instinctive reaction was silenced beneath the sound of a slap, and Bram's blood burned hot in his veins as he jumped over the iron railing to Casey's right. A few hundred feet. That was all that separated them. A few hundred feet. But even as he closed the distance, he had no idea how he would free her from the revolver pressed to her temple.

Casey whirled to face him, laughing triumphantly. "Very good, Bram! You always were the best in the service." He leaned closer to whisper in Marguerite's ear. "Except for me."

Bram saw the way that Marguerite clawed at Casey with one hand. He saw the desperation in her eyes, not just for her, but for him. *Him.* The very fact that she cared for him so deeply, even now, even like this, helped him to temper his emotions and scrape his wits about him. *Think, man. Think!*

Then he saw it—a faint glimmer of moonlight against metal—and he felt a ray of hope. The gun he'd given her. Somehow, she'd managed to bring it.

But as her free hand lifted, he knew what he had seen was too small to be a gun. Therefore, he was unprepared for Casey's shriek of pain when she drove the unknown weapon into his leg.

Bram lunged forward, throwing Casey to the ground and attempting to bash him with the gold bar, thereby releasing Marguerite from the man's hold.

"Run, damn it, run!"

But she didn't run. Ever the disobedient, willful,

defiant woman that she was, Marguerite dove back into the fray, kicking, clawing, screaming. It wasn't until Bram really heard her that he realized she was not trying to fight Casey, but was pulling Bram free.

"Come with me, Bram. Now!"

He would have argued, if not for the way her eyes glowed so fiercely. Not comprehending, he scuttled back to a point beside the doorway. Marguerite was clasping a rope crying, "Pull. Pull!"

It was then that he saw that Casey had kept her in place by tying her to the huge marble angel guarding the vault. The statue was old, crumbling, and obviously rocking on its moorings; Marguerite must have realized that fact when Casey had abandoned her here.

"Pull, Bram!"

Casey was rising to his feet, Marguerite frantically grabbing at the rope. Without another thought, Bram took the rope in both hands and tugged.

The crash of granite was overpowering, shattering the night. Then all was quiet except for the slight rain of rock and pebbles. When the dust finally cleared enough to admit a tiny beam of moonlight, it was to see that not only had the angel collapsed on Casey, but most of the facade of the crypt as well.

For some time, he and Marguerite stood there, trembling, absorbing the fact that they were alive while so many others were dead.

Unable to bear the sight any longer, Bram hauled Marguerite close, burying his face in her hair. "I should have sent you away weeks ago."

She could only laugh weakly against his shoulder. "Casey did something to my guards . . ."

"I know. I know."

"He kept talking about retrieving gold. And a list. He was going to blackmail whoever was on the list."

At long last Bram completely understood why Casey had waited until tonight before acting. He was a greedy man, wanting to claim the gold he'd stolen once before as well as a list of names that he could contact and threaten for any future revenue he might need. Why hadn't Bram seen this side of him earlier? How had Bram become so angry, so wrapped up in his own shattered hopes, that he'd failed to see how Casey had changed beneath his very nose?

Marguerite sobbed against him, a sound that was half pain, half relief.

"It's all right, Marguerite. It's all right," he soothed. She lay against him, the trembling subsiding bit by bit, the hands that gripped him becoming less frantic and much more gentle.

"Bram?" she questioned, drawing back. "I don't like this line of work you're in. Promise me you'll resign."

"Tomorrow," he whispered, touching her cheek, her lips. "I'll send a telegram first thing in the morning."

She nodded, then, without warning, clasped his hair and dragged him down for a kiss, a deep, soul-wrenching kiss that displayed the depth of her worry and the strength of her love. "Let's go home, Bram."

"Yes."

"Right now."

"Right now."

Gathering her close, he led her to his horse. Swinging into the saddle, he reached for her, cradling her next to his chest. He would send someone back to take care of the dead, to arrange for burial, to fill out the endless forms and explanations the government required. But for now, he had his wife to consider.

His wife.

His love.

"Marguerite," he said, leading the horse back in the direction of Willow Brook. "Just exactly what did you use to stab Casey?"

"A hat pin."

"A *hat pin?* Good hell Almighty, I thought I gave you a gun?"

"I couldn't hide *that* in my sleeve, now, could I?"

"I suppose not," he said, liking the way their murmured voices blended smoothly into the chirp of the crickets and the other mystical night noises. "Tell me, Marguerite, do you like Willow Brook?"

"I adore it. I almost wish we could live there instead of Solitude. It's so much more . . . approachable."

"I'm glad you feel that way."

"Why? I would have thought you'd be angry."

"No, actually, I was considering passing it on to Jackson. I'm more interested in breeding stock than the house. And now the restoration process is delayed indefinitely."

"Delayed indefinitely?"

"Yes. You just buried all our funds beneath a mountain of rubble."

"You mean—"

"The St. Charles treasure. It was hidden in the crypt."

"Oh, my."

"We'll probably have to dig it out ourselves since we wouldn't want anyone else to know about it."

"Oh, my . . ."

"But it will have to wait until much later."

"Why?"

"Because, my dear, we have a son in Baltimore—as well as your aunt, uncle, nanny, and portrait painter. It's time they came home where they belong." He grinned. "I'd say Willow Brook is about to become very crowded indeed."

"Quite wonderfully so," she sighed.

He made a low growling sound in his throat. "Therefore, I believe I'd better avail myself of your charms as soon—and as much—as possible in the interim."

This time, her response was a sigh of pleasure. "Oh . . . my . . . yes . . ."

Epilogue

"Well? Aren't they here yet?"

Marguerite would have smiled at her husband's impatient tone if she weren't just as anxious for their son to arrive.

Anxious and just a trifle frightened.

She knew that Bram had been well prepared for Jeffrey's condition. He'd listened intently as she'd relayed the information about the boy's fragile health, the medicines he took, and the treatments that awaited him when he grew stronger. But she also knew that no matter how much she told him, no matter how many times she found Bram staring at the portrait he'd hung in the parlor, nothing could prepare him for his first face-to-face meeting with his son.

"Well?"

She started when she had gone too long without responding.

Bram became immediately concerned. "What's wrong?"

"Nothing, nothing. Just nervous."

His smile was indulgent. "So am I," he admitted sheepishly. "How do I look?"

"Wonderful."

She didn't need him to hold his arms wide to show the snow-white shirt, dark vest, jacket, and trousers to see that. He had taken as much care in dressing for the occasion as he might have done for some special function—as indeed she supposed it was.

"They'll be here soon?" he asked.

Although they both knew the answer well enough, she responded, "The telegram said midday."

"Good." He strode to the window, pulling the curtain to one side so he could see the front drive. "While we're waiting, I have something I'd like to discuss with you."

The serious tone he used caused a heaviness to enter her breast. "What?" she breathed, almost afraid to ask.

"I've been thinking about Jackson a lot lately."

"Jackson?" she breathed, wondering what his younger brother had to do with them now.

"I don't think he's dead, Marguerite. I know there's no record of him, no word of what's happened, but"—he tapped his chest—"deep down I feel he's alive."

She smiled, rushing to wrap her arms around his waist and pressing her cheek to his back. "Then trus your instincts, Bram. They've served you well in the past."

He rubbed the hands she rested on his waist.

"Do you like it here, Marguerite?"

She frowned at his sudden change of topic.

"Where?"

"Here, at this house."

She smiled, nudging a little closer. "I've always loved this place, you know that."

"Me, too." He brought her fingers to his lips. "Would you mind terribly if . . . we made *this* our home?"

It took a few minutes for the meaning of his words to sink into her brain. Once before they'd discussed such a thing, but no decision had been made until now.

"You don't want to return to Solitude?"

He shrugged. "The land on this plantation is better for cultivation—I've always wanted to try my hand at growing things. And the house . . ."

"Feels like home," she murmured.

"Yes."

She chuckled softly, causing him to turn.

"What's so funny?" he asked, tipping her chin up.

"I thought you were about to reveal some deep, dark, secret, or some unresolved problem."

He eyed her intently. "But it is. You've had your heart set on Solitude ever since we met."

She shook her head, realizing he still didn't fully understand. "I never cared about Solitude one way or the other. It was beautiful, enchanting, but a place, nothing more."

"But—"

"Don't you see? I never cared about money, or position, or fame. All I wanted was a warm place for my family and means enough to feed them all. That's the only reason I would have married Algy. But with you"—she cupped his face in her hands. "You must believe me. I'm with you now because I love you, because I need you, because my life would be nothing without you. Where we live and what we do isn't important because I trust you to take care of our son and see he is provided for."

Her voice became tight with emotion.

"Other than that, my motives in the future are purely selfish. I plan to love you and be loved by you." She lifted on tiptoe. "And if you would allow such a thing to occur here, at Willow Brook, then everything I ever longed for, dreamed for, fought for, will be here. With you."

He scooped her close, laughing, whirling her in a circle. "I was so worried you would think I'd lost my mind."

"No."

"But Jackson always wanted to train horses. He's good with them. I thought he would want to stay at Solitude nearer to the paddocks, then I could concentrate more on raising feed, buying stock, and breeding."

"I think that would be wonderful."

"We'll hire someone to find him. In the meantime we'll fix the house good as new."

"And the gardens."

"Build a new barn and corrals."

"Plant some trees."

"It will be a grand welcome-home gift, don't you think?"

She grinned. "Yes. Yes, it will."

"Marguerite! Get out here at once and liberate me from this contraption!"

The distant call started them both.

"Nanny Edna?" She whirled to peek out the window, seeing the cavalcade of vehicles pulling to a stop in the drive. "Nanny Edna!"

Then she was racing outside and down the walk.

The first carriage door opened, and Aunt Aggie poked her head out, grinning in delight. "We're here, child. We're finally here."

Without waiting for her husband to assist her onto the carriage block, she hurried forward, wrapping Marguerite in a tight hug. Then she drew back to examine her.

"You're looking well."

"Thank you. I'm feeling quite well." She reached behind her to take Bram's hand and draw him forward. "You remember Bram, of course."

"As if I could ever forget the person responsible for snatching you away from Algy's side." She leaned close to confide, "So glad you did, my boy. I always thought the man was a bit of a boor, you know."

Marguerite felt her husband relax ever so slightly. "I'm glad you didn't mind the way I upset things."

"Mind! My lands, you provided enough gossip for Edna and I to live from for weeks. I've never been invited to so many places or been plied with so much rich food. Every social maven in a hundred-mile radius has been after us both—not that I'm prone to gossip, you know." Her eyes twinkled. "But I do have a weakness for a good soiree."

"Dash it all, get that man over here to get me out of his carriage!"

At Nanny Edna's command, Bram excused himself to help unload her chair. Aunt Aggie took that opportunity to ask, "How are things between you? The truth."

Marguerite leaned close to whisper, "Marvelous!"

Then she was making her own way to the carriage, searching, but not seeing her son and his nanny.

"Ma petite!" Joliet alighted from the second carriage, followed by a beaming Uncle Wilson. "So this is where we are all to live, eh? Like one big happy family?"

She shot a quick glance at her husband, but he merely grinned. "As long as you behave yourself, Joliet, and those paintings of my wife continue to be fully clothed. Otherwise, you'll be sleeping in the barn."

"The barn, eh?" He considered the idea, then shrugged. "Perhaps I will find a new model altogether; what do you say to that?"

"I think that would be a very good idea."

He began lifting Nanny Edna into her chair. "As for you, young lady. I will not tolerate any wild behavior."

Nanny Edna blushed and giggled like a girl, slapping his arm with her fan. "I always liked you, you know. Never met you . . . but I liked what I heard about you."

"Thank you, Nanny Edna."

But he was already searching. Searching for his son. "Mama?"

The call came from the carriage Joliet and Uncle Wilson had vacated.

Marguerite's limbs became weak as water as she moved forward, praying that whatever happened in the next few minutes would not have to be undone at some later date.

Please let Bram welcome him openly.

Please let Jeffrey accept him.

Resting one hand on the warm carriage, she leaned inside, seeing the child who had become more precious to her than life itself. Those strong features and tousled black curls. In his dark eyes she sometimes thought she saw the eternities.

Jeffrey laughed using his hands to scoot across the seat so that he could reach her.

"My little man," she cooed, even though she knew he was growing out of such babyish titles—a fact her son had reminded her of far too many times.

"Mama," he protested, pulling a face.

Then she was lifting him, hugging him close, absorbing his weight, his scent—gingerbread and peppermint drops.

"I've got someone I want you to meet," Marguerite said when she could.

"Papa?"

She was stunned at Jeffrey's query.

"Is he here?" Jeffrey was peering over her shoulder. "Nanny Edna told me all about him, said he'd been away fighting a war and you thought he was dead, but he came back and took you away on a wedding trip, but now you're together and ready for me to come live with you."

How he managed to say it all in one breath, she would never know, but for once his talkativeness was a blessing. It gave her time to recover, to absorb the fact that her dear Nanny Edna had prepared Jeffrey well for the meeting to come.

"Yes, sweetie. He's here. He's so anxious to meet you."

With that she turned toward her husband.

He remained by Nanny Edna's side, motionless, transfixed. His gaze clung to the boy's face, studying the features that he must have recognized as a younger version of his own.

If there was shock there, she didn't see it.

If there was distaste, he hid it well.

For all she found was complete and overwhelming pride and enchantment.

"This is your father, Jeffrey. His name is—"

"Abraham Lexington St. Charles," Jeffrey supplied.

Nanny Edna had schooled him well.

"But I will call him Papa."

"I think he would like that very much," she said, hardly able to push the words from the tightness of her throat.

"Yes." Bram's voice was no less gruff than her own.

"You're very tall," Jeffrey observed. "Do you like horses?"

The rapid change in topic didn't throw Bram.

"Yes I do. I thought we might raise some of them right here."

"That would be grand!" Jeffrey exclaimed. "Even if I can't ride them, I like to look at them."

"Can't ride?" Bram echoed. "What nonsense is this?"

Jeffrey's brow clouded. "My legs . . . I couldn't possibly stay in a saddle."

Bram reached out, taking him from Marguerite's arms. The transition was made so easily that it was as if he'd been helping to care for Jeffrey for years.

"That's because you haven't tried the right kind of

saddle yet. Let's go on down to the barn, and I'll show you what I mean. I think we could have the adjustments made in a day or two. Then you and I will begin your lessons."

Jeffrey could not have been more pleased if Bram had handed him the moon.

"Really?" He turned to Marguerite for reassurance. There had been so many things in life he'd been denied due to his poor health, it was obvious he feared this would be taken away, too. "Really, Mama, can I?"

"If your papa says so," she said, wanting to sink to the ground and weep. Not in sadness or anger or defeat. But in joy. Pure joy.

Her eyes met Bram's, thanking him, conveying a love that had grown tenfold in such a limited amount of time. But when she saw the same emotions shining from his eyes, she knew so much more had occurred than making a little boy happy.

They'd become a family.

They'd come home.

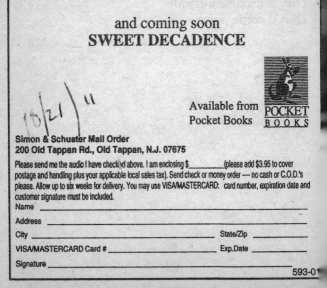